TAKE YOUR TIME

What Reviewers Say About VK Powell's Work

Side Effects

"[A] touching contemporary tale of two wounded souls hoping to find lasting love and redemption together. ...Powell ably plots a plausible and suspenseful story, leading readers to fall in love with the characters she's created."—*Publishers Weekly*

To Protect and Serve

"If you like cop novels, or even television cop shows with women as full partners with male officers...this is the book for you. It's got drama, excitement, conflict, and even some fairly hot lesbian sex. The writer is a retired cop, so she really writes from a place of authenticity. As a result, you have a realistic quality to the writing that puts me in mind of early Joseph Wambaugh."—Teresa DeCrescenzo, *Lesbian News*

"*To Protect and Serve* drew me in from the very first page with characters that captivated in their complexity. Powell writes with authority using the lingo and capturing the thoughts of the law enforcers who make the ultimate sacrifice in the fight against crime. What's more impressive is the command this debut author has of portraying a full gamut of emotion, from angst to elation, through dialogue and narrative. The images are vivid, the action is believable, and the police procedurals are authentic...VK Powell had me invested in the story of these women, heart, mind, body and soul. Along with danger and tension, Powell's well-developed erotic scenes sizzle and sate."—*Story Circle Book Reviews*

Suspect Passions

"From the first chapter of *Suspect Passions* Powell builds erotic scenes which sear the page. She definitely takes her readers for a walk on the wild side! Her characters, however, are also women we care about. They are bright, witty, and strong. The combination of great sex and great characters make *Suspect Passions* a must read."—*Just About Write*

Fever

"VK Powell has given her fans an exciting read. The plot of *Fever* is filled with twists, turns, and 'seat of your pants' danger. ...*Fever* gives readers both great characters and erotic scenes along with insight into life in the African bush."—*Just About Write*

Justifiable Risk

"This story takes some unusual twists and at one point, I was convinced that I knew 'who did it' only to find out that I was wrong. VK Powell knows crime drama, she kept me guessing until the end, and I was not disappointed at the outcome. And that's not to slight VK Powell's knack for romance. ...Readers who appreciate mysteries with a touch of drama and intense erotic moments will enjoy *Justifiable Risk*."—*Queer Magazine*

Exit Wounds

"Powell's prose is no-nonsense and all business. It gets in and gets the job done, a few well-placed phrases sparkling in your memory and some trenchant observations about life in general and a cop's life in particular sticking to your psyche long after they've gone. After five books, Powell knows what her audience wants, and she delivers those goods with solid assurance. But be careful you don't get hooked. You only get six hits, then the supply's gone, and you'll be jonesin' for the next installment. It never pays to be at the mercy of a cop."—*Out in Print*

"Fascinating and complicated characters materialize, morph, and sometimes disappear testing the passionate yet nascent love of the book's focal pair. I was so totally glued to and amazed by the intricate layers that continued to materialize like an active volcano…dangerous and deadly until the last mystery is revealed. This book goes into my super special category. Please don't miss it."—*Rainbow Book Reviews*

About Face

"Powell excels at depicting complex, emotionally vulnerable characters who connect in a believable fashion and enjoy some genuinely hot erotic moments."—*Publishers Weekly*

Visit us at www.boldstrokesbooks.com

By the Author

TAKE YOUR TIME

by

VK Powell

2018

ISBN 13: 978-1-63555-130-3

THIS TRADE PAPERBACK ORIGINAL IS PUBLISHED BY
BOLD STROKES BOOKS, INC.
P.O. BOX 249
VALLEY FALLS, NY 12185

FIRST EDITION: AUGUST 2018

CREDITS
EDITOR: CINDY CRESAP
PRODUCTION DESIGN: SUSAN RAMUNDO
COVER DESIGN BY PAIGE BRADDOCK
COVER PHOTO BY EVELYN BRADDOCK

Acknowledgments

I've been blessed to pursue two careers that brought me great satisfaction. The first, law enforcement, allowed me to help people and to work for the advancement of women in a profession that often overlooked them. In the second, I parlay that career into stories of survival, the struggle to balance love and livelihood, and the fight between good and evil. To Len Barot, Sandy Lowe, and all the other wonderful folks at Bold Strokes Books—thank you for giving me and so many other authors the chance to tell our stories.

To Cindy Cresap, many thanks for your extra time and attention on this project. Your fresh perspective and insights were invaluable. The steady doses of humor didn't hurt either.

To friends and BSB sister authors, D. Jackson Leigh and Missouri Vaun—what a ride! Thank you for lunch that day in Napa, the brainstorming that led to this project, the writing retreat at The Tower, and the many rounds of back and forth to make The Pine Cone Romances reality. Working with you guys was the best!

Jenny Harmon, friend and beta reader extraordinaire, thank you for taking time out of your busy life to provide priceless feedback. This book is so much better for your efforts. I am truly grateful.

To my friends, Paige and Evelyn Braddock, thank you for the lovely covers for all the Pine Cone books. You made this trilogy even more special with your artistic touches.

To all the readers who support and encourage my writing, thank you for buying my books, sending emails, and showing up for events. You make my "job" so much fun!

Dedication

To two friends who helped turn a "what-if"
conversation into three amazing stories and a gentle
nod to our Southern upbringings.
Thank you, D. Jackson Leigh and Missouri Vaun.
We did it!

CHAPTER ONE

Dani Wingate parked her SUV in the alley between the Pine Cone drugstore and hardware store and dashed toward the antique-looking pharmacy for a tube of toothpaste. She wasted most of her lunch hour searching for a convenience store between the vet clinic and town. Dani and rural didn't mesh, yet here she was. Not the best move, but a necessary one.

"Afternoon," the white-haired clerk called as she entered. "Anything I can help with?"

"Toothpaste." The woman pointed toward the back of the store, which didn't help at all, but Dani scanned the makeshift aisles until she found the one marked *Teeth*. Damn it. They didn't have her favorite, a recurring theme in this town. Before she decided which alternative to choose, the clerk's shriek caught her attention.

"Get over here, young lady." The woman held on to a terrified-looking teenage girl in wrinkled clothes with one hand and dialed the phone with the other. "Tell Grace to get over to the drugstore. Shoplifter. Hurry."

Dani grabbed the closest tube and walked toward the front to check out, but the clerk shook her head. "Got my hands full. Unless you want to hold this one while I ring you up."

"I'll come back later." Dani dropped the toothpaste on the counter. Any kind of drama was not on her radar. Work, keep her head down, and move on, just like she'd planned. She reached for the door handle but stopped when a sheriff's deputy got out of a patrol car in front of the store. Dani's breathing quickened, and everything about the officer blurred except the badge. Dani ducked between a row of shelves and an upright magazine rack. In her experience, small-town cops were just as power hungry and heavy-handed as their city counterparts. She wasn't about to leave this poor scared child without a sense of how she was going to be treated by the officer.

"That was quick," the clerk said when the officer entered.

"What've you got, May?"

"I think this one is hiding something inside her coat."

"Am not." The girl's voice shook and her hands trembled before she stuffed them into her jeans pockets. Dani wanted to rescue her or at least let the cop know she was watching, but this wasn't her fight yet.

Dani couldn't see the deputy's face, but she cocked her head to one side and then stooped to the same height as the girl. "Aren't you Doreen's granddaughter?"

The girl nodded and scuffed worn tennis shoes on the floor. "She'll kill me."

"Are you hiding something you didn't pay for, Emily?" the deputy asked in a voice kinder than any Dani had ever heard from a police officer.

The girl shrugged.

"Empty your pockets and put everything on the counter." She patted a spot beside Dani's abandoned toothpaste. "This yours?"

The clerk moved the tube aside. "Some lady left it."

Dani edged closer to the front. Could she sneak past without the officer noticing? She checked for a back door. Maybe she didn't need to get involved, but she'd been in this kid's place before and couldn't abandon her completely. Just a few more minutes to see where things were going. The girl obviously needed help but wasn't likely to get it. Typical cop.

Emily placed two birthday cards, a few pennies, and a single stick of chewing gum on the counter. "That's all I got."

The clerk pointed to the cards. "That's what I saw, Grace."

"Do you want to press charges, May?"

"Well," the clerk hesitated, "she *is* concealing merchandise." The woman didn't sound convincing. "Why don't you let her cool her heels in the squad car while you and I discuss the details?"

"Hold out your hands, Emily."

Tears rolled down the girl's cheeks as she stuck her hands toward the officer. *Totally unnecessary.*

"I'd really rather not do this, but it's procedure, and I'm not a fast runner." The deputy clicked handcuffs on the girl's wrists and started toward the door. "Let me know if the cuffs are too tight." She escorted the girl outside and placed her in the back seat of the cruiser. Nothing Dani could do now.

She slid out the door behind them and ducked into the alley to her car while the clerk and several bystanders watched the young girl humiliated on Main Street. She drove back to the veterinary clinic gripping the steering wheel so hard her knuckles ached. Another kid's life forever altered by inflexible laws and a cop with no compassion.

Grace Booker adjusted the handcuffs again so they wouldn't bite into Emily's wrists and eased her into the back seat of her patrol car. Arresting people was the worst part of her job, especially when the arrestee was a child. "I'll turn the AC on." When the air cooled, Grace opened the back door, and knelt beside Emily. "You be all right here for a few minutes?"

Emily nodded. "What's gonna happen to me?"

"Concealing merchandise is a crime. You know that, right?" She was already spinning through possible solutions to the situation that didn't involve criminal charges.

Emily's eyes clouded with tears again. "Yes, ma'am. I just…" She wiped her wet cheeks on her shoulder. "Sorry."

"Why did you take the cards, Emily?"

The girl's tears fell faster. "It's granny's birthday tomorrow, and my little brother and I don't have anything to give her. Daddy's out of work since the peach packing plant in Fort Valley closed, and mama isn't getting a lot of sewing jobs."

Grace pulled her into a hug. "I'm sorry, honey. Sounds like you love your granny. How old are you, Emily?"

"Just turned sixteen."

"Are you going to school every day?"

"Yeah. I'd get three whippings if I didn't."

"Because your family cares about you. I'll be right back." Grace closed the back door of the patrol car and returned to the drugstore counter. "So, May, what about those charges?"

"I don't really want to cause her family any more trouble, Grace. They're having a hard time as it is. I'm already carrying them for some essentials this month. Any suggestions?"

Grace leaned against the counter and surveyed the store. Boxes of unopened stock littered the walkways between sparsely filled shelves, and a layer of dust on everything made the store feel neglected and uninviting. "You keep saying you want to hire somebody for odd jobs. How about a sixteen-year-old who needs to work and help out her family?"

May glanced around the store. "Don't know if I can afford to hire anybody right now."

"You can't sell stock that's not on the shelves. And nobody wants to shop in a dusty drugstore that looks like it's about to close. Come on, May. The girl took the cards for her grandmother's birthday. Help us all out?"

May pulled at the tight bun at the back of her head. "You sure do come up with some interesting ideas. Fine. I'll give her a chance, but I can only pay minimum wage."

"I'm sure anything will help. And no criminal charges?"

"No criminal charges," May confirmed.

Grace started back toward the door. "And throw in the cards."

"You drive a hard bargain, Grace Booker. Send her in, and I'll put her to work."

❖

Grace parked the county cruiser in the driveway beside her barely roadworthy Corolla, shucked the heavy utility belt from her waist, and hefted it onto her shoulder. She trudged toward her small bungalow tucked behind the family-owned B and B, desperate to be clean and dry.

"I wouldn't go in there." Mary Jane, who operated the B and B, hurried in Grace's direction, her energetic approach impressive for someone in her seventies. Her voice, smooth as freshly churned butter, belied the warning tone.

"Hello to you too, MJ. Of course I'm going in. I'm tired and hot and just want to spend a quiet evening with Karla and a glass of wine."

"Good luck with that." Mary Jane caught up, brushed a strand of gray hair off her sweaty forehead, and blocked Grace's path. "She's gone, but she left you a present."

Grace's parents said Mary Jane was unflappable, prone to extravagant turns of phrase and gestures, but totally composed at all times. If her flushed cheeks and faster speech were any indication, today was testing her.

"What are you talking about? Let me pass." Grace craned her neck around Mary Jane and looked toward the cottage. "What's that noise?"

"That's what I'm trying to tell you. Right after you left for work this morning, a curvy redhead driving a pickup with North Carolina plates pulled in. An hour later, she and Karla were gone, along with her belongings. Her bird has been squawking his head off ever since." She pointed toward the cottage. "He's loose in there, and everything is catawampus."

Grace froze. "You mean he's out of his cage?" The thought of Karla leaving wasn't nearly as horrific as Dirty Harry being unconfined inside her home.

Mary Jane nodded, her eyes wide as a barn owl.

Grace squeezed her eyes shut to blot out the mental picture of the havoc the parrot could cause. "That bird hates me."

"I know, and he's been having a field day. I peeked in the window a few minutes ago, and he's trashed the place. Sorry, Gracie, but I couldn't get out here any sooner. All this happened during the busiest time at the house. People checking in and out. Repairmen everywhere. I've had my hands full."

"It's okay, MJ." The first part of Mary Jane's story registered. "Wait. You said Karla left with a redhead?"

Mary Jane nodded again. "I was afraid that woman would be trouble."

"She needed a place to live until she got back on her feet." Grace had quickly succumbed to Karla's sporty body and the time and attention Karla lavished on her, but neither of them spoke of the future, fully aware their connection was temporary.

"You're just too nice."

"So you've said." Grace thought the same thing as she considered this recent development, but she'd chosen to get involved with Karla for a short-term distraction.

"But once your hormones kicked in…" Mary Jane let the rest of her sentence drop when Grace gave her a hard stare. "Don't give me the stink eye. You know I'm right. You've got a good heart, Gracie, but you can't spend the rest of your life in dead-end relationships to keep from getting hurt. At some point, you've got to open up again." Mary Jane raised her palms and looked at the sky. "I promised your parents I'd take care of you, but the job might outlive me."

"Thanks for that, MJ." Grace hated to cause anybody trouble, especially Mary Jane.

"The truth is welcome in heaven, honey. I'm just afraid your weakness for tomboys with swagger and roaming hands will be your undoing. What you need is a nice woman—"

"—Who wants to live in Podunk with a deputy sheriff who barely makes a living. Right. Thanks for caring, but what I *really* need is to get into the cottage before that blasted bird destroys what little I have left." But Mary Jane was right. Grace did want to settle down. She wanted true love or nothing, but the last time she'd tried, a playgirl with no intention of settling anywhere but on a bed for a few hours' pleasure had broken her heart. Grace kissed Mary Jane on the cheek. "I'll be over later and give you a hand with the B and B."

"Don't worry about me. I'm in pretty good shape now." She jerked her head toward the cottage. "Should I get the broom?"

"That'll just piss him off more. I'll yell if I need backup." Mary Jane started toward the B and B as Grace edged closer to her front door. "This is what I get for trying to help a sister out." She called to Mary Jane, "If I'm not out in an hour, contact the station and have them send the coroner for my body." She wedged her foot against the door and inched it open.

"Hi, Grace."

Harry's near perfect imitation of Karla's voice was almost eerie. She edged the door open enough to stick her head inside and get a lay of the land.

"Police. Run. Po-lice." He screeched from his perch on the back of her recliner. His gray-feathered body tinged with white scalloping and bright red tail looked like someone had started plucking him for dinner. "I miss you."

"I miss you too, Harry. Like an ass misses hemorrhoids." She scanned her living room and kitchen while easing through the door, her back flat against the wall. Shredded paper, gray feathers, powder dust, and bird food confetti littered every horizontal surface of her normally pristine living space. She slowly stepped farther into the room and her shoe squished in something gooey and slick.

"La-la-la." Harry squawked louder. "La-la-la."

Grace raised her foot and wretched at the stringy greenish-white poop clinging to her shoe. "Really, Harry."

"Welcome home, Five-O."

She considered throwing her utility belt at him but placed it on the side table instead and slipped out of her shoes. Karla had thought teaching Harry a few police terms was endearing, but her attempts at humor had always been at Grace's expense. "I'm sorry your mother left you, but it's not my fault. What are the chances we could be friends, at least until I get you caged?" She mimicked Karla's actions, held out her arm and kissed at him. "Come on. Be a good boy. It's dinner time."

"I'm hungry."

"Come here, and I'll feed you."

Harry flapped his wings and launched off the recliner straight toward her head. She ducked just in time, and he looped around the room, more gray feathers floating in his wake.

"Here, Harry." She patted her arm.

He swooped again and seemed to be considering perching on her outstretched arm but surged up and clawed her head.

"Damn it."

He flew away with strands of hair clinging to his feet. "Watch your six," he cried, taking another dive at her.

"Harry, come here. Please." She kept her tone even and soft though she wanted to yell and throw a blanket over him. Loud voices and chaos only agitated him more. She slipped past him into the kitchen and opened the refrigerator. Thank God Karla had left a few slices of orange. "Look what I've got for you. Your favorite."

Harry landed on the back of a barstool, bobbed up and down, and cocked his head.

"Yes, it's for you. Come here." She patted her arm again, careful to keep the orange slice close in case Harry lunged for it.

He hopped on the bar and cautiously edged nearer.

"That's right." She waved the orange toward him and jerked it back.

Harry jumped off the counter, swiped the fruit from her fingers, taking a bit of skin with it, and landed on her arm, sinking his sharp claws into her bare flesh.

"Ouch." She almost flung her arm in pain but grabbed him first and ran toward the large aviary in the corner. She shoved him inside, picked up the combination lock from the floor, and attached it before he finished his treat and started pecking her fingers. Now she understood why he'd been flying around all day. He'd learned quickly to open the cage door, and she'd insisted on a lock for security, mostly hers. Karla never liked the idea. Why had she left this bird?

"I'm hungry."

"I know, Harry. I'm making your gourmet meal right now." She shook some pellets and sunflower seeds into a food tray and sprinkled them with bits of chopped broccoli, carrots, and orange. While Harry's back was turned, she slipped the tray into his cage and jumped away. "There. Now eat and leave me in peace."

She looked around her wrecked home. Where to start? She reached for a paper towel to clean up the poop near the door, and blood ran from her forearm down her fingers onto the countertop. She diverted to the bathroom, cleaned, and bandaged her injuries, changed out of her uniform, and returned to her disaster of a living space. The few good times she and Karla had didn't come close to making up for this mess, much less for leaving Dirty Harry unattended in her home.

She loved her small cottage set back in the trees, mostly for its short distance from the big house and Mary Jane, which afforded her both privacy and a sense of belonging. She grabbed her cleaning equipment and knelt beside a glob of poop, thinking about her parents instead of the revolting task. They had converted the old two-story home into a B and B several years earlier. Their hopes of curtailing their wanderlust with other travelers' stories failed and they were soon off again. She'd enjoyed her early years seeing the world with them but had taken the job with the sheriff's department to finally settle down and make her own life.

"Really, Karla?" Grace muttered and sprayed a poop spot with cleaner and wiped it up with a towel-covered hand. "Ugh." She gagged and turned her head to catch a clean breath.

When was her last relationship that felt emotionally, financially, and intellectually equal? Her best friends—Trip, a former basketball standout turned vet, and Clay, an accomplished artist—always said whoever bagged Grace Booker would be a lucky woman. Even after all Trip's advice couched in basketball or animal terms and Clay's attempts to paint a pretty picture of Grace's future, the possibility seemed a long shot because she just couldn't stomach the thought of hurting that badly again.

She pushed her own sad prospects aside and returned to the question of what to do about Dirty Harry. She certainly couldn't keep him though she'd grown fond of some of his antics. They just didn't get along. Karla said he needed companionship because he was a flocking bird, but now he'd be alone. Harry wasn't to blame for Karla's abandonment. The kind and humane thing was for Grace to find him another home.

Maybe Trip would take him. He'd be good company in her vet clinic and could entertain the other animals and their owners. Grace wasn't about to collect any more scars fighting him for alpha status. One of them had to go.

After a cold sandwich dinner, Grace settled in her recliner with a glass of wine. This was her first night as a deputy sergeant without new officer performance reports to write, and she wanted to enjoy doing nothing.

Harry screeched, and she nearly jumped out of her chair. He whistled and did his loudest imitation of a bus horn over and over and over.

"Trying to relax here. Could you hold it down?"

"Five-O. Five-O."

"Perfect." He wasn't usually so noisy at night, but he normally perched on Karla's shoulder, getting her full attention until they went to bed. She grabbed the blanket from the back of the sofa and tossed it over his cage. "Bedtime, Harry."

"Sex tonight?" he screeched as she walked past.

"Shut up."

CHAPTER TWO

Dani scanned the parking lot of the Beaumont Veterinary Clinic for signs her boss had beaten her to work. The horse trailer was missing from its usual spot, which meant either Trip was already on the road or she hadn't come back from yesterday's call. She sometimes slept over, depending on the client. Her new boss was quite the ladies' woman. She chuckled to herself. *Takes one to know one.*

Dani wanted to impress her new boss, so every day she worked her plan—be early, become an asset, and tactfully offer suggestions to save time and improve efficiency of the practice. A short-term plan kept her from obsessing about her stalled long-term goals of getting back to the city, finding a permanent job, and buying her first home—a moderate-sized home that would be nothing like the sprawling house on this property.

Trip's Victorian mansion sat at the end of a long, wide driveway that split off to the right, with the stables to the left. Dani surveyed the sizeable vet office with attached U-shaped stables and oval riding ring on a huge plot of land, a perfect setup for both a large and small animal vet practice. Surrounding the structures as far as she could see were flat acres of plowed fields with standing water between the rows, not a building or person in sight. Crows cawing and pecking the churned ground were the only sounds. How had she ended up in such a wasteland?

Dani slid the business key from her jeans pocket and opened the clinic back door. The building was dark and the smells of cleaning products filled the air. Thank God for high school students who'd do anything for extra credit. One less menial task Dani had to handle, more time for the animals. Brenda, the clinic's receptionist, usually turned on every light in the place when she arrived, so Dani would be alone for now, just the way she liked it.

She pulled the white Beaumont Clinic lab coat over her jeans and flannel shirt and headed to the recovery room to check on their only overnight guest. Boxer, a young French bulldog, rose slowly to his feet and watched every move as she approached. She'd neutered him yesterday afternoon, but he hadn't come out of anesthesia as quickly as she liked so she'd kept him for observation, checking on his condition a couple of times during the night when she couldn't sleep. Today his eyes were clearer and his movements, though cautious, indicated he'd recovered well.

"Good morning, Boxer, my boy. How are you? A little less baggage down below, but that doesn't mean you can't play. Trust me." She gently lifted him from the pen, removed the Elizabethan collar, and snuggled him against her neck. He nuzzled and licked the side of her face, a sure sign he was feeling better. She placed him on an exam table and checked the surgical site. No redness or elevated temperature, only slight swelling, and no discharge, all good signs. "You'll be able to go home today, my friend, but unfortunately you'll have to wear the collar of shame for a few days. Sorry about that."

Boxer shivered, and Dani tucked him inside her coat and walked through the exam area into the back where the washer and dryer were located. She threw a clean towel in the dryer, turned it on for a few minutes, and then wrapped it around her young charge. "Doesn't that feel good, boy?" Sinking to the floor against the dryer, she held Boxer to her chest. These were the moments she loved, comforting an animal and making a difference in a life. Helping animals was easy. People proved more challenging with their expectations and potential to cause pain.

She scratched the little guy behind his ears. "Are you ready to go home?"

Boxer made a small sound in his throat which she interpreted as a definite yes.

She'd give anything to be back in Baltimore. So many things in this rural practice differed from her dream job at the Maryland Zoo, city versus country being only the start. Her room at the B and B was clean, comfortable, and homey, but eating meals with strangers as if they were family was just weird. She enjoyed a more contemporary style, the vibrancy of city life, and not so much togetherness. This place was so peaceful she'd resorted to a phone app with city sounds to fall asleep. But unlike the city, everyone she'd met was nice, too nice, and too interested in her and her past.

"Are you hungry, Boxer?"

"Oh my God!"

Startled by the unexpected voice, Dani jerked and hugged Boxer closer. She was engrossed in her patient and hadn't registered Brenda's arrival or noticed when she turned on the clinic lights.

Brenda stood in the doorway, her leathery skin pale, with one hand over her heart and the other clinging to a greasy paper bag. "You scared the wet out of me. I parked in front so I didn't know anyone else was here. You should've turned the lights on to save us both the loss of a couple years' growth." Brenda shivered and pulled an elbow-patched sweater tighter, which reeked with the scent of cigarette smoke. "This place is cold enough to hang meat. The cleaner must've been having a hot flash last night." She paused long enough for Dani to respond, but when she didn't, continued. "I stopped by the Pine Cone Diner and picked up two ham biscuits for me and Trip, but it's hit or miss with her. Want one?"

"No thanks, Brenda."

"I can always eat it cold for lunch. Mind if I join you?" Without waiting for a response, she pulled a box of supplies closer and sat down. "They were busier than moths in a mitten over at the diner. Thought I'd fade waiting for this." She pulled a sandwich from the bag and took a huge bite. "Mmm…that is some kind of good. Bud is a cantankerous old hoot, but he makes a mean flaky biscuit with country ham. Chatty Jolene sends her best, whatever that means. You have got to try this at least." She shoved the biscuit toward Dani.

The still warm smell of lard and flour almost made Dani heave. She shook her head, amazed at the gusto with which Brenda attacked her food. She rivaled a ravenous dog but proved entirely capable of multitasking as she launched into questions with a mouthful of food.

"Can I give Boxer a taste? He looks hungry."

"Not just yet. I'll feed him in a bit, if Tim doesn't show up first."

"Sorry, boy." Brenda petted Boxer's head and took another bite of her sandwich. "So, tell me things about yourself, Danielle Wingate."

Dani winced. Brenda, like most people in this town, should come with a warning sign: *Have News Will Travel.* "It's Dani and there's not much to tell."

"A sweet young thing like you is bound to have some stories. This is just girl talk over breakfast, and you can trust me, unlike some of the blabbermouths in this town, say Jolene for instance. My lips are sealed." She twisted her thumb and forefinger in front of her mouth.

If only. Dani stroked Boxer's fur, suddenly needing him more than the reverse. Did Brenda really think she could simply demand her life story? What happened to Southern tact and subtlety? "I'm really not into girl talk." The front bell chimed, and Dani scrambled to her feet.

"Guess that's Tim to collect Boxer," Brenda said with a disappointed sigh.

"Would you mind reassuring him while I finish examining Boxer and make sure he's ready to go home?"

Brenda stuffed the rest of the biscuit in her mouth and mumbled something that resembled sure. She was a good vet receptionist because she knew everybody in town and the names of their pets. She was a talker, able to calm and distract anxious pet parents while their babies received treatment. But she also smoked so much her clothes stank, and it required a halo of pine air fresheners to keep the odor down in the office. Plus, she tried too hard to be everybody's friend and asked way too many personal questions for Dani.

She finished Boxer's exam, secured his E-collar, and clipped on a leash so he could walk out to meet his dad. Tim knelt on the floor as they approached, picked Boxer up, and scratched a favorite spot on his shoulders. The way Boxer's cone bounced repeatedly off Tim's face as he licked him assured Dani he was cared for and loved.

"I think he's going to be just fine. He came through the surgery like a champ. I'd keep him away from other animals for a while until he's healed a bit more. Leave the cone on so he can't lick the incision site, and check daily for swelling, redness, or discharge. If you notice any of those, bring him back in. And don't bathe him for at least ten days. Any questions?"

Tim's eyes dimmed with the fear she'd seen so often in parents who weren't quite sure they could handle such an important task. "Uh...will he be in pain? Can he eat?"

"Maybe you could offer him a boiled egg or something softer for a few days, then slowly add his usual fare back in. I was going to give him something before you arrived, but I'm sure he'd rather eat with you at home. If he's not drinking, put some beef or chicken broth in the water. You've had him since he was a pup, so you'll notice if he acts uncomfortable. I've prescribed some mild pain relievers. If you have any questions or concerns, you can always reach Trip or me. One of us is on call twenty-four seven."

Tim pumped her hand for several seconds. "Thank you, Doc, thank you so much. I just don't know what I'd do without this little fellow."

"Hopefully, you won't have to find out for a very long time." She watched as he exited with Boxer securely cradled in his arms.

"Ain't love grand?" Brenda quipped. "Wish people were as devoted to each other as they are to their pets."

Dani often wished the same thing. "Sure." She escaped to the back before Brenda launched into questions about why Dani agreed with her.

Animals were more easygoing and less complicated than humans. People could be cruel and demanding, but animals were devoted and only wanted love, attention, water, and food. She related to animals just fine, people not so much.

The residents of Pine Cone could accept her as she was or not for the brief time she'd be here. Her situation was only temporary, and as soon as possible she'd be back in a place where life made sense and technology had moved beyond dial-up. She threw the cloths she'd used on Boxer into a laundry bin and moved to her next patient who wouldn't ask questions.

Chapter Three

Grace cruised to a stop beside the old renovated house that served as the Pine Cone Sheriff's Department office and looked in her rearview mirror. "You look like Death riding a crippled spider," she told her reflection. And she didn't feel much better. Dark circles ringed her bloodshot eyes from waking too many times to Harry's screeching and scratching. By morning, the poor bird teetered on his perch close to tipping over. His feathers were thinner than the day before, and she worried for his overall health. He didn't like her much, and the feeling was mutual, but she didn't want him to suffer. She headed toward the back door, vowing to contact Trip today about bringing Harry in for a checkup and possibly leaving him with her.

When Grace entered the station, a musty, rotten egg odor crawled down her throat, and she choked back a gag. Petunia, Deputy Jamie Grant's drug-sniffing terrier-poodle, had to be close. How the animal's stench didn't scorch her own olfactory senses remained a mystery.

"Jamie, could I have a moment? Please leave Petunia on the porch."

"Aye aye, Sergeant." Petunia looked toward Grace and a fart squeaked out of her butt as she pranced toward the front door.

"Quickly, Jamie." Petunia's flatulence had brought seasoned officers to tears on more than one occasion. Neighboring departments reluctantly asked for her assistance on drug cases, but she was just so damn good at ferreting out any kind of illegal substance.

Jamie returned and brought her athletic, six-foot frame to attention in front of Grace's desk. Brown hair, neatly trimmed just above the collar—perfect regulation length—framed her youthful, olive-skinned face. There were a mess of gorgeous genes in her Hispanic family's background. Jamie's uniform pants and shirt sported a military press and lacked even one smudge or speck of lint. Something in her hazel eyes suggested Jamie was expecting a reprimand.

"At ease. Have a seat if you want. I've told you we're not so formal around here."

"It's hard to break the military training, Sergeant."

"And you can call me Grace unless we're in public or the sheriff is around."

"That might be harder." She shifted to parade rest. "Have I done something wrong, Sarge—Grace?"

"I'm just checking in. You haven't been here long, and I like to stay on top of things." She wanted her new K-9 officer to like Pine Cone because she was a good cop who followed orders, cared about the people she served, and took pride in her work. And her little dog had already rustled up a couple of drug caches. The federal forfeiture money alone could pay for both their salaries for several years. Like any smart soldier, Jamie didn't volunteer information but waited for Grace to ask a question. "So, how's it going?"

"I'm still adapting to traffic stops, community meetings, and parking enforcement. Petunia and I handled exclusively drug and bomb duties before. And having a sergeant who shows feelings, no disrespect intended, and cares how I'm doing is weird. But overall, I do like it here, ma'am."

"That's good. I love Pine Cone, but I'm prejudiced because I've lived in this time-warped town and roamed the surrounding county most of my life. Let me know if you have any problems."

She glanced toward the porch, dreading the next part of this chat. Jamie was real sensitive about her dog and took offense easily. "Now about Petunia. Have you taken her for a checkup yet? I'd like to know she has a clean bill of health in light of her...issue."

Jamie shifted and broke eye contact. "Not yet. She's perfectly healthy. I swear. Her keen sense of smell just gives her digestive problems that produce a lot of gas."

"Humor me. Let Doc Beaumont give her the once-over. She's an excellent vet. Maybe she has some suggestions to help mitigate Petunia's problem, for all our sakes."

"Is she the *only* vet in town?" Jamie's lips closed in a tight line and her jaw muscles worked.

"She recently hired a new big-city vet on a trial basis, but Trip is definitely the best I've ever seen with animals."

"I bet."

"What was that?"

"Nothing, Sarge."

"I wasn't aware the two of you had met." Grace had a hunch when they did, Trip Beaumont would be quite taken with her. She was just Trip's type—tall, athletic, and intelligent with a hint of vulnerability she kept closely guarded. But most women were Trip's type, if they had a pulse. Grace just hoped Trip didn't scare her away, because Jamie Grant and her smelly dog were providing a much-needed windfall for the Pine Cone Sheriff's Department. "Is there some history between the two of you I need to know about?"

Jamie shook her head.

"Then make an appointment. Anything else?"

"No, ma'am."

"How are you finding the B and B?"

"I really like it, but I have to be careful with Mary Jane's cooking or I'll need to be on a walking beat."

"She's a great cook for sure. Try to get out and enjoy yourself occasionally. Just because everybody in town knows you doesn't mean you can't have fun." Jamie nodded. "Now go make nice with the public." Jamie turned to leave, and Grace added, "Buy a can of air freshener for your car and bring me the receipt. Your relief is complaining about the smell."

"But we ride with the windows down."

"Guess you'd have to," Grace mumbled to herself. "Do it to keep the peace." She watched Jamie leave before returning to her paperwork.

Grace skimmed the overnight reports for anything unusual, checked in with the sheriff, and headed home to pick up Harry for a quick trip to the vet. She made it as far as her driveway before a call went out for a vehicle accident on Main Street near the edge of town. Patsy barely suppressed a laugh as she dispatched the incident, and Grace couldn't resist a quick look-see.

Eve Gardner's old black Mercedes was buried nose deep in the side of Connie's Clip 'n Curl with uprooted azaleas and a family of plastic deer scattered across the small side yard and part of the street. Several of Connie's beauty shop customers, pink hair curlers and all, swarmed around Trip Beaumont and a woman Grace had never seen who was seated under a shade tree. The self-proclaimed newspaper photographer, a recent high school graduate, skirted the edges of the carnage snapping pictures before stomping through more azaleas to get close-ups. Connie swatted him away.

Shayla, one of Trip and Clay's mutual fuck buddies, pressed as close to Trip as public decorum allowed, but Trip shook her loose and knelt in front of the stranger. Grace chuckled. Trip had absolutely earned her CB handle, Fast Break, when they were in high school. Trip swore the distinction came from her prowess on the basketball court. She'd also slept with and left more women than Grace and Clay put together, but when it came to true love, the three shared a common trait—when they fell, they fell hard and fast. Too early to tell where this new woman rated on the potential spectrum, but Trip was testing the waters.

Grace climbed out of the patrol car, tucked her clipboard under her arm, adjusted the uncomfortably heavy utility belt, and walked toward the stranger who was holding a hand to her forehead. "I'm Sergeant Grace Booker. Are you okay, ma'am?"

The woman nodded.

"Had a bit of an accident I see."

The woman looked at her like she wanted to say, *duh.*

"Can you tell me your name?"

"River Hemsworth. I'm afraid it was my fault."

"I assumed the building didn't jump out in front of you." She tried to suppress a smile because the scene was quite a sight. The local paper would spin headlines from this for days. *Woman hits Clip 'n Curl with car and survives perm fumes. Stranger steals dead woman's car and kills deer family during escape. Accident interrupts gossip marathon at Clip 'n Curl and starts another in the street.* The possibilities were endless in a town whose highlights included monthly celebrations like crazy hat contests, popcorn stringing, plarn weaving, and vegetable carving, in addition to the more traditional peach festivals and church bake sales.

She glanced at Trip and shook her head. "I see you've got things in hand, as usual." Trip's deep blue eyes sparked, full of mischief and interest. She was on a fresh scent, and why not? River Hemsworth was gorgeous, feminine, and dressed like she shopped on Fifth Avenue. Not Grace's type at all, but the women Trip and Clay often competed for did absolutely nothing for her, and that worked.

"I'll call one of my deputies to fill out an accident report while we wait for Clay." Grace spoke into her walkie-talkie before squatting beside River. "Are you sure you don't need an ambulance, Ms. Hemsworth? That blow to your head could cause a concussion or possibly a small brain bleed."

"I'm fine. Really. Who's Clay?"

"Clay Cahill drives the tow truck," Trip said.

"I'm afraid your car is inoperable. Do you know what day it is? Where you are?" Grace assessed River's physical condition and tried to distract her.

River answered the questions correctly and seemed calm and composed, until the tow truck pulled up behind her car and Clay stepped out. River's face flushed and she licked her lips repeatedly.

Clay looked at River, took one stutter step toward her, and froze. Clay had never been this obviously affected by a woman. Grace had a feeling Trip might have to fight for this one. Grace didn't take sides when Trip and Clay vied for a woman's affections, but Ms. Hemsworth seemed different somehow. Time to disperse the crowd and give Clay a clear path.

Shayla elbowed her way through the onlookers closer to Trip and handed River a glass of sweet tea. She took a long drink and got a funny look on her face.

"Connie, would you take your clients back inside, please? Clay needs room to work. You've all been real helpful. I'll have the officer come inside when she's done here and get statements and your insurance information." She stood and motioned for the other bystanders to move away. "Nothing else to see here, folks."

Grace glanced down at River, but her attention was squarely focused on Clay as she scanned her from head to toe.

"Clay, this is River Hemsworth. She's having a bit of car trouble." Grace pointed toward the crumpled Mercedes, unsure if Clay had heard her or even seen the accident yet. "River, this is Clay Cahill. She'll take care of you as soon as we finish the report." She checked her watch. "Where the heck is my deputy?"

"Clay can take care of her *car*," Trip said, squatting in front of River again and wrapping her fingers around her wrist. Trip looked at her watch as she checked River's pulse. "I'll be happy to escort River to her destination in case she has a delayed reaction to the accident and needs medical attention." She grasped River's chin. "Look at me for a moment, so I can check your pupils."

River obediently looked into Trip's eyes, and she flashed one of the sexiest smiles Grace had ever seen. Trip was definitely on the make.

"Your heart rate is a bit elevated," Trip said softly.

River shook herself, withdrew her wrist from Trip's grip, and took another sip of the sugary tea. "I'm fine. Really. But I appreciate your help, Dr. Beaumont."

Clay snorted and Grace barked a laugh.

"Trip might have *played* doctor with a few women around town," Clay said, "But she's actually our local veterinarian."

River almost choked as she swallowed a mouthful of tea. When she regained her breath, she stood, looking back and forth between Trip and Clay. Grace could almost hear the internal dilemma over them.

"Thank you for your assistance, Trip, but I'm fine. I should go with Clay and make the necessary arrangements to have my car repaired."

Clay pulled a paint-splotched rag from her back pocket and wiped her hands repeatedly, her eyes never leaving River. Clay used the nervous habit to disguise her attraction, and Grace hadn't seen the behavior recently. She really wanted both Clay and Trip to be happily settled with great women, but she'd have to pull for Clay where the sexy newcomer was concerned. The chemistry between them was as thick as the sugar settled in the bottom of Connie's sweet tea.

"Were you trying to make a quick getaway when the Clip 'n Curl cut you off?" Clay asked, tipping her head in the direction of the car.

"Excuse me?"

"That's Eve Gardner's car. I've worked on her vintage Mercedes before."

"Eve was my aunt."

"Oh, I'm sorry, my condolences." Clay's face paled.

Trip cleared her throat. "Eve was a fine woman. I'm sorry for your loss."

"The best," Grace added.

"Thank you all." River looked from Clay to Trip and back.

Clay elbowed Trip while Grace just shook her head. They were in a standoff to see who relinquished the girl first, and Grace hoped they didn't start marking territory. She couldn't resist the urge to help Clay along. "Hey, Trip, can I talk to you a second before you leave?" She inclined her head toward her patrol car.

"That wasn't subtle or anything," Trip said as she followed Grace. "What's up?"

"Karla left Dirty Harry at my house yesterday when she vamoosed with a redhead. I think he's having a meltdown. Any chance you could look at him for me?"

"You're not thinking about keeping him, are you?"

"Probably not."

"He hates you."

"I just need to make sure he's physically okay before I decide anything."

Trip gave her a hard look that quickly melted. "Grace, when are you going to stop settling for scraps and grab some real happiness for yourself? Karla mooched off you for three months. I say good riddance to her."

"Don't blame Karla. I went into that with my eyes open. There was some mutual using going on."

"I'm just saying you deserve better. You're Glitter Girl. Find someone who deserves you and be happy. The three of us aren't called Fast Break, Paint Ball, and Glitter Girl for nothing. We have reputations to uphold."

"Yeah, like women grow on trees around here." Grace pulled at her utility belt. While she appreciated Trip's concern, she couldn't turn her back when someone needed help any more than Trip could. "I'm talking about Harry right now. He'd make a nice addition to your waiting room. He's very entertaining."

Trip backed away with her hands up. "No way."

"I have to do something before he completely wrecks my place. Please?"

"No can do, my friend, but I'll check him over. Bring him by the clinic sometime."

"Right after I observe my new deputy's first accident investigation."

"Okay, whenever, I have to get these horses home and out of that hot trailer." She started toward her truck but turned back to Grace. "And have your damn pen-happy deputy stop papering my truck with parking tickets every time I stop somewhere." She gave Clay a good-natured shove on her way past. "River, I look forward to seeing you again under better circumstances."

"Catch you later, pal." Clay gave a casual wave and focused on River again. "Let's get your things out of the car while we wait for the accident report."

"Things?" River looked confused.

"Well, I assume your dress came with shoes at some point."

River looked down. She seemed surprised to be barefoot. "Yes, my shoes. I can't drive in heels so I took them off." She shrugged, smiling as if she'd amused herself. "I'll just get them and my purse. I also have a small bag in the trunk."

Grace felt like a voyeur as she watched Clay follow River to the open door of the car to retrieve her shoes. Clay stood behind River with one hand on the doorframe and another on the roof enjoying the view of the dress stretched tightly over River's shapely rear as she bent over.

River grabbed her shoes and pulled back quickly, bumping her butt against Clay's crotch. Her cheeks colored.

Clay quickly stepped back. "Sorry, I didn't mean to crowd you."

Good first contact, pal. Grace smiled. "New love. Nothing better."

Chapter Four

Cindy, one of Trip's veterinary technicians, struggled to hold Churchill in a headlock while Dani bent over the massive English bulldog with her finger in his anus attempting to force his backed-up anal glands to drain. Dani hated this task, and Churchill was making it nearly impossible. He clawed the metal table trying to get away and dragged them both to the edge.

"Hold him still, Cindy," Dani said, her teeth clenched so tight her jaws ached. "I can't do this with him moving."

"I'm trying, Dr. Wingate. He's just too big. I don't know how Dr. Beaumont does this without any help."

Dani was wishing Trip had shared her secret when she appeared in the doorway just in time to see Churchill leap from the table, scattering medical supplies and taking both Cindy and Dani to the floor with him. Not a good impression to make on her new boss.

"Is Churchill giving you a hard time?"

"Is it true you handle this dog by yourself? I've had larger zoo animals easier to manage than Churchill, but they were tranquilized."

Trip chuckled. "Actually, I always call out the troops to help." She brought an orange tabby cat from behind her back and set him on the floor at her feet. When the battle-scarred old tom saw Churchill, he bowed his back and growled. Churchill, who was about to lift his leg on a box of cleaning supplies, froze and then cowered. "He's scared to death of Otis. Put him back on the table. He won't give you any more trouble."

Dani and Cindy lifted the heavy dog onto the table where he remained still as a statue, his eyes never leaving the cat. Dani quickly performed the required procedure and looked up at Trip. "All done."

"Excellent. Another battle won, Otis." Trip scooped Otis off the floor and headed toward the door. "I've got some lunch for you in my office as soon as you get Churchill and Mrs. Swenson on their way."

Dani's face reddened when her stomach growled loudly. "Thanks. I didn't have time for breakfast, and I'm starving, but the waiting room is full of patients." Besides, she wasn't used to leisurely lunches with the boss. The lines were clearer in her last job, but like other things she'd noticed in the South, boundaries blurred here. Was it the heat that made everything feel hazy and undefined or the overfamiliarity of the people?

Trip shrugged. "The longer they wait, the more they'll have to talk about when they see their friends in the grocery aisle tomorrow. Besides, most of them are on their cell phones gathering gossip about the woman who drove Eve Gardner's old Mercedes into the side of the beauty shop this morning. You'll just interrupt them."

Dani chuckled and shook her head. "I am hungry."

Cindy popped into the office. "Here you go, Doc. All reheated." She placed two plates on the desk between them.

Dani stared at the mound of food. Each plate held an oversized bun stuffed with pulled pork dripping with barbecue sauce and surrounded by finger-sized corn fritters.

Trip added two Styrofoam containers of potato salad and extra large cups of sweet tea.

"Eat up. It's the best barbecue in this half of the state. The only thing better is Friday's special—Bud's fried flounder sandwich."

They ate in silence for a while, Dani still mulling over the morning's tasks and comparing them to her former job. How much more would she have to endure before she returned to real life, and how many times a day would she ask herself the same question? She preferred the anonymity of city life—in the workplace, people on the street and in businesses, and in casual relationships. No one asked about her past or questioned why she liked or disliked things.

"You know, I always block off Wednesdays for surgeries and only see emergency patients. Next week, I have to castrate two yearlings in the morning, but since you're taking care of the small animal neuters I would have done in the afternoon, how about you and I ride out together to check on some of my special clients?"

Dani hesitated. Was Trip reading her mood and trying to assure her there was more to rural veterinary medicine than she'd seen so far? "What if there's an emergency—an animal hit by a car or something?"

Trip waved a dismissive hand. "Cindy's a licensed vet tech and will be in the clinic all day. She'll triage and call us if anything serious comes in."

Dani's expression was wary. "Special animals or special clients?"

Trip licked her fingers, then stuffed the trash from her lunch into the plastic carryout bag from the diner. She held out her hand for Dani's trash and stuffed it into the bag before tying it up. "Got a mastitis case to check and a mare to ultrasound, so I'll throw this in the dumpster on my way out. Ants love Bud's barbecue sauce as much as I do." She paused in the doorway and looked back at Dani. "Special? Both the animals and their owners. But don't worry, I'm not shoving my difficult customers on you, just my unusual ones."

Dani wasn't sure which would be worse but decided anything was better than draining anal glands.

"Pig, pig, pig!" Harry screamed so loud Grace placed a hand over her right ear and drove with the other.

"Could you *please* calm down? I'm taking you to the vet. You should be happy."

"Mama. *Mama!*"

"You're seriously annoying me right now, bird. I'm trying to be patient because your mama abandoned you, but you're acting like a temperamental toddler."

Harry shrieked and lobbed a piece of orange that landed in Grace's hair. Another volley hit the side of her face and fell in her lap.

"Thanks." She pulled into Trip's vet clinic but didn't see her horse trailer. She hadn't mentioned going anywhere else on her way back from the accident scene. Grace had been clear the situation with Dirty Harry was urgent. Maybe the new vet had taken the trailer on another call. At the very least, she'd leave Harry in the air-conditioned clinic until she got off work.

Grace draped the bath sheet over Harry's small travel cage, scooped it up in her arms, and walked into the clinic. Nobody staffed the reception desk, which was unusual. "Hello?" If Brenda was out, a vet tech usually checked clients in and regaled them with the latest gossip, a requirement of any public job in Pine Cone. "Hello?"

"A moment, please," a disembodied voice called from the back, not Brenda's smoke-thickened one or Trip's.

Harry flapped impatiently against the sides of his cage, and Grace folded the towel back. "Can you just wait?" He squawked at his highest pitch, and two feathers landed on the towel covering her right arm.

"What have you done to that poor bird?" A tall androgynous woman stood in the doorway leading into the examining rooms and inclined her head toward Harry's cage. Her eyes sparked with flecks of gold as she glared at Grace with a chastising look that made her cringe.

"I...nothing."

The woman casually raked her hand through short ebony hair, a gesture that relayed confidence in her appearance and in her assessment of Grace. "Looks like something." She tugged at the collar of a flannel shirt that peeked from under the Beaumont Vet Clinic smock and continued to stare. Heat and curiosity leapt from the depths of her eyes, and Grace's gaydar pinged all over the place. She opened her mouth but nothing came out.

"Jail bait," Harry called. "Jail bait."

"Quiet, Harry." She tried to think of something clever and charming to say.

"Is that your parrot?"

Grace nodded. "I mean no."

"Then I repeat, what have you done to him?"

The implication registered, and Grace slipped into cop mode. "What have *I done to him*? I'd like to see Trip. She told me to come by. Without an appointment. We're friends. And you are?" The woman walked toward Grace but stopped within touching distance, towering over her by at least three inches, which both intimidated and tantalized. Her stomach did a tumble.

"Dani Wingate, the new vet."

Grace breathed a long sigh, releasing some of her annoyance and a bit of sexual tension as well. "I'm sorry. I just assumed—"

"Figures."

"I beg your pardon?" Dani Wingate seemed determined to insult her.

"Where I come from law enforcement types make a lot of wrong assumptions." Dani stepped to Harry's cage and cooed at him in a soft melodious tone, totally different from the strident one she used with Grace.

She considered firing off an equally snarky remark but chose the high road. "I hate to shatter your image of brutal police officers, but in this case, I'm the victim." She removed her right arm from beneath Harry's towel and offered it for Dani's inspection. "He doesn't like me very much either and he's known me longer, but please don't take that as a character reference. His owner abandoned him, and he's taking it out on me. I'm Grace Booker by the way." Dani stared at the scratches and bites on Grace's arm until she could've sworn they started to tingle and burn under the scrutiny.

"Keep antibiotic ointment on those until they start to heal. Bird bites can become infected if not properly treated. Sorry I jumped to the wrong conclusion."

Dani's voice had softened and settled into a sultry calming timbre that Grace enjoyed. She shook herself, realizing she'd been staring, and that Dani's apology required a response. "No problem. It's easy to get the wrong impression. Look at us." She motioned between her arm and Harry. "So, you're the newest guest at the B and B. Sorry I haven't met you before, but the last few days have been crazy at work with new officers, training…" She trailed off, realizing she was rambling and that Dani probably had no interest in anything she was saying.

Dani ignored the comment. "Why doesn't he—what's his name?"

"Dirty Harry. Again, not my doing. His ex-owner thought it was cute."

"Why doesn't Harry like you?"

Dani's eyebrows drew together creating railroad tracks between her inquisitive eyes, a look Grace associated with more suspicion or at least disapproval. "I really wish I had an answer. I don't know what's going on with him, but something is obviously wrong." Maybe if she distracted Dani from her suspicion of Grace as a bird abuser, she'd lighten up a bit. "By the way, where's your receptionist?"

"Got an emergency call from her cousin. Seems her beauty salon was under attack."

Grace laughed. "Guess you could call it that. A car ran into the corner of the shop. I forgot Brenda and Connie are related. Now you know how small-town gossip gets started."

Dani grinned just enough to expose a tiny space between her front teeth revealing a softer side to her stoic exterior. Not quite as flawless as Grace initially thought, but Dani Wingate was the most enticing woman Grace had seen in Pine Cone in years, which probably meant she wouldn't be staying long, if Grace's luck with women held out.

"Where did you say you're from?"

"I didn't."

Grace stepped closer. "I've lived in Pine Cone most of my life and never want to leave."

"How nice for you." Her tone indicated she thought it was anything but. Dani took Harry's cage and started toward the back. "I'll need some background information. Come with me."

Gladly. Grace followed close enough to detect a clean soapy fragrance as Dani walked and a hint of dog when she brushed dark hairs from her smock. "So, how did you end up in Pine Cone, Georgia?"

"Not a very exciting story. Can you tell me about Harry? I'm expecting the afternoon rush any minute with Trip doing farm calls."

"Sure." Grace reminded herself she was on the job and probably shouldn't be flirting quite so freely, but Dani's evasiveness spiked her interest. She wanted to know everything about her before Trip or Clay homed in on her. Trip had mentioned getting someone on a trial basis but had been stingy with details. If she wanted to bed Dani, she'd probably already done it. Maybe that was why Dani was avoiding personal details or perhaps she was just shy. Grace placed her hand over her stomach at the thought of Trip and Dani together.

"Spread 'em," Harry cried. "Spread 'em, perp."

"Quite a vocabulary," Dani said as she set Harry's cage on an examining table and edged closer.

"My ex thought it was funny to teach him police terms to annoy me. Well, she's not exactly an ex, just a woman I let move in. I mean we did have—"

"Probably less awkward if we stick to the facts about Harry."

"Right." Grace brushed the front of her prickly uniform shirt, and nervous perspiration tickled her underarms. "His owner moved out yesterday. He never liked me and that's gotten worse since she took off. I don't know anything about parrots or what they need."

"Did she spend a lot of time with Harry? Parrots are loyal and usually attach for life."

"She was with him all day."

"No job?" Dani gave her a glance that made her feel foolish. She'd gotten the same you-dumb-ass look from Trip, Clay, and Mary Jane when she let Karla move in temporarily.

"She lost her job, and I gave her a place to stay during her transition."

Dani openly stared, her eyes pinpoints of scrutiny. "Why? Not that it's really any of my business."

Grace was suddenly self-conscious. She'd sound pathetic if she told the truth, that she couldn't bear for anyone to suffer or struggle unnecessarily. Dani would think she was a bleeding heart with no business in law enforcement. If she tried to make up something, Dani would know immediately because Grace was a terrible liar. So she shrugged and said nothing.

"You're either really nice or very naïve, which is hard to believe for a cop."

That was the second time Dani maligned Grace's profession as if being in law enforcement explained who she was. "Bad experience with cops?"

Dani hesitated as she reached for the door to Harry's cage. "Just the usual stuff." She inched the lock open without making a sound.

"I wouldn't do that." She wanted to know more about Dani's comment, but safety took priority. "He looks friendly enough, but he can be vicious. You *have* seen my arm."

Without looking up, Dani opened the cage door. "The key is to approach slowly. If Harry is used to being handled, I could towel him inside the cage without any trouble, but I prefer to let him come to me."

Harry turned toward Grace, squawked loudly, and flapped his wings. "Five-O, five-O."

"He's obviously disturbed by you. Would you step outside please?"

Grace left but poked her head around the door. Harry immediately calmed. Damn. Dani easily soothed Harry while stirring riotous emotions in her.

"Interesting," Dani said and opened the cage door wider. Harry hopped onto her outstretched hand. She breathed deeply and refocused. With Grace Booker on the other side of the door, Dani concentrated on her patient instead of the way Grace scanned her body and scrutinized every move. Grace was direct, unfiltered, and never stopped talking—Dani's exact opposite.

"I've never seen him take to anyone except his owner...my ex...err...you're amazing," Grace said.

If she'd met Grace in Baltimore, out of uniform, she might've pursued her. What wasn't to like about that package? Grace was attractive, compassionate, and personable. She took a woman into her home because she lost her job and looked after her parrot when she didn't have to. But Dani wasn't looking for a woman like Grace. Her job alone eliminated her from the fling list, especially after Dani witnessed her arresting the girl at the drugstore. Besides, Grace was probably a forever type, and Dani wasn't staying in Pine Cone one minute longer than necessary.

Losing her ideal job at the Maryland Zoo because of budget cuts and low seniority had been an unexpected blow. Fortunately, she'd seen Trip Beaumont's ad online. Some varied animal experience couldn't hurt while she waited for the next perfect job up North. Rural life did not agree with her—too many bad memories, too much gossip, too little to do, and not nearly enough women to go around. The sooner she got out of here the better off she'd be. Keeping her distance from Grace would be a priority.

Dani concentrated on Harry and mentally clicked off each part of him as she checked them with her fingers. He didn't have any injuries she could detect by feel, but the poor bird was traumatized by his abandonment. Dani disliked people who got pets without knowing how to properly care for them and then shoved them aside when they proved inconvenient. At least Grace was concerned enough to bring Harry in, which spoke well of her, despite what Dani had seen at the drugstore.

"How did you do that? Where did you study?" Grace's eyes were wide and curiosity lit her face.

She felt a swell of pride and softened in response to Grace's awe. "I'm not really an avian vet, but you learn to deal with most animals in school and a variety of others in a zoo." How much longer would she have to dodge Grace's questions? Eventually, she'd get the hint that small talk was not Dani's forte and sharing life histories wasn't going to be part of their professional relationship.

"What was your favorite animal in the zoo? I know it's probably not PC to have favorites, but everybody does."

Semi-professional question, requiring no personal information. Dani could do this. "The giraffe, I guess."

"Why?"

"He's tall, obvi, and sort of regal, but he also seems happy all the time. Kids can get close and feed him without worrying he'll have a bad day and snap at them or worse. And I had a stuffed giraffe when I was a kid." *Why did I say that? No personal details, Wingate.* "Besides, who can argue with a tongue that long?" Damn, that was a bit out there. Her skin heated and she shifted back into work mode.

Grace chuckled. "I see."

Dani felt Grace's gaze follow her as she lifted Harry's wings, turned his head from side to side, and palpated his chest. "Has he been sick at all?" Grace was obviously not listening, her attention focused entirely on Dani's hands. "Hell—o?"

"What?" Grace shook her head and finally made eye contact, her eyes adjusting slowly.

Dani forced her attention back to Harry. Grace examined her too closely, and if encouraged, could potentially divine much more than Dani wanted to reveal. "I asked if Harry has been sick. Throwing up? Diarrhea?"

Grace shrugged. "Maybe a bit more poop than usual. I wasn't the one who took care of him, so I didn't really notice things like that."

"Do you cover him at night?"

Grace stared directly at Dani's mouth as she spoke, but Dani wasn't sure she'd heard the question. "Are you all right?" Dani brushed back the loose strands of hair falling across her forehead, and a heated flush crawled up her neck and ears. Grace followed the movements with her eyes. Grace was attracted to her. Normally that would've set Dani on a conquer-and-release mission, but not this woman, this *cop*, and not in this town. "Grace?"

"Uh-huh."

"I'd like to keep Harry overnight to conduct a more thorough examination and possibly run some blood tests."

"Sure." Grace eased into the room, and Harry launched toward her head. She ducked and back-stepped behind the door again. "Can you figure out why he hates me?"

Dani shrugged. "I deal with physical conditions, not mental ones, but he is seriously hating on you."

"If you can't help, I'll probably have to get rid of him. It wouldn't be healthy for us to cohabitate the way things are."

"Maybe we'll figure it out." *We'll figure it out*? What the hell was the matter with her? Choosing the right words was everything. Women like Grace—small town, big plans—were far too prone to hear a promise where none was intended. "I mean I'll do my best." After all, she was a professional and prided herself on being a problem solver. Her ego demanded that she try.

"Thanks." Grace started toward the front door. "By the way, are you going to Trip's cookout on Saturday?"

"Doubt it. I don't know anybody."

Grace's broad smile transformed her face, and her cheeks colored. "Well, Dr. Wingate, you'll meet plenty of folks there. That's the idea of a get-together, along with keeping in touch with folks you already know. The entire local sisterhood will be there, and it's a larger community than you'd think for a town our size. Will you come?"

Dani swallowed hard, her throat dry from the unwanted attraction. "Probably not." The last thing she needed to do was encourage Grace. It wouldn't be fair to either of them.

Grace reached to touch her arm, but Dani stepped back. "I *really* hope to see you there. In the meantime, guess our paths will cross at the B and B. Gotta run. Meeting some friends at the river." And after providing more information than necessary, Grace left.

Dani enjoyed watching Grace's movements from the clinic door to her car—the swing of her round hips, which Dani chose to believe was for her benefit; the casual flip of hair off her collar, another flirtatious habit; and a friendly wave to a passerby. She'd never seen a woman in such an unattractive, drab uniform look so sexy and feminine. And she was an absolute sucker for femmes.

Chapter Five

G race rested her pounding head in her hand. Why had she drunk so much wine at the river with Clay and Trip last night? She took another bite of a ham biscuit and prayed it would absorb the bitter taste in her mouth. She chased the food with coffee and forced a smile as River Hemsworth came into the dining room and eyed the pastry platter. Despite her head, her duty as a representative of the B and B forced her to sound cheerful and welcoming. "You should try one. MJ's cinnamon rolls are not to be missed."

"If they taste half as good as they smell, I'm in serious trouble." River placed one of the generously sized buns, oozing icing on all sides, onto a small china plate and turned, scanning the room.

"Please join me." Grace motioned toward the empty chair across from her. "Unless you're less of a morning person than I am and prefer to be alone."

"Not at all. Thank you for the invitation." She glanced at Grace's uniform and quickly back down at her plate.

"Don't let the uniform scare you off. I'm really quite docile."

"You were very helpful and not at all scary yesterday." River's cheeks flushed a lovely shade of pink. "It's just...you're so...I better shut up before I sound prejudiced and uncivilized."

"It's okay. I've heard the gamut. 'You're too cute, too sexy, too feminine, too nice, blah blah blah to be a police officer.' No offense taken."

"I imagine you have." River sipped her coffee and hummed with approval.

"How is your head this morning?"

"Excuse me?"

"Where you bumped it on the steering wheel."

"Oh. Fine. MJ was kind enough to give me an ice pack yesterday. That really helped."

"Good." Grace studied her. "It doesn't even show."

River smiled and forked a small bite of the pastry into her mouth and groaned. "Hmm, you weren't kidding. These are deadly. So yummy."

"Hmm, yes. Yummy indeed." Grace could barely whisper the words. The view over River's shoulder had sucked the breath from her lungs. Dani stood by the serving table pouring coffee into a paper cup. She was totally wearing the hell out of those jeans, and the plaid shirt made Grace drool. Dani glanced in her direction shyly and then left.

River turned to follow Grace's gaze. "I was talking about the pastry, not tall, dark, and handsome over by the coffee pot."

Grace laughed. "You saw that, huh?"

"Was that your attempt at subtlety?" River smiled and took another bite of the pastry.

"Maybe I need more practice." Grace sighed.

"Do you know her?"

"I wouldn't say I *know* her." Grace leaned forward, holding her coffee cup between both hands, and spinning it on the saucer. "But I'd like to. That's Dani Wingate. She's the new veterinarian at Trip's clinic."

"Well, she's super cute." River's eyes glazed over for a second, and Grace tried to decide if it was from the sugary pastry, how cute Dani was, or if she was thinking about something else. "This is the best cinnamon roll I've ever had."

"I warned you." Grace laughed.

"Does MJ make these every morning?"

"Thankfully, no. If she did, I'd be as big as this table."

"Do you...do you live at the B and B?" River seemed almost shy about asking Grace anything personal. "I don't mean to pry. I blame it on the sugar rush."

"If you don't ask personal questions around here, you'll be tagged as an outsider for sure. You can ask me anything. Everybody's life is an open book in this town. I own the B and B, but I live in the cottage out back." Grace motioned with her thumb over her shoulder. "I took over the place from my parents."

"Wow, you're a police officer and you run a B and B? When do you sleep?"

"I probably wouldn't if it weren't for MJ. She keeps everything going smoothly, and I get to eat breakfast and dinner here every day. That sounds like I get all the benefits. Don't tell her I said that, or we'll be renegotiating terms."

"Well, it's a beautiful place. Very charming and inviting."

"I hope you don't feel pressured to say that because I'm armed."

River laughed. "Not at all. Wait. Dani is staying here? At your B and B? My brain is finally waking up."

"Yes," Grace said cautiously, not sure where River was headed.

"So, you get to see Dani coming and going every day?"

"She just moved in. When she took the job, she was staying in a hotel a few miles outside of town, according to MJ. But yes, I'm sure it'll be torture going forward now that I've met her. Thanks for pointing that out," Grace said.

"I'm so sorry."

They both laughed.

Grace waited until River finished her cinnamon roll and coffee before scooting her chair back. "Guess I better get to work. I have a boss too."

"I don't suppose you know where I could get a rental car?"

"The closest rental office is in Savannah."

"Oh," River said.

"But I think they might have a loaner you could use at Cahill's garage, where Clay took your car."

"Really? I'm supposed to meet the Realtor today to go over my aunt's property. I suppose I could call her and see if she'd pick me up—"

"I don't think that'll be necessary. I'm sure Clay can find something." Grace finished her final sip of coffee. "I can drop you off on my way if you like."

"If it's no trouble."

"None at all. Then you'll have a chance to see Clay again."

River's face flushed bright pink. "I suppose I need some lessons in subtlety too." River followed Grace toward the door.

"Heightened observational skills are part of my job."

"Noted."

Grace turned partway to look at River, and she had a quizzical look on her face. "Something you want to ask, River?"

"So, you know Clay well?"

"We've been close since high school. She and Trip are my best friends."

River sighed and suddenly couldn't meet Grace's eyes. "Is she single?"

"Yes." Grace could tell by the way River fidgeted with her handbag strap that she had other questions, but maybe wasn't ready to ask them. River Hemsworth didn't seem like the kind of woman who beat around the bush for long.

Grace gave River the nickel commentary on the town as she drove toward the garage. She had a feeling if River stuck around the two of them would become friends. It would be great to have another femme to talk to. She dropped River in the garage parking lot and sped away before Clay made it to her car. If Clay didn't see her face, maybe she wouldn't know Grace was purposely putting River in her path, just like she and Trip had agreed yesterday at Mosquito Alley. Besides, Clay had a fancy Italian motorcycle that she adored, all black and chrome badass with some fancy name. She could loan River her truck.

Grace was fixing her second cup of coffee at the station when Clay badgered Patsy into putting her through to Grace. "You know we don't have rental cars, Grace Booker." Clay's tone said she wasn't nearly as upset as she wanted Grace to believe.

"The woman needed a car, Clay. You have two vehicles. You should at least try to be a full-service business. And invite her to the night market. She's new in town." Clay hung up before Grace could say more. Clay and River would work it out. Grace was too busy with arrangements for this evening's market to play full-time matchmaker.

❖

Dani searched for a parking spot near the Pine Cone Diner for lunch and finally stopped on the street behind a truck with a hound dog sitting in the open bed and black smoke belching from its tailpipe. A group of men smoking cigarettes watched a deputy release the windshield wiper of Trip's vet truck with a slap to secure the ticket she just wrote. The deputy, definitely not femme Grace Booker, rested her hand on the holstered gun at her hip for a moment shaking her head as if Trip's truck had somehow personally offended her.

Everything about the scenario chafed—polluting the environment, endangering a dog not properly secured in a truck, and a cop with an attitude, just like the authoritarians who'd harassed the residents in her low-income housing neighborhood as a child. One year in this town tops, less if another decent zoo job opened. She hoped something materialized before she lost her mind or started drawling her words.

She walked toward the diner and frowned at the memory of her newest patient, not a hound dog or a farm animal, but an exotic bird with health challenges. The owner, to her surprise, was the proprietor of the B and B where she was staying, and very easy on the eyes. But Grace already had three strikes against her on Dani's scorecard. She was obviously unqualified to care for her parrot, she was a cop, and she'd admitted never wanting to leave Pine Cone—unlike Dani whose hopes and dreams, along with most of her possessions, awaited her in a storage unit in Baltimore.

Dani pushed Grace from her mind and entered the diner. Too many people crowded the tiny space, their voices competing, reminding her of the nightly shouting matches in the apartment high-rise of her youth. And the décor, if it could truly be called decorative, consisted of antique cups, saucers, and coffee pots on shelves, and pictures of livestock tacked to the walls, all covered with a thin layer of dust. In the civilized world, this place would fail a health inspection and be closed as a public hazard. She turned to leave. Contracting a disease from an unclean restaurant occupied last place on her list of new things to try. She should've eaten Mary Jane's semi-healthy breakfast before rushing out this morning, but Grace had been eyeballing her like a tasty cinnamon roll causing an unwelcome spike in her hormones.

"There's a spot at the end of the counter," a waitress yelled and pointed to the far side of the room.

"Never mind." Dani held onto the door, but everyone stopped talking and stared as if leaving was a social faux pas. "Well, okay." She folded to the pressure, slowly released the door handle, and wound her way through the throng of people to the vacant barstool.

"Hey, everybody, this is Danielle Wingate, Trip's new vet," the waitress, whose nametag read Jolene, called out.

Jolene, the town crier Brenda warned her about. Great. Dani hated being in the spotlight for any reason. "It's Dani," she barely whispered and covered her face with the menu.

"I was beginning to think you were never coming in. What can I get you, darling?"

Dani held the menu firmly in front of her, refusing to make eye contact or encourage conversation with the brash stranger. "Coffee."

Jolene placed a finger on the edge of the menu and slowly lowered it, forcing Dani to look at her. "Didn't quite catch that. Did you say coffee?"

Dani nodded.

"Something to eat?" She smiled and warmth lit her face.

Dani perused the offerings for something that required high heat and was hard to mess up. "Can I still get breakfast?"

"All day long." Jolene cocked her hip against the edge of the counter.

"Special, please, wheat toast instead of biscuit."

"Gotcha." Jolene turned around and shouted toward the kitchen. "Special breakfast, deep six the biscuit, lay on the wheat."

Now that the whole town knew who she was and what she ordered for breakfast, they resumed talking in low tones that quickly built to a loud drone. She pulled her cell phone from her back jeans pocket to ward off any unwelcome conversation, pleased with the two bars of signal strength. She searched Google for lesbian bars in the area and watched the color wheel of doom spin.

"Is this seat taken?"

Dani recognized Grace Booker's low, sexy voice and the combination of sweet flowery perfume before she saw her, annoyed that she could already identify both. When she spotted the leg of Grace's uniform pants from the corner of her eye, she shifted on her stool to put distance between them but didn't answer. Grace attracted people and conversations like Dani repelled them and being near her raised the risk of more talk and sharing. Not good.

"Hi, Jolene, Diet Coke and a BLT with Duke's, please."

"Coming up, Sheriff."

Grace shook her head. "Still just a deputy."

"You'll always be the sheriff in my book." Jolene placed a Styrofoam cup of Coke and crushed ice in front of her.

Grace waited for the bubbles to settle before taking a healthy swig. "Oh my God. This is a lifesaver." She turned sideways to face Dani, her knees brushing Dani's thigh and producing a jolt of sensation. "Haven't seen you since the breakfast bar. Busy morning?"

Dani sucked in a quick breath at the contact and tried to parlay the unusual sound into a question. "So, what's Duke's?"

"Seriously? You *must* be a city girl. Duke's Mayonnaise. No self-respecting Southerner eats any sandwich without Duke's. What do folks put on sandwiches where you're from?"

"Baltimore and Hellman's."

Grace leaned in conspiratorially, and Dani caught another whiff of her delicious-smelling perfume, and her skin tingled. "Don't say that too loudly or you'll be run out of town."

If a job came with her exile, Dani would gladly run through the streets of Pine Cone declaring her love for everything above the Mason-Dixon Line. If only escape were that easy.

"How's Harry today?"

Dani fought the distraction of Grace's continued contact with her thigh. Grace was very touchy-feely, and that kind of person was too hard to figure out. Touch equaled sex for Dani. She pressed her knees together and refocused on Grace's question. "Seems okay." She finally glanced at Grace but looked away before they made eye contact. Her eyes were clearer today, and she looked rested and sounded more chipper, but Dani shouldn't be noticing any of those things.

As if somehow intuiting what Dani had been thinking, Grace said, "I should thank you for a great night's sleep."

Jolene placed their food on the counter at the same time. "What? The two of you slept together? Already?"

Dani slapped her napkin over her mouth to stop a spurt of coffee.

"No, Jolene, we did not," Grace said. "She kept Dirty Harry at the clinic overnight, and I finally got some peace and quiet."

"I like my version of the story better. I heard Karla dumped you for some redhead from North Carolina who drives a pickup. Redheads are always trouble. What are you going to do about

Harry? He hates you." Without waiting for a reply, Jolene sashayed to the other end of the counter, pouring coffee, and talking all the way.

"Thanks for cutting her off." Dani nodded and stirred a glob of something that vaguely resembled oatmeal but was whiter. "What's this?" Grace laughed again, and it vibrated into Dani where they touched, producing warmth and discomfort. She scooted farther away until her ass barely clung to the barstool.

"Grits, a delicious Southern delicacy. You really should try them."

Dani spooned the strange mess to the side of her plate. "Hard pass."

"Jolene, an order of hash browns for Dani please." Grace slid Dani's plate closer and scraped the grits onto hers. "Never met a grit I didn't like. It's an acquired taste."

The way Grace took care of her, removing the offending food from her plate and ordering hash browns for her, both pleased and annoyed Dani. She wanted to know things about Grace besides her preference for grits and propensity for touching but filed her curiosity under not a good idea and dug into her eggs, which were surprisingly good. "Weather report says rain this afternoon." Lame, but keeping things simple and impersonal was necessary around Grace.

"You weren't listening to WPCG radio, were you?"

"Not sure. My clock radio alarm—"

"Yep, Cloudy McClain. Don't believe a word he says. Last winter he predicted only a few clouds one day, and we got over five inches of snow, the first significant snowfall in these parts in twenty years. You'd think he would at least be in the ballpark."

"Thus, the Cloudy nickname?"

"Exactly. Folks around here are unforgiving about flagrant infidelity, crops, livestock, and weather. Trust me, it's going to be hotter than a goat's butt in a pepper patch all day."

Dani muffled a chuckle in her napkin. "Thanks for the tip, but back up. Flagrant infidelity?"

Grace crooked her finger for Dani to come closer, but they were already too close. She felt the heat from Grace's body tumbling and stirring her insides. She held her ground, but Grace leaned in slightly and said, "Just between you and me, there's probably more infidelity in this town per capita than in the entire state of Georgia, but if you keep it on the DL, nobody bothers you. Southerners take pride in their public reputations."

"I see. And how's the dating pool around here?"

Jolene slapped a saucer of hash browns in front of Dani. "Here you go, sport. If you're asking about available women of your persuasion, there's a nice selection, but—"

"Seriously, Jolene? We're having a conversation." Grace shooed her away. "Don't you have other customers?"

"None as interesting as you two, all cozy and getting to know each other."

Dani stood and dug into her pocket for some cash, her face burning. She didn't want the whole town thinking she and Grace had something going. In fact, she didn't want these people thinking about her at all. Grace touched her arm and heat penetrated before she pulled away and slapped her money on the counter.

"Don't leave, Dani. Jolene has a big mouth, but she's harmless."

"Maybe, but I'm—"

"You're a private person. I get that." Grace followed her toward the door but stopped at the checkout to pay. "Hold up a minute."

But Dani couldn't wait a second longer. She exited the diner, eager to put distance between her and Grace, and noticed a man with ragged clothes standing near the door watching each person come out. A baseball cap pulled low over his forehead shielded his eyes, and weathered lines on his face hinted at middle age. She pulled a twenty from her pocket and slipped it into his hand.

"Bless you," the man said as she crossed the street to her car.

"Wait." Grace fast-walked toward her and stopped beside her car, eyes wide. "Wow. We can see you coming for miles in this thing, midnight blue, Acura SUV. Won't find another one like this around here. Cool."

Dani shook her head at the outdated slang. "Need something, Grace?"

"You asked about the dating pool."

"Yeah?"

"Like I mentioned about the cookout, we have a lot more lesbians in town than you'd think, and there's also a contingent of straight and married women who'd take you on just because they're bored. You won't have any trouble amusing yourself."

"What about you, Grace?" Damn, that sounded like she was asking if Grace was available, which she didn't want to do, but might've been and didn't want to be quite so obvious about. "I mean, are you able to amuse yourself?"

"Amusement isn't what I'm looking for, but is often exactly what I find," Grace said.

"Still pining over Karla?"

"Hardly. We both knew what we were getting into." She gave Dani a crooked smile. "So, you've been asking about me, Doc? I don't remember mentioning a name when I told you about my ex."

Rookie mistake. "Brenda might've mentioned it." Totally believable. "If you're not happy with your dating results, maybe you should adjust your expectations."

"I do all right, but thanks for your concern. You'll probably have more luck," Grace said.

"Why's that?"

"I get the feeling we're not after the same things."

"Probably." Grace was definitely right, but Dani couldn't pretend she wasn't a little disappointed. Grace was physically attractive, with only a few negative traits Dani was willing to overlook in the short-term, but no amount of Southern charm could convince her to abandon her dreams and settle in a rural area like Pine Cone. She needed the pace and variety of the city.

"Well…I enjoyed having lunch with you. Next time, I'll give you a rundown on the townsfolk, if you'd like. They all have a story, and everybody has an opinion about everybody else's story."

"What's the general opinion about Grace Booker?"

"I'm impressed, Doc. See, this is how it's done, back and forth, questions and answers. That's how we get to know each other." Grace studied her for a second before answering. "They'd probably say I'm ill-suited to be a sheriff's deputy because I'm too kind and don't like to fight, and I should've been a social worker or nurse instead." She shifted the heavy-looking belt around her waist as if to emphasize the weight of her words.

"Do you agree?"

"Sometimes. And what about Danielle Wingate? What do people say about you?"

"What you see is what you get." Dani unlocked her car door. "You can come by the clinic and check on Harry anytime."

"Thanks."

Dani got in her car and rolled down the window, the heat inside already like a pizza oven. Grace offered her hand, unusual under the circumstances, but Dani was learning that touch was important to Grace and dangerous for Dani. She shook Grace's hand quickly to be polite, but the brief contact was enough to set her insides roiling and her mind spinning through a list of possible encounters that could never happen. She sped off toward the clinic, willing away the lingering sensations and the desires they stirred.

Grace stared at Dani's car until it disappeared at the edge of town, sparks from their handshake still shooting up her arm like static from a summer lightning storm. No doubt about it, she was attracted to Dani, but Dani was a bad bet in the future department. A familiar question tumbled over in Grace's mind. Was she willing to get her heart broken again by a woman who was not long for her small part of the world? Her pain from the last time wasn't fresh, but it still lingered making her wary.

Dani had been stingy with any personal information at lunch, fueling Grace's curiosity. Maybe Dani's city upbringing just made her overly cautious. Jolene's suggestive comments embarrassed her, something Grace hadn't expected from a city woman. But she'd seen another side of Dani when she slipped money to Beetle Bledsoe, the homeless town drunk, on her way out of the diner. Grace doubted Dani would've helped Beetle if she'd known anyone was watching. What did that say about the kind of person she was or about her past?

Grace wanted to know what made Dani tick, about Dani's past, her family, her likes and dislikes, and how she ended up in Pine Cone. Everything. The process required time, and she'd tread carefully, probe discreetly, and hold her heart in reserve for now. But Dani Wingate might prove a challenge in the sharing department, a walking cautionary tale in every aspect.

She glanced down Main Street and saw Trip jogging in her direction. "Hold up there, hoss. You could get heat stroke. Where's the fire?"

"Sorry. I was looking at your car. I thought it was my stalker until I noticed the scratch on the fender. When are you going to let Clay fix that?"

"I haven't had time. I had a new officer I needed to drive around for orientation, then…well, other stuff happened. I'll probably get it over to the garage later this week. Anyway, what's this about a stalker?"

"Your new cop—"

"Officer Grant?"

"Yeah, I definitely think Grant is stalking me."

"Stalking you?"

"More than twenty parking tickets in the past two weeks."

"You poor thaang." Grace drawled the word just enough to let Trip know she didn't feel any sympathy at all. She'd warned Trip several times about her parking habits.

Trip glared at her sarcastic tone. "It's not funny. It's police harassment."

"Why don't you try parking in a legal spot?"

"Grace."

"What do you want me to do? Tell Officer Grant she shouldn't enforce the law because you're my friend?"

"You can explain that I'm usually on important business. I have emergencies and...did you say *she*? Does she play on our team? Is she hot?"

"Down, girl. I've been trying to get the town council to allot money for a drug detection dog for the past five years, but they're expensive. I got a two-for-one deal with Officer Grant. She owns a detection dog she trained personally, and I need for them to stay. What I don't need is Fast Break bird-dogging her, breaking her heart, and running her out of town."

"I was just going to suggest you bring her to the cookout this weekend. If she knows how charming I can be, maybe she'll stop slapping tickets on my truck every time she sees it." Trip wiggled her brows suggestively.

Grace frowned. "I'm pretty sure she's a lesbian, so I'll see if she wants to come to the cookout so she can meet some people. But *you* stay away from her."

Trip waved off Grace's last comment and opened the door to the diner. "See you this weekend. Oh, and go check on your damned bird. I caught Brenda sharing her ham biscuit with him this morning. If those two bond, I'm going to let Essie roast him for dinner."

"Headed there now." Grace smiled broadly, gave Trip a mock salute, and rushed to her car. The radio was quiet and the street mostly deserted because of the noon heat, so it was the perfect time to check on Harry. Doctor's orders, nothing to do with Dani Wingate. She ignored the little voice in her head snickering at the fib and sped toward the clinic.

"I surrender, Deputy." Brenda raised her hands when Grace entered the front door. "If you're going to arrest me, please search me thoroughly. I could use a good groping." Her throaty laugh descended into a hacking cough as Grace headed to the exam area.

"One of our new techs is back there with Dani right now working on an injured shepherd. Her name's Michelle, the tech not the shepherd, and she's gussied up like she's at a beauty pageant. Her britches are so tight her legs look like cased sausages. Lord knows what she's up to besides work."

Grace kept walking, unwilling to engage in Brenda's speculation about Michelle's motives, but noted her disappointment that Dani wasn't alone. No way around it now. She followed Dani to the clinic to spend more time with her. She wouldn't deny it, and she couldn't blame Michelle for disrupting a foolish plan she knew nothing about. Maybe they were sniffing after the same quarry. "Dani, it's Grace." She announced her presence because Dani didn't strike her as the type who liked surprises.

"Room three, near the back," someone, not Dani, replied.

Grace peeked through the observation square in the door and saw Dani and Michelle hunched over a large German shepherd. Michelle's T-shirt plunged just this side of indecent, long blond hair hung loosely around her face, and her strong perfume wafted under the door and into the hallway. She wouldn't attract any of the local boys wearing that fragrance because her smell would interfere with their dog's scent-tracking abilities and scare off any game. Maybe Brenda was right and Michelle wasn't hunting male prey. Grace shook the thought from her mind along with a twinge of discomfort.

She returned her attention to the scene inside the examining room as Dani explained the procedure for treating the shepherd's injury. If Michelle asked questions, Dani described what she was doing and why the process was necessary. She was kind, and her tone patient, unlike the clipped exchanges they'd shared earlier at the diner. Where animals were involved, Dani was caring, devoted, and communicative, but her view of humans had seemingly been skewed along the way making her suspicious and untrusting. Grace felt a desire to help change Dani's opinion.

Michelle edged closer to Dani, and Grace noticed the right side of the dog's coat was shiny with fresh blood. Dani held a needle with stitching in one gloved hand and a syringe in the other. She lowered the syringe toward the dog, and Grace looked away. She didn't tolerate pain well, hers or any other creature's. "I'll just wait out here."

"Harry is in room one, right next door, if you want to visit while I finish up. I'll join you in a few minutes," Dani said.

She turned toward Harry's room, leaving the shepherd in Dani's capable hands and Dani too close to Michelle. Grace did a peekaboo into Harry's room and watched him enjoying a feast of orange and seeds. He hopped from the food dish to the higher perch and back, twisted his head around, and squawked new, tamer words. He looked nothing like the anxious bird she'd brought in, except for the bald patches on his body.

"What do you think?"

Grace jumped away from the door, and Dani grabbed her waist just above her utility belt to keep her from falling backward. Dani's solid body pressed into hers, and excitement scuttled across her skin. She might've actually wilted a little before Dani released her.

"Jumpy for a cop, aren't you?"

"You shouldn't sneak up on someone like that, especially when she's armed." Dani grimaced and the tiny space between her top teeth looked so sexy Grace almost swooned. She reluctantly returned her attention to Harry. "He seems better."

"I took blood and checked for contagious diseases, anemia, parasites, organ failure, basically everything, and didn't find any problems. He was dehydrated, but that's better today."

"How do you take blood from a bird exactly? Stupid question, I guess, but I've never really thought about it."

"Same way you do in a human. Needle in, blood out." Her grin widened.

She enjoyed teasing Grace, and that was just fine—at least she had a humorous side. "Cute, Dr. Wingate. Maybe I should be more specific. Where do you draw blood from a bird? And please don't say veins."

"Neck or wings, but I prefer the feet for easier access, and the bird tolerates it well. Shall we go in?" Dani opened the door and held it for Grace, the little courtesy a welcome change from her speedy retreat from the diner.

"Good morning, Harry," Grace said. "How are you?"

"Five-O," Harry shrieked, bobbed up and down, and furiously beat his wings. "Watch your six."

"Harry, what's wrong?" Grace moved closer, and he flapped harder.

"Grace, why don't you step away?" Dani edged in front of her. "Harry, it's okay. She's not going to hurt you."

"Of course I'm not going to hurt him. I don't understand why he behaves like this every time I'm around."

Dani glanced at her, suspicion oozing from her eyes. "There has to be a reason."

"Well, it's not *that*. I'd never hurt anyone or anything, intentionally."

While they chatted, Harry flailed, feathers and dust swirling into a mini tornado around the small cage. "Police. Run. Po-lice."

"You should probably wait outside so I can calm him down."

"Dani, I don't want you to think—"

"Please, Grace, just go."

She shot Harry a parting glare. Now she understood how a wrongly accused suspect felt. "I'll wait in the hall, but we need to talk before I leave."

Michelle swished by Grace on her way out, giving her a pointed stare before joining Dani in the room with Harry. Soothing voices mingled with Harry's screeches until they eventually tapered off and quieted. When they exited Harry's room, Michelle touched Dani's arm. "Want me to stay?"

Dani shook her head and waited until she walked away before turning to Grace. "You wanted to talk?"

"Seriously? You can't possibly believe I abuse that poor bird."

"I don't know what to think, Grace. I can't find any organic reason for his behavior, but he definitely dislikes you. I don't believe it's a good idea to take him home when he has such a bad reaction to you. It's not healthy."

"You might want to clear keeping him with Trip. She's anxious to get rid of him before Brenda turns him into the Beaumont Clinic mascot." Grace hesitated before asking her next question, unsure of her motives. "What if you come by my place one evening and check it out?"

"What good would that do?" Dani asked.

"Maybe you'll spot something that's offensive to him or birds in general that I'm not aware of. And you are right next door."

"That wouldn't account for what happened just now."

"True." She could let Dani find Harry another home, cut her losses, and celebrate, but having Dani believe she was an irresponsible pet owner set her teeth on edge. "Please, help me figure out what's going on with him." She might not want the bird, but she cared, particularly if she'd inadvertently done something wrong.

"I'm not a bird psychologist, but maybe he associates you with his missing mother. Leave him another day, and I'll watch him closely, see how he responds to other people. He seems okay with Michelle."

"Of course he does," Grace mumbled.

"Sorry?"

"Whatever you think." Michelle was the one who should be caged, if only for Dani's protection and Grace's peace of mind, not that she had any more right to Dani's attentions.

"I'll see what I can arrange," Dani said.

"Great. I'll be at the night market this evening, but any time after that should be fine." She stomped out of the clinic toward her car without acknowledging Brenda's parting comment, annoyed with her own ungracious thoughts and possessive behavior over a woman she didn't even know. Damn it. She wasn't some clichéd small-town girl who lusted after the first attractive stranger who came along. She'd had that heartbreak before and wasn't anxious to go back. She simply wanted to figure out Harry's problem... and spend a little more time with an interesting woman. Nothing complicated about either.

CHAPTER SIX

Dani gasped on her predawn run, sucking in hot, sticky air. She checked her watch, only two more minutes of the sameness of flowers and old buildings along Main Street. She hadn't passed another soul, unless she counted a purple Siamese cat that was probably a sleep-deprived hallucination. To distract from the boredom, she'd relived her too-easy hookup in a Savannah club last night. The hour-and-a-half drive for companionship wasn't ideal, but it kept her from totally losing her mind in a town with too few options or thinking about Grace, a woman she could not get involved with for reasons too numerous to count. She glanced at her watch again, slowed, and finally stopped at the steps of the B and B to cool down.

She stretched her right leg against the bottom step, and an image of the woman she'd chosen last night emerged—soft, curvy body; red hair that filtered through her fingers like silk; eyes the color of wet moss; and a bubbly personality—a lot like Grace. She froze mid-stretch. No. The woman was a lot like any number of other women in the world. Her choice of sexual partner had nothing to do with Grace. She slumped onto the steps. Had she unconsciously chosen this woman *because* of the similarities? She hadn't imagined Grace in place of the woman, whose name escaped her.

After a second of panic, she decided so what? Nothing wrong with a healthy fantasy. What was harmful was thinking about Grace too often, wondering what being with her was like, or wishing for things that couldn't happen. Dani was a one-and-done kind of woman, and Grace deserved more. Dani pulled the tail of her T-shirt up and wiped the sweat from her face. What did Grace look like under her drab brown and beige uniform? She jumped from the steps and almost bumped into someone walking toward her.

"You were seriously gone," Grace said. "I called you twice."

"Sorry. Just finished a run. I zone out sometimes. Did you need something?" Seeing Grace in the flesh after fantasizing about her only seconds before seemed weird and caused her body to heat even more. The fresh scent of recently showered skin and lightly fragranced perfume reached her and she almost moaned aloud. Grace would probably taste as good as she smelled. *Stop it, Wingate.*

"On my way to breakfast before my tour." She paused, possibly giving Dani an opportunity to ask to join her, but she didn't take the bait. "Anything interesting on your run?"

"Does hallucinating a purple Siamese cat count?"

Grace grinned. "Not a hallucination."

"Seriously? Who dyes a cat?"

"Doreen Divine-Dot."

Dani shook her head. "Am I suffering heat stroke or are you messing with me? Who has a name like that?"

"The same person who dyes a cat purple. Doreen Divine is our local florist. She married Bob Dot thirty years ago and insisted on hyphenating her last name. They call their shop the Divine-Dot Florist. Original, huh? She's a great florist though, if you ever need flowers, and she's a responsible pet owner. She uses organic food dyes to color Snowball."

Dani shook her head. "Only in a small town. Does Snowball come in any other colors?"

"You'll have to wait and find out with the rest of us. Doreen bathes and colors her every Saturday so she'll look good for church on Sunday."

"Unbelievable." Dani started toward the house.

Grace placed her hand lightly on Dani's arm. "Would you join me for breakfast?"

"No time." Dani's skin came alive under Grace's fingers, a physical invitation to stay but an emotional warning to move, quickly.

"We always make time for the things that matter."

Grace was exactly right, but Dani couldn't afford to let Grace matter to her at this point in her life. Her career and future depended on keeping her eye on her goals. Her physical attraction to Grace was strong but irrelevant. She needed to establish a firm boundary. "Grace, I—"

"Did you have a good evening? I saw you heading out of town on I-95. Savannah?"

She couldn't discuss her personal life with Grace, especially not her sex life. That would open a door that could only lead to pain for both, and while she wanted to keep Grace at a distance, she had no desire to hurt her. "I really have to go. I'm running late, and Trip and I are working together today." She didn't wait for Grace to respond but could feel her eyes on her as she climbed the steps. She could easily seduce Grace, but it would be so unfair. Dani only went after women who were at the same place she was, and Grace was definitely not there. A sharp twist in her gut registered her disappointment.

Dani's tight ass looked yummy in Lycra shorts as she climbed the stairs of the B and B. Her legs were lean but muscular and rippled with definition Grace could never hope to achieve. Dani had lowered her T-shirt and Grace got a whiff of her exercise sweat, a scent track Grace couldn't help but follow. What was happening to her?

Why had she asked Dani about her visit to Savannah? She'd crossed a line. Despite Dani's reluctance to talk about anything personal, Grace sensed protectiveness in her tone instead of rejection. Maybe she should listen to Dani. If you listened, people told you who they were when you first met. Maybe Dani was warning her against getting too close, but why?

Grace's body slowly cooled and she joined Mary Jane in the kitchen. "Smells good in here. Need any help? I've got a few minutes."

Hands covered with lard and flour, Mary Jane glanced up from her biscuit making. "Are you okay?"

"Sure." Grace quickly turned and reached for a Diet Coke from the fridge.

"You're flushed. Not getting sick, are you? There's a nasty bug going around."

"No, MJ. I'm good."

"Wouldn't have anything to do with our new guest, would it? The one who just came in from a run? The one you were sniffing around on the steps?"

"I was not sniffing. Don't get any wrong ideas in your head."

Mary Jane kept kneading the biscuit dough. "It's not me who's getting a wrong idea. Danielle seems like a nice woman, accomplished, with a decent job, but she's not staying."

"How do you know? Has she said something?"

"Doesn't need to. I see the light in her eyes when she talks about her life in the city and her job at the zoo. She can't wait to leave."

Grace clutched the Coke bottle tighter. She'd told herself the same thing, but hearing the words aloud made the situation more real. "I'm aware, MJ." She gave Mary Jane a hug from behind. "Thanks for worrying about me, but it's really not necessary. Are the other new guests okay? Jamie and Ms. Hemsworth?"

"Jamie is settling in nicely, but we're going to need more air freshener for her room if she stays much longer. Little Petunia has a real problem. I had to ask Jamie to keep her out of the kitchen and dining room during meal times. She'll put the guests off their food. River checked out yesterday and moved over to Eve's place until her car is fixed. She's anxious to get back to her life in the city too."

Clay would be sorry to hear that. "Sure I can't help before I go?"

"Nope. Everything's under control, but I got the bank statement yesterday. You could balance the checkbook and pay the bills when you have a chance. You know I hate numbers."

"Will do."

Mary Jane gave her a quick glance. "And grab a ham biscuit. Can't work on an empty stomach."

Grace lifted one of the ham-stuffed biscuits from the platter, held the flaky delicacy out from her uniform shirt, and bent over to take a bite. She moaned as she savored the chewy, salty, floury goodness. "These are the best biscuits in the county. I don't care what Bud says."

"Where do you think he got his recipe for the diner?" She nudged Grace's shoulder. "Any news from your parents lately? I just remembered today is their wedding anniversary."

"Last I heard they were still in Thailand, working on a building project, doing exactly what they love."

"Do you miss them, honey?" Mary Jane stopped working the dough and pierced her with one of her tell-me-the-truth stares.

"Sometimes. You know how it is. Always miss what you don't have, but I wouldn't interfere with them living the life they love any more than they'd interfere with me."

"This question may come a little late in the piece, but do you ever wish they'd been more traditional parents, more homebodies?"

She and Mary Jane had talked about most things through the years but never touched on her folks' parenting style. She rolled the question over in her mind, checking for flaws in her logic. "I don't believe so. We traveled the world working in underprivileged areas, and I learned a lot about people, their motivations, and things that really matter in life. And I always knew my parents loved me. So, I'm good with all that."

"I'm glad. You turned out to be quite an exceptional woman." Mary Jane winked and nodded toward the door. "Now, you better get going. I don't want the sheriff to fire you."

"Right. How about saving future heavy conversations for evening cocktails and not first thing in the morning?" She scarfed up the rest of her biscuit, washed it down with Coke, and then grabbed another before heading for her patrol car. "See you later, MJ."

Grace checked in with the sheriff at the station before beginning her rounds with a quiet walk down Main Street. She enjoyed the intimacy of small-town policing where she knew everybody, helped with more quality-of-life issues, and worked few serious crimes. She'd made her way to the center of town in front of the library when she spotted Beetle Bledsoe arguing with the librarian.

"I've told you not to come in here when you're liquored up, Beetle. Now get out. And go by the shelter for a shower and some clean clothes before you come back. You reek." The stocky man urged Beetle out the door and onto the steps, but he resisted.

Beetle shook his fist with his usual drunken flare, emphasizing a point but not really threatening. "You got no cause to shove a man out of the library. I'm seeking knowledge."

Grace walked up behind Beetle before he realized she was there. She looked toward the librarian to make sure he was okay and, when he nodded, she focused on Beetle. "Hey, man. What's going on today?" She lightly touched his elbow and helped him navigate the steps to the sidewalk.

"Nothing, Grace, 'cept I might be a little tiny bit drunk." He raised a hand and spaced his thumb and forefinger apart slightly, squinting to get the proportion right.

"Remember what you asked me to do the next time I saw you drunk in public?"

He pushed a dirty John Deere tractor cap back on his head and scratched his forehead. "Prob'ly not right this minute."

"We'll talk about it on our walk to the station."

Beetle pulled away from her and squared off. "No. I ain't going to jail."

Grace let her hands fall unthreateningly to her side. "You're not going to jail per se, just taking a break."

He shoved Grace backward and wobbled away, but she regained her balance and caught him quickly, careful to steady him when she grabbed his belt and tugged. He swung at her, but she ducked, and folks from the library and other shops along Main gathered to watch the highlight of their day.

"Stop struggling, Beetle. This doesn't look good. I don't want to hurt you."

He swung again and connected with her ribs between the panels of her vest. The air gushed out of her lungs, and she took a minute to recover while Beetle staggered off. "That's it." She caught up to him, yanked his arms behind his back, and clicked the cuffs in place. "I tried to do this the easy way." Her car was at the other end of town, and she reached for her walkie-talkie, but before she could make the call, Jamie slid her patrol vehicle up to the sidewalk.

"Need a lift, boss?"

Grace handed Beetle off to Jamie and stood back while she carefully searched and placed him in the back seat. "Let him sleep it off. No charges."

"But I saw him hit you, Sarge. That's assault on a government official," Jamie said.

"He'd never do that if he wasn't drunk. When he sobers up, I'll talk to him."

"Okay. You're the boss." Jamie made a U-turn on Main and drove toward the station.

Grace brushed the front of her uniform, and when she looked up, Dani Wingate stood across the street staring at her, a mixture of anger and total disgust on her face. Grace started toward her, but before she could cross the street, Dani got in her fancy car and sped out of town in the direction of the vet clinic.

Great. She already had an attitude toward cops, and Grace's manhandling of Beetle probably hadn't softened her perception.

❖

"Dani, you here?"

"In the back," Dani said.

Trip opened the door to the laboratory where they did everything from nail clipping to anesthetizing for simple surgeries. "Should've known. I can follow Michelle's scent through the whole building." She stepped back, fanning the air with her hands. "Jeez, Michelle, I told you about wearing a ton of that crap to work. We'll have lawsuits coming out our backsides for traumatizing the animals. Go wash that mess off, right now."

Michelle huffed and rolled her eyes before strutting toward the restroom.

"Thanks for that," Dani said. "My eyes were starting to water. I felt bad for the animals."

"I like to run a relaxed but professional business. I told that girl when I hired her to leave that odor and her flirting at home. How's that going?"

Dani shrugged, unwilling to jeopardize Michelle's job because of her own discomfort.

"She obviously didn't listen to the first part of my advice, so I'm guessing she's been on the prowl and you just don't want to say." Trip patted Dani on the shoulder. "Never figured a Northern girl for tact and diplomacy."

"She's pretty good with clients, and I can handle myself. But that eau de awful perfume she bathes in has to go." The small Boston whose wound Dani had been checking sneezed in agreement before she lifted him off the table and put him back in his kennel.

Trip nodded toward the back door. "Let's take a walk and get some fresh air." She held the door for Dani, then led them toward the barn where the horses were stabled. "So, how are things going?"

"Fine."

Trip let the silence hang between them, but when Dani didn't say anything else, Trip prodded. "You're not much of a talker, are you?"

"If I have something to say."

"And you don't have anything to say other than fine? I hired you because of your extensive experience and great references. I'm asking you for an evaluation. The large animal part of the practice is my main interest, but the small animal clinic is the moneymaker. Any changes you'd recommend for efficiency and better care in that area? Any other equipment or supplies we need? Do we have enough staff? I value your professional opinion."

"Oh…you mean work things."

Trip stopped halfway to the barn. "Look, Dani, I like you, but I don't get involved in my employees' lives, unless they ask for advice. And it's obvious you're not asking. So yes, as a vet, any suggestions?"

Dani's shoulders relaxed and she felt less stressed as she answered. "It's a good clinic. You've got plenty of exam rooms in the main building and sufficient stalls in the barn. You could even expand if you wanted. Your equipment is top-of-the-line, and you're located conveniently to facilities in Savannah if you need a specialist. It's all good."

Trip smiled, nodded toward the barn, and started walking again. "Thanks. Do you have time to help me with a castration before you head out?"

"Sure." Dani collected the necessary equipment and followed Trip into the stall.

When the anesthesia buckled the knees of the six-month-old colt, Trip pushed him over, and Dani shoved the ten-inch surgery pad against his feet from the other side. The smoothly coordinated maneuver felt like they'd been working together for years. The rest of the surgery was quick and equally synchronized. Trip's technique was efficient and confident, handling this family pet as gently as she'd managed a show horse days before. She never cut corners or lost focus, and Dani admired her professionalism.

The colt slept soundly on his side, with Dani monitoring his vitals while Trip performed the routine surgery and then fed the medicine into his vein to wake him. Trip stepped back to wait for the moment they'd help the colt to his feet.

"So, are you going to come?"

Dani blinked up at her. "Sorry?"

"My cookout. Tomorrow. It's an annual thing. Lesbians from two states will be there, along with some of the gay-friendly community."

"I'll probably go to Savannah. You know, for the clubs and women."

"Grace will be at the cookout." The comment floated like a pleasant aroma waiting to settle. "Jolene at the diner said you two had a nice chat the other day."

Dani rolled her eyes. "We sat beside each other at the counter. Only seat in the place."

Trip raised her hands in surrender. "I'm just saying, she'll be there and she's good people. You couldn't do better if you're looking to make friends around here, and I hope you will. I'm only suggesting friendship because she's a close friend of mine, and I'm protective."

"Don't worry. Grace is safe. I'm not exactly the relationship type."

"Your loss, but that's probably a good decision. You likely see this job as a step in your career, so you wouldn't be right for her. But come to the cookout anyway. You'll know at least a few people—me, Grace, and Michelle. There'll be lots of women, and several of the clinic's best horse clients I'd like you to meet. Grace and I can introduce you around."

Dani shook her head. "Thanks for the offer though."

"My cookouts are a huge event. The Savannah crowd will all be here so the clubs are likely to be shy on prospects. Think about it?"

Dani nodded and started toward the clinic. "I better get back to work."

Chapter Seven

Grace took a quick shower after her shift then walked to the B and B for supper and to work on the books. She'd tried to convince Mary Jane that a B and B only provided bed and breakfast, not supper as well, but she argued cooking for everyone was as easy as cooking for just the two of them. Grace had given up the fight a year ago, and the B and B had been fully booked ever since.

The smell of Mary Jane's delicious meatloaf welcomed her when she opened the back door, and her stomach growled. She'd skipped lunch, using her meal break to check on Harry at the clinic. When she rounded the corner into the large eat-in kitchen, Mary Jane and Dani were the only ones at the table. "Where are the rest of our guests? Don't they like meatloaf?"

"Day trips, visiting, eating out, and dating." Mary Jane started to get up, but Grace waved her down.

"I've got it." She kissed Mary Jane's head, retrieved a place setting and cutlery from the china cabinet, and sat across from Dani. "How's it going?" She lobbed her query in no particular direction hoping the question might prompt Dani to comment, but she glanced up at Grace with something akin to distaste and kept eating. Dani had been almost nice this morning, but tonight the deep freeze was on again.

"I hope that sour look isn't about my food," Mary Jane said.

"No, ma'am. This is great." Dani offered a half-smile and returned to her meal again.

Mary Jane shrugged at Grace while she filled her plate. "I'm fine. Dani was just telling me about her challenges with that crazy bird of yours."

"He's not my bird." Grace crowded a lump of mashed potatoes between the meatloaf and green beans on her plate and ladled a generous helping of gravy in the middle. "I stopped by twice today to check on him, and both times he went psycho. Do you have any idea what's going on with him?"

Dani didn't look up. "Not really."

Dani hunched over her plate, irritation rolling off her, and Grace didn't understand why. Their morning chat hadn't been unpleasant, except for the part where she'd nosed into Dani's night out. Then she remembered. Dani had witnessed the scene with Beetle, and her expression had spoken loudly from across the street.

Mary Jane gave Grace a questioning look, and she shook her head. "Any other news?"

"I planted more flowers in the back garden to attract butterflies. You?"

"Beetle Bledsoe showed out at the library, and I had to take him in."

Dani shoveled a forkful of potatoes into her mouth and her teeth clamped on the tines.

"Did you do what he asked this time?" Mary Jane asked.

Dani suddenly looked up at Grace, her eyes searching, questioning.

"Not yet. He was too drunk to remember our conversation. Maybe tomorrow."

Dani swallowed her food and washed it down with sweet tea. "What did he ask you to do?"

Grace took a second to consider her response. Was it a violation of trust to divulge her promise to Beetle? And even if it wasn't, should she have to justify her official actions to a transient guest? On the other hand, maybe honest communication and transparency could change Dani's mind about her profession and alter her opinion of Grace. But which should take priority, the professional consideration or her personal one? "I'm not sure I should say."

"Why not?" Mary Jane asked. "He told everybody in town."

Grace could be generous with her own personal details, but her profession and moral code required her to be judicious with others. Still, Mary Jane made a valid point. She returned her tea glass to the table and met Dani's gaze. "Beetle returned from Afghanistan with problems like a lot of other veterans. After losing his wife and kids because of PTSD and drug addiction, he downgraded to alcohol. So far, he hasn't kicked the habit completely. He made me promise a few months back that the next time I saw him drunk I'd have him admitted to a rehab facility. I carry his signed consent in the glove box of my patrol car."

A strange look crossed Dani's face as she rested her fork on the side of her plate. "So, when your deputy hauled Beetle off, where was she taking him?"

"A holding cell to sleep it off. He was still out when I left this evening."

"You didn't arrest him? I saw him hit you."

"What?" Mary Jane clutched her chest. "Are you hurt, honey?"

"I'm fine, MJ, just a light punch in the ribs. No harm done." She patted Mary Jane's hand before addressing Dani again. "He didn't know what he was doing, so assault charges hardly seemed fair."

"And the young girl at the drugstore?" Dani's eyes blazed anew and her skin flushed.

"What?"

"I saw you snap handcuffs on her and put her in the back seat of your car without a second thought just because she took a couple of birthday cards."

Grace leaned across the table, unwilling to shrink from Dani's ardent but inaccurate assumptions. "Is that what you saw?"

Dani nodded, seeming quite satisfied with herself.

Mary Jane waved her hand to settle Grace back in her chair. "Was that Emily, Doreen's granddaughter?" When Grace nodded, she added, "You persuaded May not to press charges, released Emily, and got her a job to boot if memory serves. Her family was so grateful."

Dani's eyes locked on Grace, and she saw a glimmer of something different in their depths and couldn't resist clarifying, "What's wrong, Dani?"

"It's just...I thought..." Dani mumbled while nervously folding her napkin.

Grace controlled her growing irritation and spoke calmly. "You thought I harassed a homeless man and a teenager for the fun of it. Is that the impression you have of me?"

"Grace would never—"

"Stop, MJ. Dani has only known bad cops and doesn't want to give anyone else the benefit of the doubt. She's marked the entire law enforcement profession with a big black X. Isn't that right?"

"Excuse me, please. Dinner was very good, Mary Jane." Dani didn't look at her again as she slid her chair back and left the room.

The large kitchen was quiet for several seconds before Mary Jane spoke. "Well, guess I should get her bill ready."

"I'm sorry, MJ. I really dislike people who judge others before they even know them."

"And you really want her to like you."

"Yeah," she answered without overthinking. "Guess so, but that's obviously not going to happen. Probably just as well because she's leaving soon." She cupped Mary Jane's hand where it rested on the table. "Sorry if I embarrassed you."

"You didn't embarrass me, honey. I was proud of you for standing up for yourself." She slid her chair back and retrieved two pies from the sideboard. "How about pecan or peach pie?"

"Not right now, thanks. Maybe after I balance the books and pay the bills I'll have a slice with some coffee." Grace started gathering dishes, but Mary Jane shooed her away. "I can help."

"You can help me more by getting those blasted accounts in order. Go crunch numbers."

Grace moved to the small hutch in the corner of the kitchen that served as the business hub of the B and B and pulled the checkbook and bills out of the center drawer. She automatically entered the purchase receipts in the checkbook and then organized the bills from highest to lowest, a habit she'd picked up from her dad. The sounds of Mary Jane clearing the dishes and preparing for breakfast the next day faded into the background.

When she looked up later, two hours had passed and a slice of pecan pie along with a coffee carafe sat on the butcher-block island behind her. She stood, stretched, and poured herself a cup before returning to her chair. The to-do stack on her left was gone and a pile of addressed and stamped envelopes rested to her right. She smiled, satisfied with her progress. Then she remembered her unfinished dinner and the sense of accomplishment faded.

She'd been a bit harsh and overly defensive with Dani earlier, but she had nothing to lose with this woman who judged her unacceptable because of her job. Why not be brutally honest? Nothing to lose except her future business at the B and B. Why was she trying so hard with Dani? The answer came swiftly from Grace's gut. She had a feeling Dani Wingate was worth the effort, and her instincts about people were seldom wrong.

Dani stood in the kitchen doorway and watched Grace for several minutes as she worked at the small hutch. Her hair brushed her shoulders and swept forward concealing her face and expression, but the sideways tilt of her head was adorable. She flipped through a stack of papers, her foot tapping to some silent rhythm, before making an entry in a checkbook. Dani tried to reconcile this softer, more domestic image of Grace, which she much preferred, with the drunk-wrestling one she'd seen earlier today.

Intoxicated family members brawling with cops had been a given during her childhood, but warm familial scenes like the ones at every B and B meal were practically nonexistent. She'd learned the hard way that getting close to people, including her parents, only led to pain. She hadn't allowed a partner to even try. A calm feeling settled over her as she watched Grace, adaptable, easygoing Grace, as comfortable in one scenario as the other. Dani had jumped to the wrong conclusion and needed to apologize.

"Excuse me."

Grace jerked, and her pen flew out of her hand, landing on the floor near Dani's feet.

"Sorry. I didn't mean to startle you." Dani retrieved the pen and handed it back.

"I was wrapping up anyway." Grace turned her attention to the hutch, gathered her paperwork, and stuffed it in the center drawer. "Did you need something?"

Grace parroted the question Dani had asked that morning. Fitting she should get a dose of her own surly medicine. "Do you have a minute?"

Grace gave her a look that lasted just long enough to make Dani squirm before finally saying, "Sure. I was about to have a slice of pecan pie. Can I tempt you?"

The problem was she'd tempted Dani since the moment they met, but Grace was talking about food. Her stomach growled. She'd left dinner in a huff before finishing her meal, and pie sounded perfect.

"Your stomach says yes. Peach or pecan?"

"Peach, please." Dani settled on the opposite side of the butcher-block island while Grace retrieved a saucer from the cabinet and sliced the pie.

"If you'd like, I can heat that up and top it with French vanilla ice cream."

Dani licked her lips, as much from the stare Grace was giving her as the idea of peach pie a la mode. "That would be magic, if it's not too much trouble."

"No trouble. I'm heating mine anyway. Coffee?"

Dani nodded, and Grace slid the pie in the microwave, hit the button, and pulled the ice cream from the freezer. She handled the domestic tasks with the same consideration she'd shown Beetle Bledsoe on the street, and Dani felt a wave of admiration for her consistency and kindness. Grace poured the coffees, scooped the ice cream on top of the slices, and presented both to Dani at the same time. "You're pretty much perfect in the kitchen."

"But despicable everywhere else? That sounds a little judgmental, Dr. Wingate."

Damn, she couldn't say anything right around Grace. "That's not what I meant. I actually wanted to apologize for earlier."

"Which part?"

Dani respected Grace for holding her to task. "Assuming you were a cop who mistreats people...and likes it."

Grace's stare pinned her, and a whirlwind of warring emotions bowled through Dani, just like when Grace touched her arm the other day. "Thank you for that, I think." Her cautious tone was less than convincing.

"Seriously, Grace, I'm really sorry."

"Okay, I appreciate it. Making such a sweeping assumption about an entire profession is sort of like judging all pit bulls by the one that bites someone or all raccoons by the one that catches rabies, isn't it?"

Grace took a forkful of pecan pie into her mouth and when her lips slid over the tines, Dani swallowed hard. "Valid point, and well made using my field."

"There are bad cops. I can't argue, but there are also bad veterinarians, dentists, cooks, politicians...every profession has some undesirables. I just like to think I'm not one of them."

"Again, I'm sorry."

They ate quietly for several minutes, each glancing up periodically until their dishes were clean. "More coffee?" Grace asked.

"No, I'm good." Dani collected the saucers and placed them in the dishwasher. With her back turned to Grace, she asked, "Why police work?"

Grace slowly poured herself another cup of coffee, as if considering her answer. "I needed a job."

Dani waited, hoping she hadn't completely alienated Grace and that she'd say more because she really wanted to know. The realization startled her. Being interested in someone, asking questions, and exchanging life stories were the first steps on a road Dani didn't usually travel, but in Grace's case, she couldn't stop herself.

"Most of my childhood was spent traveling the world with my parents, going from one missionary project to another. Not that they were religious, they just enjoyed seeing other places and doing something meaningful. They finally settled here for several years, where I was born, but it didn't take. After I finished school, they decided their traveling days weren't over and took off, leaving me the B and B. I enjoy people and cooking, to a point, but not as a full-time job. Mary Jane ran the place when we were traveling, so we struck a deal. She manages the B and B, and I help out as needed, but I had to find a job with benefits." Grace wiped nervously at the countertop. "Guess that was more than you wanted to know."

"Not at all." Grace had barely skimmed the surface of her life, making Dani even more curious about how a person so compassionate and non-violent would choose a job as a cop. "And why law enforcement?"

"I wanted to be a nurse or social worker—suits my personality better—but I didn't have the formal training or the time to go back to college. I needed to work. The sheriff was looking for deputies, major crime is practically nonexistent in our community, and I know everybody, so fighting didn't seem too likely."

Dani gave her a skeptical look. "Seriously?"

"Maybe not the best logic, but I missed my parents and had just broken up with someone. And so far, it's been okay. Most days I feel like a social worker. Wielding authority, power, whatever you call it, doesn't really appeal to me. I'm more of a mediator or negotiator." She sipped her coffee. "Enough about me."

Grace licked her lips before bringing them to the rim of her coffee cup again. She had the most delicious-looking mouth, plump lips that usually settled in a partial smile. Dani felt another round of unsettling feelings tumble through her.

"Now can I ask you a question?" Grace asked.

She nodded.

"Why such a bad opinion of cops?"

Dani hated this you-show-me-yours-and-I'll-show-you-mine back-and-forth. The exchange felt too personal, something she purposely avoided in most situations, but Grace's vulnerability touched her, and she deserved an honest answer. "My story is a pretty common one. I had an unpleasant childhood in low-income housing with drug dealers and users, robbers, and child abusers, all the prime targets for cops. I saw more than my share of excessive force and corrupt police before we moved." Grace studied Dani's face for several seconds and the scrutiny calmed and unsettled her.

"And that's how you see me?"

"No, but some images are hard to get rid of, like a flashback when I see a uniform. I come from a different world than you. I never had a real home, more an addict's version of a B and B without food, and I believe that colored my view of the world going forward." She stared at the countertop, unable to meet Grace's eyes.

Grace trailed her hand slowly up and down Dani's back, her voice soft and comforting. "I'm so sorry. But you made it out."

Dani resisted the urge to bolt. If she wasn't careful, she could find herself in real trouble—confiding more about her childhood and being comforted by a woman she couldn't afford to become attached to—but Grace's hand felt so warm, so vital next to her skin. She couldn't remember the last time she'd been caressed in anything but a sexual way. For a few seconds, she relaxed and allowed Grace's intimate touch to imprint on her body. What was happening to her?

"Are you okay?"

The words shattered their connection, and Dani stood and backed away. "Fine." She couldn't look at Grace for fear she'd see hope, desire, or some other unfulfillable emotion in her eyes.

"Can we—"

"Have to go." She pointed to the stairs leading to her bedroom, still too affected by Grace's closeness to form a complete sentence. "Tired."

CHAPTER EIGHT

Grace spent the morning getting Beetle Bledsoe presentable and transporting him to the substance abuse clinic in the neighboring county. On her way back into town, she stopped by Trip's place to check on Harry with the same unpleasant result as before. She intended to ask Dani again about a home visit, but she wasn't in, so Grace parked at the station and walked toward the diner. The noon rush was over and she could have a nice leisurely lunch with few interruptions.

As she reached for the door handle, she spotted Dani heading toward her car. "Hey, wait up." She sprinted across the street and cupped Dani's elbow, falling in step. Her skin dimpled with goose bumps even though the weather was hot enough to blister the bottoms of bare feet on the blacktop. Why couldn't she keep her hands off this woman? "Walk with me?"

"Why?"

"If you really need a reason, it's a beautiful day, nice scenery, and I've been told I'm pretty good company."

Dani slid her arm free and gave Grace a suspicious look.

"I promise not to ask any personal questions." She'd seen the fear in Dani's eyes last night when they'd talked about her family and childhood, but she'd also felt Dani's body relax into her touch as if starved for real affection. Dani was afraid to get close, and Grace felt her resistance like a barrier between them.

"No, thanks. I'm on my way to the Clip 'n Curl for a haircut. Another time." She started back toward her car at a rapid pace.

"Okay, I won't push on the walk, but I can't let you go to Connie's for a haircut." Grace ushered Dani into the alley between the drugstore and the old hardware store where Clay's latest mural adorned the walls.

"Grace?" Dani gave her a what-the-hell-are-you-doing look. "Why not? Brenda said they're the best in town."

"Brenda said that because they're the only place in town and Connie is her cousin, not because they're actually any good. Most of the hairstylists belong to Hair Whackers Anonymous. They don't know when to step away from the scissors. I don't want you to come out with a shaved head or worse."

"Is it really that bad?"

"You *have* met Doreen Divine-Dot at the florist's."

Dani's eyes widened in comprehension. "Bowl haircut slash mullet. Where do you go?"

"Savannah. I wouldn't trust these tempting tresses to just anyone." She flipped the hair off her shoulders, and Dani stared at her neck. They were almost toe-to-toe in the tight alley and their proximity felt intimate, the air between them thick. Grace's body hummed like a taut string stretched between the tuning head and bridge of a guitar. She eased back but had nowhere to go.

"Backed yourself into a corner, Grace?"

Dani's grin was pure mischief, an expression Grace hadn't seen before, but rather enjoyed. "Very funny. I was only trying to be helpful."

Dani leaned closer, gazing into Grace's eyes. "How can I ever repay you?"

Grace enjoyed being close to Dani more than she wanted to admit, but an alley in the center of town while she was in uniform wasn't a good idea. "Come to my place tonight?"

"What did you have in mind?"

Grace could tell by Dani's grin that she was enjoying her discomfort. The grin turned into a full smile, and Grace wanted to trace the space between her front teeth with her tongue. "To check me...my place...out...for Harry."

"Of course, for Harry. What time?"

Grace swallowed hard, the idea of Dani in her small cottage too provocative. "After six?" She placed her hand on Dani's chest to ease her back so she could leave but liked the feel of Dani's heart galloping between her breasts.

Dani edged closer and stared at Grace's mouth. Any minute she was going to kiss her, and Grace was so ready. She opened her mouth slightly and licked her lips in invitation.

"Grace? Are you all right?" Clay Cahill stood at the entrance of the alley with her arms crossed over her tight T-shirt scanning Dani suspiciously.

Grace debated throwing her arms around Clay to thank her for the save or yelling at her for the interruption. She was flustered being so close to Dani and needed a way out but didn't really want one. She hated when her head and heart gave her mixed messages. "I'm good."

"You sure?" Clay's aw-shucks demeanor hid her depth of passion and protectiveness for the people she loved. She eyeballed Dani again.

"She's sure, sport," Dani said as she pushed her way past Clay.

Clay moved aside, and when Grace headed toward the street, fell in beside her. "Mind if I walk with you a bit?"

"Course not. I'd love the company." Grace looped her arm through Clay's, and they walked slowly down Main Street like a couple out for a Sunday stroll. She started to explain what Clay had interrupted but wasn't sure how to decipher something that had been so emotionally charged and unexpected.

"Wasn't that Trip's new vet you were trapped in the alley with?" Clay smiled in her handsome way that had captivated several hearts since they were in high school.

"Yes, but I wasn't exactly trapped. I sort of pulled her in there, by accident, to warn her about the Clip 'n Curl. Love your mural by the way."

"Thanks. I'll be painting a few more around town once the council chooses the scenes. Pre-drawn works are the only thing I can paint right now. It's like color by numbers, no creativity required. So…just doing your civic duty with the new girl?"

"Exactly."

Clay stopped and turned to face her. "Be careful, Gracie. She's a player and not long for our little town."

"What have you heard?" Grace wasn't naïve, but she wanted Clay's impression of Dani because her interest was definitely piqued. And after their chat in the kitchen last night and the teasing bout in the alley, she felt Dani was warming to her as well.

"A friend called from Savannah yesterday and went on and on about a woman she'd met at a club, a vet from up North, currently living in Pine Cone. She asked if I knew her. Do I need to spell it out?"

"I'm not the innocent kid you and Trip protected in high school."

Clay nudged her, and they continued to walk. "But we still try. That's what friends do."

"And that's one of the reasons I love you both like sisters."

"I'm serious, Grace. I know your instincts about people are good, but any one of us can be fooled when our hearts are involved."

The sadness in Clay's tone reminded Grace how badly Veronica had hurt her when she was in New York. Her recovery had been lengthy and agonizing. She squeezed Clay's arm tighter. "So, how's it going with sexy gallerist River Hemsworth?"

Clay looked away as color painted her cheeks. "Slow."

"Well, it's not because she's not attracted to you. Chemistry poured off you two like August heat in Georgia."

"She's just passing through too, so I should probably take my own advice. But we're going to Howard Station for dinner."

"Excellent news. You haven't been that attracted to a woman since…when exactly?"

"Can't remember," Clay said.

"Right. My advice, as one of your dearest friends, is to go for it. You've got nothing to lose." Grace tried to quiet the voice in her head telling her the same thing, but she wasn't rushing into anything with Dani. If something happened between them, it'd be because they both wanted it and understood the consequences. She'd learned her lesson about chasing women who didn't want her. Bad for her health, self-respect, and future. Not again. Thank you very much.

"Nothing to lose except my heart when she leaves," Clay said.

"Isn't love worth the risk?" The question echoed inside, but Grace refused to consider her response.

Dani rushed back to the B and B after work, showered, and pulled on a clean pair of jeans and a fresh T-shirt. She loved the smell of her patients, but what if Grace wasn't an animal person? She certainly had a hard time getting along with Harry. Anyone who couldn't tolerate animals was a definite red flag date-wise. *Snap out of it, Wingate.* Grace was never going to be a viable dating option. Maybe Dani could downplay her attraction into a friendship or possibly friend with benefits situation. Would Grace settle for that? Would she? Dani dabbed a bit of styling gel in her hands and tousled it through her short hair for the desired messy effect.

As she bounded down the stairs two at a time, she reviewed her behavior with Grace in the alley and in the kitchen last night but couldn't explain either. Grace threw her off kilter with her compassion, soothing tone, and casual touches, touches that seeped under her skin and burrowed into her soul. She'd wanted, no, she'd needed, a touch like that for ages, but it also terrified her. Why had she practically invited herself to Grace's tonight? That damn alley. Being so close. Her first glimpse of nervousness in Grace emboldened Dani and brought out her softer side. And feeling Grace's hand on her chest, she'd wanted it everywhere else.

On her way through the kitchen, Mary Jane said, "Supper in five minutes."

"I appreciate it, but I'm not hungry."

"I'll leave a plate warming in the oven in case you change your mind later."

"Thanks." She marched across the backyard toward the cottage. This visit was all about Harry, a professional assessment. This wasn't a date and she couldn't forget it. The turmoil in her stomach was nothing more than the usual case of nerves she got with any challenging case. She tapped lightly, then more forcefully.

Grace opened the door wearing a pair of shorts that revealed shapely legs and a sleeveless blouse that accented her breasts but not in a slutty way like Michelle's clothes. Dani's mouth dropped open as she ogled Grace's body once and then twice. She'd never seen Grace out of uniform and never wanted to see her in it again.

"So, you approve of the outfit?" Grace's voice cut through her lusty haze.

She nodded, unable to find words that didn't sound like a pickup line or a cry for mercy.

Grace waved Dani in and preceded her into the small space, but she couldn't move, her gaze fixed on the cheeks of Grace's ass when she walked. "Damn, you look great."

Grace grinned over her shoulder, obviously enjoying the effect her attire was having on Dani. "It gets hot, as you've probably noticed, and I don't like air conditioning, so I raise the windows in the evening and use the ceiling fan and a small portable." She shrugged. "Do you plan to come in at some point?"

"Oh, yeah." Dani stepped awkwardly over the threshold, closed the door behind her, and shoved her hands in her pockets. The small space shrank around her, and no matter where she stood, she was too close to Grace's tempting body. Her earlier thought of friendship vanished in favor of friends with benefits.

"Would you like a cold drink? I have beer on ice or several choices of wine."

"Beer, please."

"I figured you for a beer woman, like Clay and Trip. They won't go anywhere near a glass of wine but put an ice-cold beer in front of them and you're friends for life. You've met Clay, right?"

Dani accepted the beer and took a long swig to lubricate her parched throat, a recurring condition when Grace was close. "Not officially, but doesn't she work at the service station? And wasn't she the one who rescued you in the alley this morning?"

"Yeah, but don't let the grease monkey gig fool you. She's an accomplished artist, made quite a splash at her first New York show."

"Then what the hell is she doing—" Dani stopped before insulting Grace again.

"What's she doing in Pine Cone? I get how you wouldn't understand, but that's her story and she'll have to tell it." Grace poured a glass of wine, took a sip, and waved her hand around the room. "So, let's deal with business first. I don't want you thinking I lured you here under false pretenses."

Dani's mind blanked. She took another gulp of beer and made an obvious show of studying the room. Focusing on Grace's outfit or her auburn hair that shifted provocatively around her face when she moved wasn't why she was here.

"Do you see anything particularly offensive…to an African gray parrot?"

Oh yes, Harry. "Not really, but as I've said, I'm not a bird psychologist." She pointed with her bottle to the large aviary against the wall between the living and kitchen areas. "Is that where he is most of the time?"

Grace nodded.

"So, no view outside?"

"I keep the blinds closed during the day because it gets so hot."

"Do you keep the air conditioning on in the daytime?" The minute the question was out she regretted it and the accusatory tone of her voice.

Grace propped a hand on one of her shapely hips and glared. "You still don't have a very high opinion of me, do you? I don't know much about birds, but I wouldn't leave any animal in a confined space during a Georgia heat wave without some type of relief."

"Sorry, I didn't mean it that way." She turned up her beer bottle, got nothing, and placed it on the kitchen counter. "I'm in assessment mode, just asking questions. Can I get another one of those, please?" She nodded toward the empty bottle.

Grace seemed to relax and gave her a partial grin before bending over the cooler to pull out another icy beer. Dani didn't even try to look away. She zeroed in on Grace's well-rounded ass and felt a jolt in her center as she imagined grabbing Grace from behind and bringing their bodies together. When Grace turned around, Dani felt heat rush to her face.

"Are you all right?" Her wicked grin said she knew exactly where Dani's mind had wandered.

"Yeah...fine."

"Other suggestions? About Harry?" Grace offered Dani the beer but held on to the bottle when Dani reached for it, purposely grazing her fingers over Dani's when they separated.

The touch was a match, fiery and dangerous, and Dani wanted it over and over again. No more touching, she reminded herself. "Music?"

"You'd like some music? What kind?"

Dani shook her head, still reeling from Grace's soft skin against hers. "No...for the bird...for Harry. He might enjoy music or television during the day when you're gone."

"Hadn't thought of that. Good idea, Doctor, but this whole me and the bird thing is probably not going to work out."

"Why?" Dani guzzled her beer and started feeling a buzz. Drinking plus Grace equaled trouble. She had to focus on the bird situation, not on how delicious Grace looked or how much she wanted her right now.

"As you've said, he needs interaction, stimulation, and I'm not here to provide that for him. Maybe we should consider other options. Surely someone would enjoy a communicative addition to their home."

"Perhaps, but he'll still have a tough transition. Michelle said he's thriving in the clinic, enjoying the comings and goings, and isn't bothered by anyone..."

"You mean the way he's bothered by me."

Dani nodded.

"The clinic is out. I've already asked Trip and got a definite no."

Dani finished her second beer and placed the empty beside the other on the counter. "Hey, I've got an idea. It might not work, but it's worth a discussion."

Grace moved to her side of the counter and placed her hand on Dani's forearm causing an immediate surge of arousal so strong she flinched. "Let's hear it. Why don't we sit?" Grace pulled the sofa cushions onto the floor, settled cross-legged, and motioned for Dani to join her.

Dani told herself not to let Grace touch her while praying she would. She swallowed hard, fighting the chemistry between them as she lowered herself a few inches from Grace on the cushions. She'd never been around anyone who made her feel equally aroused and comfortable. "How about the B and B sunroom?"

"Could that actually work?" Grace leaned back, resting with her arms behind her and exposing an easy view of the pale flesh at the tops of her breasts. Dani focused on the pulse point at Grace's neck and then shifted her gaze to her cleavage. "Having trouble concentrating, Doc?" Grace's voice was light and teasing, but Dani felt like she'd been stroked.

"Serious trouble." Dani forced herself back into professional mode. Her idea had possibilities, and she wasn't sure if she was more pleased about it for Harry's sake, Grace's, or her own because of Grace's interest. "Think about it. He'd be around people almost all the time. He'd have a great view of nature, and when those massive French doors are open, he'd practically be outside."

"I'd have to talk with MJ." Grace took a slow sip of wine and licked her lips, and Dani had to look away. "I couldn't ask her to take on more responsibility. Harry can be a handful."

Without thinking, Dani inched closer to Grace and heard a rapid intake of breath. The beer had dulled her control and spiked her libido or maybe she just needed an excuse for her actions. "You really are a very thoughtful person, Grace. And so damn hot." Grace's light flowery perfume filled Dani's senses and accelerated the slow burn in her body. She could seduce Grace right now, and the dreamy look in her eyes said she wouldn't resist.

Grace stroked a finger down the side of Dani's face and traced her bottom lip with the pad of her thumb. "I try."

"Grace...I—"

"Don't talk." Grace leaned in and angled her head for a kiss.

Grace's kissable mouth mesmerized Dani, and she licked her lips as Grace opened slightly.

"Dani," Grace whispered.

Her name sounded so heartfelt, so intimate, that Dani jerked away just before their lips met. Getting involved with a woman who wanted so much when she could give so little just wasn't fair. She couldn't do that to Grace or to herself. "I have to go."

Grace rested her hands on Dani's chest just above her breasts, and the touch burned Dani's skin, just like it had in the alley this morning. "Okay, I understand."

What did Grace understand? That Dani wanted her so much her insides ached? Or that she'd promise anything to have sex with her right now? Or maybe she somehow knew she made Dani want things she'd never considered possible. She was afraid Grace saw all those things, and it terrified her. "I can't." She stood, hoping Grace knew why they could never happen, but certain she didn't. "I'm sorry, Grace." As she ran from the cottage, Dani heard Grace's frustrated response.

"So am I."

Leaning against the doorframe, Grace watched Dani sprint across the backyard like a rabbit chased by a fox. One minute they were discussing possible solutions for the Harry problem, and the next Dani bolted. Maybe Grace's touch and the near kiss made her skittish and scared her into escape mode.

Grace sighed, closed the door, and settled back on the cushions with her wine. Dani was definitely conflicted, but Grace sensed a connection the first time they met, and it kept growing stronger. Dani had initiated their closeness for the first time in the alley this morning and inched within kissing distance tonight. They'd both leaned into that kiss, both wanted it. But Grace probably shouldn't have touched her, but the pull had been so strong.

She didn't want to let Dani push her away like she probably had other women when they got close. And Grace didn't want another fling with a passerby. She needed something deeper and believed Dani did as well, but they'd both have to be willing to embrace their feelings. She sat quietly for a while, finished her wine, and then walked to the B and B.

Mary Jane closed the dishwasher as Grace entered and gave her a raised eyebrow. "You're a little late, but I've got leftovers if you're hungry."

"No, thanks, MJ."

"Guess I know why our guest bolted through the kitchen like a cat with her tail on fire." She waved toward Grace. "Look at the state of you."

Grace poured herself a glass of tea and sat at the island opposite Mary Jane. "What's wrong with the state of me?"

"You're not exactly trying to cover your assets. You probably scared the poor woman half to death." She shook her head but stopped short of tsking.

"Trust me, she can handle it. Besides, these are perfectly presentable clothes for a stroll down Main Street." She tried for a contrite look, but Mary Jane's expression said she wasn't buying it. "Okay, maybe I was testing the waters a bit."

"You know what they say about horses and water."

"The same thing *they* say about fish and worms? You can't make them take something they don't want. And just for the record, I think you're right. I probably came on a little strong."

"Then why do I sense a but at the end of that sentence?" Mary Jane asked.

"Because I don't want to give up on her yet. I can't really explain why. I just know I'll never forgive myself if I don't try."

Mary Jane hugged Grace and swayed like she used to when Grace was a kid. "I've seen people come and go in your life, honey, and you've never gone wrong listening to your gut."

"Thank you. I'll probably need a few more of these heart-to-heart sessions along the way, but right now, I need to talk to you about something else." She took a sip of tea and caged the glass in her hands. "It's about that crazy bird Karla left at the cottage."

Mary Jane nodded. "I wondered what was going to happen to him."

"Dani and I discussed the sunroom as a possibility. What do you think?"

She was quiet as Mary Jane glanced toward the sunroom and then walked through the space. She waited patiently until Mary Jane was ready to deliver her decision, knowing that either way Harry would have to adjust to a new environment.

"I think it can work, with one condition," Mary Jane said.

Grace wasn't sure if she was relieved or disappointed. "What?"

"He has to learn some new words and forget the colorful ones Karla taught him. I can't have him alienating the guests."

"I'm not sure parrots can forget words, but I'm willing to give it a try if you are."

Mary Jane grinned. "He'll be a unique addition to the place, something people will talk about and that could draw others in. This might be good for everyone, especially Harry and you."

"Me? He's a bird, MJ."

"He's a living thing that deserves a happy home and someone to care for him."

Mary Jane was right, as usual. Grace hadn't been able to turn her back on Harry at first, and she couldn't do it now. He was becoming part of the family like it or not. "Of course."

Mary Jane started toward her room but stopped and turned back. "You going over to Trip's tomorrow to help with the cookout preparations?"

"Yeah, I'll direct cars to the house with traffic cones, cordon off the stairs to the second floor, and schlep a ton of food from downtown. You need something before I go over?"

"Nah, just checking on my girl."

"Thanks, MJ. And thank you for Harry too. I was running out of options."

"We always seem to manage, but in this case, you should probably thank Dani."

She might not have the nerve to face Dani again after tonight. It hadn't been a calculated move, but once Dani scooted closer and leaned into her, she hadn't been able to resist trying for one kiss. Now that Dani knew she was interested, Grace could slow down and let things progress naturally.

CHAPTER NINE

Dani walked slightly behind Michelle from the clinic to Trip's house for the cookout. She'd grown weary of the long drives to Savannah for companionship and decided to check out the local options. She chugged a beer, enjoying the view of Michelle's firm ass in bikini bottoms and the pale expanse of skin between the top and the flare of her hips. The woman was hot and knew it but tried too hard for Dani's taste, unlike Grace who highlighted her assets without flaunting them. Dani didn't want to show up at the cookout with Michelle, but didn't want to arrive alone either, not after almost kissing Grace last night. Despite her attempts at distraction, she'd thought of little else since. She enjoyed the excitement Grace brought to a room, the way she looked at her, and the compassion in her voice when she talked about townspeople or Harry.

Michelle reached back for her hand as they approached the house. "Ashamed to be seen with me?"

"Of course not. I just don't want to give anyone the wrong impression. And I don't do handholding. Go on in, and I'll see you in a minute." Michelle hesitated, but Dani walked away to gather her courage before facing Grace.

She'd behaved like a scared novice when Grace leaned in to kiss her. She'd hungered for that kiss too, but not the fallout. Grace would've made more out of it, and Dani couldn't afford to leave any damage when she left, especially not involving Grace. Grace and Trip were good friends, and Dani needed an impeccable referral when she applied for her next job.

Decision made again to keep her distance, Dani walked up the front steps of Trip's large two-story house. People crowded the front porch and the screened porch on the right side, overflowing into the backyard around the pool. She hadn't expected so many people, but that could be a good thing. Maybe she'd meet someone who made the frequent trips to Savannah unnecessary.

When she entered the living area, two massive seating areas off to each side were flooded with mostly women and a smattering of men already drinking and competing to be heard. She caught the glance of a couple of potentials and gave a quick smile. When she entered the combination dining, kitchen, and sunroom area, Trip and Clay walked toward her.

"Glad you made it," Trip said, patting her on the back. "I was beginning to wonder if you were going to blow me off."

"Wouldn't think of insulting my boss. What a crowd."

"Greatest show on earth." Trip jerked her thumb toward the woman beside her. "Don't think you've been properly introduced, but this is Clay Cahill, resident artist extraordinaire and part-time tow truck driver and grease monkey."

"We've bumped into each other," Dani said.

Clay shifted a paper plate loaded with quesadillas, chips, and salsa to her left hand and offered a half wave. "Welcome to the best cookout in three counties. I see you brought a date." She nodded toward Michelle who was getting a drink at the bar.

"Not a date," Dani said.

"Good to hear. I'd hate to bust your chops for dating the underage help." Trip nudged her as she passed on the way to greet other arrivals.

"Underage? But she looks—"

"Looks can be deceiving, but she's not really underage, just acts like it sometimes. See you around," Clay said.

"Yeah, see you." Dani scanned the room but didn't have time to register if she knew anyone else before Michelle was by her side, sliding her arm through Dani's.

"I missed you," Michelle said.

Dani edged away. "Listen, I like you, but I'm not interested in anything else. I agreed to come with you to the cookout as friends and colleagues. Whatever you're hoping for beyond that isn't happening. Understand?" Why couldn't she be as straightforward with Grace?

Michelle's smile altered only slightly as she slowly released Dani's arm. "Sure. I just thought you'd like a good time. Obviously, I misjudged you. I'll be around if you change your mind." Then without warning, she cupped Dani's face and kissed her before heading toward another woman standing alone in the kitchen.

When Dani looked up, she met Grace's incredulous stare across the room. Great, she'd alienated two women at the same time without even trying, a personal worst. She couldn't do anything right with Grace, which was probably a good thing considering her earlier resolution to stay clear. She needed a drink in the worst way, scanned the space for the bar, and walked to the outside patio near the pool. "Beer, please."

She took two long pulls from the bottle, turned back to the crowd, and came face-to-face with Grace. She gasped and sucked beer down her windpipe, which caused a coughing fit. Sputtering, she grabbed a napkin from the bar and wiped her mouth. Grace slapped her on the back, and Dani felt her face heat.

"All right?" Grace asked nonchalantly before addressing the cute bartender. "Can I get a glass of zinfandel, please?" She retrieved her wine and turned back to Dani with an amused smile on her face.

"Yeah, fine, just went down the wrong way."

"Karma perhaps?"

"For?"

"Dissing your date so publicly."

"Why does everybody assume we're dating? We just walked over together after work."

Grace held up her hand. "You don't need to explain to me. Just an observation about how it looked to an outsider. And you can bet there will be a big breakup story going around town before nightfall."

"Doesn't the truth matter?" Dani took a smaller sip of beer mainly to distract her from Grace's focused gaze.

"Not usually."

Grace raked her fingers through her wavy hair and let it fall to her shoulders, making Dani wonder if it felt soft and fine or course and thick. Grace's white shorts and bright green sleeveless blouse were crisp and summery like an exotic flower, and Dani caught a whiff of her floral perfume on the light afternoon breeze. The sexy fragrance sent her stomach into a tumble.

"Well, guess I'll see you later. A couple of people are trying to crash the emergency tape and escape upstairs," Grace said and turned to leave.

Dani's startled exit from their near kiss last night had sent normally cordial and engaging Grace into cautious mode, and Dani didn't like the cooler version. "Wait…I…" She grappled for something, anything to get Grace to stay.

Grace stopped but searched the room as if she was looking for someone before she called out to the couple near the stairs. "Hey, upstairs is off limits. Don't you see the tape?" She returned her attention to Dani, pinning her with an amused stare. "You were saying?"

"I was…just wondering how you, Trip, and Clay became such good friends." Lame, but impersonal and engaging. Grace's expression said she was enjoying her discomfort.

"We've known each other since we were kids. Growing up in a small town has that effect. And we came out to each other one Christmas when we were freshmen in high school and went caroling together."

"How did singing Christmas songs bring up being gay?"

"Not Christmas caroling. We were all dating women named Carol. Sort of became obvious when we showed up at the seasonal play arm in arm with other girls."

Dani almost sucked another mouthful of beer down her throat. "I see."

"I should mingle. I'm one of the cohosts. Have a good time, Dani."

She wasn't ready to let Grace go, and before second-guessing herself, she brushed Grace's arm. "Could we talk a bit more?" The heat from their touch surged through Dani, and she jerked away. She didn't reach out first. She didn't chase women. And she certainly didn't ask to talk, ever. What was going on with her? Grace's cheeks tinged pink and she licked her lips. She'd felt the connection too. Dani raised her hands and backed up. "Yeah, see you later."

She watched Grace walk away, and the sway of her ass made Dani's throat dry and the rest of her wet. What was it about Grace that tempted Dani to chase after her, drag her to bed, and never let her leave? But Grace wouldn't allow anyone to drag her anywhere. Maybe the challenge was part of Dani's attraction.

She'd been such a coward not to kiss Grace when she had a chance and now Grace wanted nothing to do with her. As Grace worked her way through the crowd talking and laughing with guests, Dani felt an unfamiliar sense of loss.

"Not exactly what we talked about, Grace," Trip whispered in her ear. "You're supposed to be your usual charming and charismatic self, not some slightly muted version of an ice queen. I felt the chill way over here."

"Charming and charismatic Grace sent her running for the hills, so I've just toned it down a notch. You don't chase a spooked horse, do you, Trip?"

"Depends on the horse, and that one is definitely in heat. Her eyes were tracking you the whole time Clay and I were talking to her and she's still watching every move."

"But when I'm around, she's standoffish and weird."

Trip steered her toward a group of other women. "Maybe you need a teaser."

"For God's sake, stop talking in animal terms and speak plainly." Grace tried to free her arm from Trip's grasp, but she held firmly and aimed them toward a particularly cute butch with buzzed hair and a buff body accented by swim trunks and a tank top.

"Jay is the best teaser in the county. She flirts with everybody, acts like she's the biggest whore dog around, but is basically harmless."

"What *are* you talking about, Trip Beaumont?"

They stopped just out of earshot of Jay, and Trip continued. "A teaser is a horse that breeders use to stimulate the mare, but he's not the stallion that will ultimately mate with her."

"Seriously, Trip? You're comparing me to a breeding mare?"

"You're missing the point, Gracie. Dani is a stallion with eyes only for you. Trust me, she won't like some other stud sniffing around. Just go with it. Talk with Jay for a bit and let this play out. I know what I'm doing."

Grace shook her head but refused to move when Trip nudged her closer to Jay. "I don't like games, Trip."

"You're just being my very sociable cohost. Clay and I have our hands full working the femme side of the crowd."

"Hey, Grace." Jay had walked up behind them while she was debating with Trip. "I've been trying to get a minute alone with you since I got here. Walk with me?"

"See you later," Trip said, winking at Grace, and disappearing in the throng of women.

Grace sighed, still uncomfortable with the situation, but she could at least be friendly. "How've you been, Jay?"

"Not too bad." Jay offered her arm, and Grace looped hers through as they walked toward the backyard away from the pool and the noisy crowd. "You might've heard Cynthia and I broke up a couple of months ago."

Grace rubbed her hand down Jay's arm. "Are you okay?"

"Getting there. She was cheating with a woman in Savannah."

Savannah, sin city to the folks in Pine Cone. Any kind of deviance you wanted thrived there, and those temptations had ended many good marriages and relationships—hers included. "I'm so sorry, Jay. What a horrible thing to do to another person."

Jay's eyes glistened and her bottom lip quivered. "Yeah, never saw it coming." She took a couple of deep breaths trying to contain her emotions.

Grace put her arm around Jay's shoulder and felt the slight trembling of her body. "It's okay, Jay. Let it out."

"Can't...afraid I...won't stop. I loved her...so much."

Grace pulled Jay close and guided her head onto her shoulder, blocking her face from prying eyes. "You're a good person who deserves better."

Jay bit back a sob, but then cried softly. "But we don't always get better, do we?"

"No, we don't. Sometimes life just sucks big green donkey dicks."

Jay chuckled against Grace's shoulder. "You're one of the best people I know, kind, considerate, optimistic, but you still got hurt." She slapped her hand over her mouth, her eyes wide. "I'm so sorry, Grace. I shouldn't have said that."

"Nothing wrong with telling the truth. But if we don't push through the pain and disappointment, we'll never find true love." Good advice but she hadn't managed to follow it yet either. She scanned Trip's backyard and spotted Dani leaning against the fence staring right at her. Grace started to release Jay, but she held firmly, her tears soaking the front of Grace's blouse. She couldn't leave a friend hurting no matter how Dani might interpret their embrace. She held Jay until her crying stopped and looked around again, but Dani was gone.

After a few more minutes, Jay straightened and wiped her eyes. "Thanks for listening and for letting me cry on your shoulder. I'm not usually like this, bad for my butch image."

"Your secret is safe. You know where to find me if you want to talk again."

"Maybe we can go dancing in Savannah one night, as friends. Might do us good."

"Sure, Jay. Give me a call sometime." Grace left her by the back gate to compose herself and headed toward the bar. "Could I get another zinfandel, please?" She reached for the glass, but Dani cupped her elbow and guided her into the house and down the hall. "What the—?"

"Will you please come with me?" Dani asked, leading her toward Trip's office door. "We need to talk."

Clay spotted them and started toward her. "You okay, Grace?"

"I'm fine. Really. Go back to River."

Trip elbowed her way through the room toward them as well, but Grace waved her off with her free hand.

Grace finally pulled her arm loose, stopped abruptly, and just stared at Dani. "What do you think you're doing?"

"I want to talk to you." Her voice was a low raspy growl, as if the words pained her.

"Well, this isn't how it's done. You ask a woman if you can talk to her or you just talk. You don't put your hands on her. That behavior is called assault, not to mention rude."

Dani stepped closer and lowered her voice. "I'm sorry. Please, Grace, can we talk?" Dani's eyes turned dark, and she inclined her head farther down the hall.

Grace hesitated, trying to name the odd look on Dani's face, then nodded and followed her into Trip's office. The women outside the door were too loud for Grace's liking, so she led Dani into the adjoining half bath, and waited for her to close the door. "What is this about?" The space was so small with Grace's heels against the wall and Dani's butt touching the sink they were almost nose-to-nose.

"Who was that woman?"

Grace assumed she was asking about Jay and considered not answering, but she wasn't cruel and didn't play games. "A friend."

"A friend-friend or lover-friend?"

"Just a friend, Dani, but I don't think that's any of your concern because you've made it perfectly—"

Dani dipped her head and kissed Grace, lightly, awkwardly, but the heat of her lips made Grace tingle and grow weak. For a second, she couldn't move as shock surged through her followed by the clumsy tenderness of Dani's kiss. What was happening? When Dani pulled back, Grace pressed her hand to her lips to stop a jumble of feelings from pouring out. "That's not how it's done either, Ms. Wingate."

"I just wanted to show you how I feel."

"Which is what, exactly?"

"I'm...not sure."

Grace shook her head. "And I'm not a toy you can play with when you feel like it and discard when you don't. You wanted to talk, so talk or I'm leaving."

Dani gripped the sides of the sink, her knuckles white. "I saw you with that woman...and I..."

"I know it's hard to talk about this stuff, but you can tell me, Dani." Grace waited while Dani looked at her body, lingered over her breasts and lower before focusing on her lips. The hard set of Dani's jaw slowly loosened and she pushed away from the sink.

"You were holding her. She had her arms around you. You looked...intimate."

"And how did that make you feel?" Dani's expression shifted from vulnerable to scared in a matter of seconds, and Grace knew she wouldn't get an honest answer.

"I have no right."

She reached for the door, but Grace caught her hand and brought it to her waist. She'd never seen a woman so afraid of being close, of caring, and she ached to know why. "Rights come with time and respect, and we don't really know each other. I'm willing to learn. Are you?" She leaned in and kissed Dani, probed her lips gently with her tongue, and then eased inside. Grace guided her back against the sink, pressed her thigh between Dani's legs, loving the fit of their bodies, wanting to live in that kiss until she couldn't breathe.

Dani's response was immediate and hungry. She ran her hands down Grace's back to her butt and tugged her even closer. Grace relaxed, certain that for a moment the feelings between them were real even if Dani couldn't express them in words. And then Grace stepped back, opened the door and forced her trembling legs to walk casually away.

"But, Grace…" Dani's voice faded in the noise of the party as Grace shouldered her way to the front door.

Walking away was the hardest thing Grace had ever done, but she refused to give her heart to another woman who couldn't love her completely.

CHAPTER TEN

Grace poked her head around the corner of the B and B looking for Dani. She hoped she was already gone, because she desperately needed lunch without a side of drama.

"She hasn't come down yet," Mary Jane said. "She came in around three this morning. Heard that was quite a party."

"Lunch ready?" Grace grabbed a Diet Coke and purposely avoided the reference to the cookout. Mary Jane would spill the rest of her news soon enough without encouragement.

"Finishing up. Have a seat." Mary Jane pointed to Grace's usual spot.

She'd just settled when cautious footsteps sounded on the squeaky stairs followed shortly by Dani standing in the doorway looking flushed and too appealing for someone who'd been up most of the night. "Hi," Grace said.

"Morning." Dani turned and walked out the front door without another word.

"Well," Mary Jane said. "Guess I don't have to wonder if the gossip was true. You two definitely had a moment at the cookout, and it appears not all warm and fuzzy. It's colder than a witch's tit in a brass bra in here."

"Please, MJ, you know better than to believe town gossip." She paused and took a few sips of Coke, hoping Mary Jane would fill in the blanks. When that failed, she couldn't resist. "So, what exactly did you hear?"

Mary Jane grabbed her coffee cup and sat across from her at the table, lowering her voice for effect. "At church, I heard the new vet, that's Dani, and some young girl named Michelle had a very public breakup right in front of everybody. And there was speculation that Michelle might be under age, but Clarabelle said she knows for a fact Michelle is at least twenty-one because she went with her grandson to an event where alcohol was served and had to show ID. May overheard talk that you and Jay Griffith were making out near the pool. Then, not five minutes later, one of the visiting choir members said she saw you and Dani sneak into a bathroom together…and you didn't come out for ages." Mary Jane gave her the equivalent of the stink eye. "Thought I taught you better. Two women in one afternoon? Any truth to the rumors? Want to comment on what went on?"

Grace heated, whether from her irritation with Trip at throwing her into the uncomfortable situation with Jay or at Dani's behavior or their kisses, she wasn't entirely sure. "No."

"That's all I get? No? How will I hold my head up in this town when I live with one of the main characters in these juicy stories and can't even get a firsthand account?"

"Don't gossip."

"Exactly my point. If you told me what happened, it wouldn't be gossip, and I could set the record straight."

"Nope."

The room was quiet for several seconds before Mary Jane whispered, "You know you can talk to me." She reached across the table and squeezed Grace's hand.

"Thanks, but we need to revisit something relating to the B and B. Are you still sure about Harry living in the sunroom? I'll be responsible for feeding him and cleaning his cage."

"How will you do that? He hates you."

"I'll try, because I don't want you taking on any more work, and he's going to be part of the family. We have to figure out how to get along."

"I'll clear out a spot in the corner of the sunroom this afternoon."

"Thanks, MJ. You're the best."

"Of course I am." She looked down at her hands before one more attempt to get Grace to open up. "Did Dani do something to you, something rude?"

She didn't know how to explain what had happened between her and Dani. She'd run the scenario through her mind since last night with no new revelations. "Nothing I can't handle, MJ. Dani is just a little confused right now, and I'm letting her work through it."

What else could she do? She liked Dani a lot, and something about her forced Grace to stand up for herself, which wasn't a bad thing. If this was Dani's lesson to her, the message was worth an unrequited attraction.

"That's probably best, honey. Now, can I get you some lunch?"

"I'll make a plate in a bit. Thank you for looking out for me."

Mary Jane grabbed her in a hug and squeezed until Grace kissed her cheek and pulled away. They'd played that game since she was a kid, and Grace still loved that the comfort of Mary Jane's arms felt like home.

❖

Dani couldn't face Grace after her unchivalrous behavior at the party, much less sit across the table from her and eat a meal pretending nothing significant had happened between them. Her jealousy had been unexpected and totally uncharacteristic, and when Grace called her on it, Dani balked. She couldn't even tell Grace how she felt—that she was starting to care for her and was afraid of hurting her. So, like a coward, she'd snuck out of the B and B. Work was what she needed, so she'd decided to relieve some of Trip's Sunday workload at the clinic. She'd taken in the alcohol steadily last night and might need a hand.

Dani was inserting a new IV in the leg of an Irish setter who'd pulled his previous one out during the night when Trip walked into the treatment room. "Hey, haven't you read your contract? You're not scheduled to come in on Sundays. That's my job because you cover Saturdays while I go to horse shows."

Dani glanced up and smiled as she finished taping the IV securely to the setter's leg, then ruffled the dog's ears affectionately and softly scolded him. "Now leave that one alone or you'll get a cone of shame next time." The dog wagged his tail, oblivious to her threat.

"I don't think your scolding penetrated his thick Irish setter skull," Trip said in a teasing tone.

Dani shrugged. "You know what they say in vet school..."

"Some dogs have brains and others have red coats," they quoted together.

"This is his last bag of fluids, anyway," Dani said, hefting him from the table and walking him back to his cage. "He's feeling a lot better. I'll call his owner to pick him up tomorrow. I doubt we'll have to worry about them being careless with antifreeze again once I show them their bill."

"Their teenager was the careless one, but it won't happen again. Not only did he come close to losing his best friend, he'll be working off most of that bill slinging hay bales for my property manager, Jerome. Trust me, that's hard work he won't soon forget."

While Dani gently checked the IVs and administered medicine to a pair of Yorkie pups suffering from parvo, Trip pulled a terrier mix from a smaller pen and checked the multiple stitched wounds he'd earned in a fight with a dog five times his size. "This guy looks like something out of a horror movie, but he should be good to go home tomorrow, too."

"You were right about the cookout, by the way."

"How so?"

"I met a lot of great people and even picked up a new client."

"Do tell," Trip said.

"A terrier mix with a gastric problem. She was a shelter pup, so her medical history is sketchy. It's a chronic issue, and several visits to specialists have helped the owner manage it somewhat. But she's worried because the pup seems to be having some abdominal pain and has lost interest in food."

"Could be intestinal cancer," Trip offered, closing the terrier back in his pen. "Who's the owner?"

"Jamie Grant. It'd be a shame if it is cancer. The terrier came from a program that turns the most unwanted shelter dogs into service animals. Jamie works for the sheriff's office and trained the dog herself to sniff out drugs and explosives."

Trip stood by the terrier's pen staring off in the distance.

"Trip? Are you all right?"

"Fine. My brain just sidetracked to something else for a minute. It's still a little foggy. What were you saying?"

"I've already been through the cat room, so we're done."

"Oh, right. Remind me why you're here on a Sunday?"

Dani ducked her head. "Well, I saw you, uh, napping in the chair on the front porch and had an idea you might not be up for dealing with clogged drainage tubes and double diarrhea from the Yorkie twins."

Trip couldn't meet her gaze. "Yeah. Not usually my style. At least, not since I graduated vet school a decade ago." She rubbed her temples. "And it'll be two decades, if ever, before I'll do it again. But thanks for having my back."

"No problem," Dani said.

Trip started to leave but stopped in the doorway. "Did Jamie make an appointment for her dog?"

"Tomorrow. Nine o'clock. Before they start their shift."

"My morning is flexible. I'll handle that one if you don't mind. Jamie and I were teammates on the basketball team where I did my undergrad. I'd like to take this one personally."

"Sure, no problem. Jamie didn't mention you were friends. I sure hope it isn't cancer so you don't have to give her bad news."

"Yeah. Thanks. See you tomorrow morning."

"Glitter Girl to Fast Break and Paint Ball, do you copy?" Grace tried a second time to reach Trip and Clay on her CB radio.

Texting or calling would've been easier, but she still enjoyed using their high school method of communicating, a reminder of simpler times. She hadn't talked to Dani since their kisses at the cookout and needed their advice. "Come in, guys."

"Paint Ball here. Go, Glitter Girl." Clay's concerned voice sounded crisp and loud over the radio, and Grace breathed easier.

"Where are you?"

"On a pickup near the county line, about thirty minutes outside town. Are you okay?"

"Fast Break, I copy. What's up?" Trip cut in.

"Any chance you guys could meet me at Mosquito Alley for a powwow?" They'd adopted a portion of the Altamaha River as their private meeting place and dubbed it after the pesky occupants.

"Paint Ball ETA about five thirty."

"Fast Break same."

"Thanks. I'll bring some food and drinks. Glitter Girl out." Even though they saw each other almost daily somewhere in town, the alley gatherings were special, just the three of them.

She packed the beer into a cooler in the trunk of her battered Corolla, covered them with ice, and gathered some of their favorite snacks on the way out of town. When she arrived at Mosquito Alley, she parked behind Trip's clinic truck and Clay's wrecker but didn't see either of them. "Hey, where are you guys?"

She glanced out across the water at the rope swing swaying from the mammoth old oak tree. They were in the water already. Those two could probably recite exactly where the Altamaha originated and the path it took to the Atlantic, but she didn't really care as long as it came by Pine Cone.

Trip's voice drifted up from the river, "Taking a quick splash. Bring your mosquito spray."

"I could use a hand with the *food*," she called back. She emphasized the magic word that assured both would show up quickly. Clay and Trip scrambled up the riverbank, their shorts and tank tops dripping and their hair plastered flat from swimming. They both had bodies to die for, and if they weren't such great friends, she could go for either of them, but that ship had sailed years ago with a pact to never cross that line, drunk or sober.

"Did somebody mention food?" Clay grabbed Grace and gave her a big wet hug. "Where's your swimsuit, woman?"

Before she could answer, Trip hugged her from the back, effectively soaking her from both sides. "Who needs to swim when I have you two?"

Clay grabbed one side of the cooler and Trip the other in a time-honored act of chivalry that always made Grace feel special. At the water's edge, they set it down on Grace's favorite flat rock, and Trip gave Grace a mischievous grin.

"Don't even think about it, Trip Beaumont. If you throw me in the water, neither of you will get anything from that cooler."

Trip shrugged, nudged Grace closer to the water, and then darted around her and jumped in, splashing just enough to cool Grace's legs. "Chicken," she called to Clay.

"No can do, pal," Clay said. "She threatened my energy source." Clay helped Grace spread a picnic blanket on the rock and then stared across the river toward the sunset. "Isn't this view just amazing? All the texture, colors, and the light...the light is so good."

"You're such an artist, Cahill," Grace teased her. She glanced at Clay's hands and saw fresh paint stains around her nails. "Painting for real again?"

"Yep. Had an image in my head that wouldn't go away."

"I'm so glad, Clay. You were born for it."

"I know, right?" She blew Grace a kiss before jumping back in the river.

Grace poured herself a plastic cup of wine and rested against the slick-sided rock while watching Trip and Clay splash and dunk each other. She usually joined them, but today she was too pensive to play. She needed to talk. When Clay and Trip showed no signs of letting up, she reached into the cooler and rattled the beer bottles loudly. Clay's and Trip's heads popped out of the water and looked toward her. "Cold one?" Before she could twist the tops off two bottles, they were beside her.

"Okay, hand over my money." Trip held out her hand to Clay.

"What did you bet on this time?" Grace asked.

Clay riffled through her dry clothes until she found her wallet and handed over a ten-dollar bill. "How long you'd wait to talk. I said thirty minutes, and Trip guessed fifteen. So, what's up, Gracie?"

Grace reached toward the food containers. "Are you hungry? I brought all your favorites. Chicken wings, ribs, cracklings, and potato salad."

Trip cocked her head. "You're stalling. We know where the food is. What's up?"

"Dani Wingate."

Clay and Trip stared at each other for several seconds, but neither spoke. Finally, Clay fished another ten from her wallet and handed it to Trip.

"Seriously, guys?"

"I'm a sucker for a sure bet," Trip said and gave Grace her cutest femme-slaying smile. "Besides Jolene at the diner is telling everybody the two of you've already slept together."

"*What?*" Grace glared at her. "I hope you set her right."

Trip shook her head. "She could know something I don't."

"She *is* your type," Clay said shyly, taking another swig of beer.

"And what exactly is my type?"

"Over to you, pal." Trip looked out over the water.

Clay shrugged. "You know, like…us." She wagged a finger between herself and Trip. "Handsome, butch, sporty…did I mention handsome?"

Trip added, "Yeah, what Clay said. In other words, if we weren't like sisters, we'd probably be dating each other."

"There's a significant difference between the two of you and Dani. She doesn't even want to be around me half the time."

"Explain," Trip said.

"She barely speaks to me one day, almost kisses me the next, shies away if I get too close, can't talk about her feelings, and goes to Savannah twice a week, probably to get laid."

Trip frowned. "You mean when I send her to the airport to ship or pick up semen?" She tossed her chicken bone into the woods. "This is breeding season and frozen semen is big business in the horse world. I've been sending Dani to Savannah to keep her from feeling so isolated in Pine Cone."

Grace considered Trip's comment and studied the river. She'd basically just met Dani and already had the hots for her, but Dani was running hot and cold. She took another sip of wine, and when she glanced back at Clay and Trip, they were both studying her with a look she knew too well. "No, no, no. I'm not falling for her. Really."

"Then why can't you look at us? You're a crap liar," Trip said.

"And what were you doing in the alley with her the other day?" Clay waved a rib in front of her face like a magic wand.

"Yeah. Wait. What?" Trip looked back and forth between them. "What alley?"

Clay gave Trip the abbreviated version of finding Grace and Dani practically tit to tit between the hardware and drugstore. "She said nothing was going on, but it looked cozy to me."

"You're seeing things." If Clay imagined their coziness, so did Grace because she'd felt the connection too.

"Did I imagine seeing the two of you heading into my office yesterday?"

"She was upset because she saw me with Jay but couldn't talk about it. I'm not falling for her. She's afraid of getting involved, I mean *really* involved."

"What do you want, Grace?" Trip waited while Grace twirled her wine glass.

"I can't stop thinking about her, but I refuse to chase her. I tried that once, and we all know how that turned out. Am I doing something wrong?"

Trip washed down some potato salad and turned to Grace. "Dating is a dance. If you yank on the lead rope to force a horse to follow, he's either going to balk or his flight instinct will kick in and he'll drag you off your feet. So, instead, you guide the horse to go where you want by teaching them to give in to pressure. It's how a stallion moves a herd, or a boss mare leads it. Before you know it, she'll be following you around like a puppy."

"I thought we were talking about dating, not dancing or riding lessons." Clay shook her head. "Seriously, dude, how did you ever get a woman, much less bed half of Pine Cone, with advice like that?"

"Dancing, training horses, and dating—a lot of the same techniques apply. That's why I'm so good at all three." Trip blew on her fingernails and brushed them against her T-shirt.

"Okay, I get it, maybe," Grace said. "But you know I've got no game."

"Absolutely none." Trip scooted closer.

Clay draped her arm around Grace's shoulder on the other side. "The important thing is to just be yourself, Gracie. You're a people person who enjoys chatting and spending time. Let Dani see the real you."

"Yep," Trip added, reaching for another chicken wing.

"The other night, she bolted from the cottage like her butt was on fire." She realized her error too late.

"Your cottage?" Trip eyed her.

"What night?" Clay rolled her hand, encouraging Grace to say more.

She shook her head. "It wasn't like that. She's trying to figure out why Harry hates me, so I asked her to come by and check out my place. We had a couple of drinks and…"

Two pairs of eyes locked on her like sights on a target.

"And we almost kissed. We moved together at the same time, and it almost happened, but it didn't. All I saw were elbows and dust shooting up from her shoes on her way back to the house." Grace paused, her face heating. "But then she kissed me at the cookout. Totally clumsy. It just happened because she was upset or something. Who knows?" She gave Trip a shy glance.

"Yes." Trip pumped her fist in the air. "And what'd you do?"

"Well, it was awkward. Sort of like, 'There. I did it.'" Grace ducked her head and grinned. She'd been so moved by that simple, clumsy kiss that she'd initiated another. It had been sizzling and emotionally arousing. "Then I showed her how to really kiss."

Clay hooted, and Trip reached behind Grace to bump fists with Clay.

"Sounds to me like she's coming around," Trip said.

Grace frowned. "I don't know what to do next."

"Cook for her," Clay added, her stomach never far from any conversation.

"Screw her brains out at the first available opportunity," Trip said. "She can get good food at a dozen restaurants, but great sex—"

"Worthless I say, totally worthless. She's probably had more sex than all of us combined, and I'm not going to sleep with her to try and convince her to stay. She either wants me or she doesn't. End of story." Grace poured another cup of wine. "Let's talk about something else. Like maybe Clay scoring with the gorgeous River Hemsworth?"

"Wait, what?" Trip looked at her.

"Nothing," Clay said.

"Come to think of it, why did you leave yesterday in such a hurry? You didn't even say good-bye. And you left River poolside looking kind of upset." Trip's attention was fully focused on Clay now.

"I don't want to talk about me. We're here for Grace, remember?"

"Too late," Grace chimed in.

"So? What happened yesterday?" Trip wasn't letting this one go.

"We had a misunderstanding," Clay said.

"And?" Her answer clearly hadn't satisfied Trip.

"We spent last night sorting it out." Clay's cheeks turned pink under the scrutiny.

"All night?" Grace's high-pitched question ended in a giggle.

"And this morning." Clay couldn't stifle a big grin or stop the deeper flush of her cheeks.

"I knew it." Grace was smiling too, her own worries forgotten for the moment in the presence of Clay's happiness. "I knew she was into you that very first day under the maple tree, sitting on that stupid fake plastic deer."

"Yeah, well, it just took me a little longer to figure it out."

"Maybe you'll finally cheer up. I miss my pal, Clay." Trip reached over and playfully punched her shoulder.

"And what about you, Fast Break?" Clay asked. "Anybody catch your interest?"

"Not really." Trip shook her head. "It's...complicated."

"Oh, do tell." Grace rubbed her hands together.

Trip peeled at the label on her beer bottle before finally answering. "I sort of like someone from my past, but she's not the forgiving type."

"Ouch," Clay said. "Did you sleep with her girlfriend or something?" Trip's look said it all. "Oh shit, dude, really?"

"The girl from college?" Grace asked. "You were all friends until...She told us about that, Clay. Remember?"

"But she's not *here*, is she?"

Grace couldn't recall the girl's name, but there weren't that many new women in town, only River, Dani, and... "Jamie? My Jamie?" Trip looked vexed. "I don't mean *my* Jamie, just my officer Jamie."

Clay shook her head. "I'm confused. The one who's been laying parking tickets all over your truck like she's hanging wallpaper?"

Trip nodded. "The girl knows how to make an impression."

"She's just doing her job, Trip. I've asked her to use more discretion, but she's military."

"I'd be happy to pay every single ticket if she'd just talk to me."

"We're a sorry bunch," Grace said.

Trip sighed. "Pathetic."

They were silent for a few long moments, staring out at the river while they contemplated their woman issues.

Then Grace threw her head back and laughed. "You can sit down here and sulk if you want, Trip Beaumont." She turned both her thumbs toward herself. "Glitter Girl is putting her heart out there again." She pointed to them. "Clay has River now. When you're done with your little pity party, Trip, go home, put on your big girl pants, and go courting like the Fast Break from our high school days. Show Jamie you've still got what it takes to sweep her off her feet."

Chapter Eleven

Dani tapped on Trip's open office door, hoping her desire to be in on Petunia's examination this morning didn't reflect a lack of trust in her abilities. She'd gotten the impression Trip's interest was more personal, more in the direction of Jamie Grant. Before they finished the examination, she'd know for sure. If she knew one thing, it was women, with the exception of Grace, who left her a tangled mass of nerves and emotions. "They're in exam room three," Dani said.

"Thanks." Trip put her pen down and rose from her chair. She wiped her hands on her jeans and looked a little unsettled, though nothing like Sunday morning after the party.

When she brushed past, Dani stopped her with a hand on her arm. She reached around Trip and neatly slipped the white lab coat from the hook by the door. "I'm told that a white coat with doctor on the name tag always impresses." She handed the coat to Trip with a smile.

Trip's uncustomary response was a nod and a weak "thanks." Something was definitely bothering her, but now wasn't the time to broach it.

Michelle stepped out of exam room three, pulled the door closed, and gasped for breath. "Oh my God," she said, her voice carrying down the hallway. "I should've put that one in a room with a window that opens."

Trip clenched her jaws, and Dani jumped in. "Michelle, can you give me a hand with the Hollister beagle in the back?"

Trip stopped her. "Actually, Dani, I'd like you to see the Grant dog with me. Two heads will be better than one." Trip glared at Michelle. "And I want you to wait in my office. We're going to have a little chat about your continued lack of professional decorum."

Michelle opened her mouth to say something but checked herself and went directly to Trip's office. Dani didn't say another word.

Trip sucked in a deep breath and opened the door to exam room three, and Dani trailed silently behind. "Hey, Jamie."

Jamie looked from Dani to Trip, her expression questioning. A wheat-colored, wire-haired terrier mix sat on the exam table, watching them with wary eyes and pressing herself against Jamie's chest. "I thought we were seeing Dani this morning."

Dani was smart enough to know when to let the boss take the lead.

"Dani and I talked about what you told her Saturday and agreed that two heads would be better to figure out your pup's problem." Trip spoke in a soothing tone for Petunia's benefit. "Will you introduce us?"

Jamie seemed to consider her options briefly, but finally stroked the terrier's head and nodded. "This is Petunia." Jamie's face twisted in a grimace. "I just call her P. Some joker at the shelter probably named her that because of her gastric problems."

"Hello, P." Trip held out her hand for Petunia to sniff while Dani made notes in Petunia's chart. "Hey, girl. I understand you've got a bit of a bellyache." Petunia's lips curled into a silent snarl.

Jamie cleared her throat. "It might help if you ditched the coat. She was rescued from a research lab, and they probably wore white lab coats."

"Damn. You didn't tell me that," Dani said, shucking her coat and taking Trip's as well. "I'll toss these in my office."

"While you're doing that, will you send Michelle out back to help Jerome for the rest of the morning?" Trip kept her voice nonchalant so she didn't upset Petunia, but Dani could tell she was still troubled by Michelle's earlier comment. "Then call Jerome and let him know she needs to strip some stalls."

Shoveling out the bottom layers of urine-soaked wood chips was the worst job in a stable. Dani grinned. "Sure thing, Trip."

But Jamie frowned. "You don't have to do that for me. I'm used to people saying crap about P's gastric problem."

Trip looked up sharply. "Not in my clinic. Not about my sick clients."

Dani ditched the lab coats, delivered the bad news to Michelle, and called Jerome before heading back to the exam room. When she slipped back inside, Trip and Jamie were ending a hug. From Jamie's flushed face and Trip's starry-eyed smile, both had enjoyed it.

"Now, let's see if Petunia is buying it," Trip said.

Petunia's dark eyes went from Jamie's face to Trip's, and she sniffed at Trip's scent on Jamie. Trip tucked the diaphragm end of her stethoscope inside her shirt to warm it and held out her hand to the terrier again. Petunia snuffled Trip's hand, then stood on the table to thoroughly examine Jamie's scent on her. Trip scratched behind Petunia's ears like Jamie had done, then knelt next to the table to put herself at eye level with the terrier, but not so close as to be in Petunia's personal space. Dani was constantly impressed with her skills with animals.

"So, P." Trip worked her scratching fingers around Petunia's neck to her chest. "Your mom and I go way back to when we were both baby dykes strutting around the college campus like we thought we were special. Actually, Jamie is sort of special."

That explained the familiarity between them, Dani thought, but not the tension.

Petunia thumped her tail against the metal table as if agreeing with what Trip had said, then her back foot when Trip scratched a particularly itchy spot along her spine.

Trip continued. "Jamie upped my game on the basketball court so much, we were both being scouted to play pro." She kept up the running monologue while scratching turned to a massage before she slowly stood. "But things happened and she ran off to join the Army. I didn't even get to talk to her before she left. I was really scared when I found out she was doing tours in Iraq."

Trip finally glanced up at Jamie, who was watching her with an unreadable expression. Dani sensed definite chemistry between them but returned her attention to the chart.

Petunia sighed and rolled onto her back, releasing a long expel of flatulence as she relaxed into Trip's gentle massage of her belly. Trip continued, keeping her voice low and even, and Dani scribbled notes as Trip dictated. "Possible neuter scar along the belly crease, but since she came from a research lab, it could be from a different, more extensive surgery. Significant bloating, but flatulence odor is indicative of incomplete digestion rather than fetid bowel. Tenderness apparent in the upper quadrant upon palpation and a thickening of tissue which could indicate a number of things—intense inflammation, blockage, scarring from previous surgeries, intestinal cysts, or tumors."

Trip pulled her stethoscope from her shirt, keeping up the massage with her other hand. "Jamie, can you rub her lightly while I do some listening?" Jamie trailed her fingers along Petunia's chest while Trip listened to her bowel sounds, then along her belly while Trip listened to her heart and lungs. "Heart and lungs sound good, but her gut is definitely painful and producing a lot of gas." She held the stethoscope out to Dani and stepped to the side. "How about you take a listen just in case you hear something I didn't."

Dani couldn't suppress a moment of pride that Trip wanted her opinion as well. She put her notes aside and rubbed her hands together to make sure they were sufficiently warm. Petunia's only reaction when Dani's hand replaced Trip's was to let out a long snore. She was a picture of relaxation. They waited in silence for Dani's verdict.

"Heart and lungs good," Dani confirmed. "And I concur on the tenderness." Petunia's hind foot twitched when Dani pressed against her lower belly.

Trip gently rolled Petunia onto her side when she began to sneeze from lying on her back. The terrier stood and shook herself, then looked to Jamie.

"So," Jamie said.

"I understand that Petunia has a history of bowel problems, but let's talk specifically about why you brought her in today."

"She's been reluctant to eat lately. I've been feeding her prescription food that a specialist in New York prescribed, but she's either tired of it or doesn't feel like eating at all."

"If her intestines are tender or she's feeling too bloated, that could discourage her appetite," Trip said. "Dani, let's draw some blood and get a panel on her."

"I brought stool and urine samples," Jamie said, pointing to a pair of plastic containers by the exam room sink.

"That's great." Dani gathered what she needed from the cabinets over the sink's counter.

"I know the drill. I've taken her to a dozen specialists, trying to fix this for her." Jamie's voice broke on her last words, and the muscle in her jaw worked while she watched Dani.

While Dani collected the samples, Trip took the chart, and when she spoke again, her voice was thicker and quieter as if she were fighting deep emotions. "So, can you give me some background on Petunia? You rescued her from a research lab?"

Jamie shook her head. "I got her from a kill shelter. She'd originally come from a research lab. The people who left her there said their son had adopted P from the SPCA after the lab gave in to public pressure to stop animal testing. Then he dumped her on them when he decided to travel overseas after graduating college."

"If we could track down the type of research they were doing, it might give some clues about her problem." Trip was in full problem-solving mode, and Dani just watched her work.

"The shelter asked, but the couple didn't know and their son was overseas and unreachable. I asked for information on the people who turned her in, but the shelter said that was private information they couldn't give out."

"What was the name of the shelter? I'd like to talk to the vet they use to see if they can give me any history on her."

Surprise showed in Jamie's eyes, then a glimmer of hope. "Nobody, none of the specialists we've seen, ever asked me that before."

Dani patted Jamie's shoulder. "I promise Trip and I will leave no stone unturned. Trust us."

Jamie looked down at Petunia, her throat working. When she looked up, she searched Trip's face, not Dani's, and Dani hesitated to break their connection.

She finished collecting and labeling the specimens and held them up. "I'm going to get these off to the lab. On the way back, I can pick up lunch." Trip pulled her attention away from Jamie long enough to nod, and Dani couldn't get out of the exam room fast enough. Whatever was happening between Trip and Jamie was personal and none of her business.

She drove into town slowly, giving Trip and Jamie time to finish the intake forms and have a real talk if they wanted. She could kill some time before collecting their lunches. She parked near Main Street but sat in her car for a while with the windows down. Seeing the interaction between Trip and Jamie had spun her thoughts down that emotionally uncomfortable but physically pleasurable path of thinking about Grace again, until a loud commotion across the street distracted her.

"I'll only be here a minute, Grace." A hulking, hairy man flying Hell's Angels colors on his leather vest squared off with Grace beside a cherry apple red Harley.

"I can't let you park here, Will. We've had this conversation before. My new deputy has a hard-on for illegal parking. I'm just doing you a favor."

"All right then, Grace, you know what has to happen." The man stepped closer and reached around her waist at the same time Grace placed her right hand on his left arm.

Dani imagined the cop in Grace flying hot at having her warning ignored and her personal space violated, and the big man protecting his machismo by standing up to a woman. Dani ran across the street, grabbed the man's right arm, swept his feet from under him, and threw him to the ground. She jammed her knee in his spine and wrenched his arms behind his back. "Cuff him." When Grace didn't move, Dani looked up. "What are you waiting for?"

"What are you doing, Dani?"

Grace's irritated expression said Dani had done something stupid. Again. What was wrong with her? She didn't overreact, except where Grace was concerned apparently.

"Grace, will you get this person off my back before I smash her like a bug."

Dani looked from Grace to the man under her. "What's going on?"

"Let Will up, Dani. He's not going to hurt me or anyone else."

Heat rose up Dani's neck as she released the man and slowly stood to face Grace. "He put his hands on you."

Will brushed off his clothes and grinned at Grace. "This your new girlfriend?"

Grace shook her head. "Go get your mother's lunch. I'll watch your bike." When Will walked away, Grace turned back to Dani. "Care to explain?"

"I thought he was going to hurt you." Grace stepped closer, and Dani thought she was about to touch her but stopped short.

"I appreciate your concern, really, but maybe you should ask next time, especially if I'm on the job."

Dani tried for nonchalance, but she burned with embarrassment. "He grabbed a deputy sheriff. You grabbed him. Where I come from that means things are going to get ugly. What was happening if you weren't going to arrest him?"

"It's an old shtick from our teens. When we disagree about something, Will and I dance it out. The first one to step on the other's toes loses."

Dani shook her head. "You're one strange law enforcement officer. Excuse me for overreacting…and for caring." She glanced at the ground. She'd admitted that she cared for Grace, but out loud this time.

"You care about me? That's certainly news." The lines around Grace's eyes and mouth softened, followed quickly by a wide grin.

"We had breakfast together at the diner, with the rest of the town. You stopped me from getting a bad haircut. I practically live with you at the B and B. I've been in your home. We almost kissed at your place once, sort of kissed, twice, at the cookout. Guess I must like you a little, right?" She tried to make light of her blunder, but Grace slid her hand down Dani's arm creating a deep stirring.

"I'm just surprised you admitted it. I'm flattered but also having trouble keeping up with the back-and-forth. Do you want to talk about what happened at the cookout?"

"Not really. Sorry." Dani looked around and their little scene had attracted more than a few curious bystanders. "I apologize for my macho bullshit, then and today. Every time I'm around you, I get…"

"What?"

"Never mind." Grace stood up to Dani when she lashed out, gave advice about small town survival, and offered emotional comfort. Grace mesmerized and pulled Dani in, made her feel safe and cherished, like family only better. But Grace also gave her hope for a love and home she'd never imagined, and that was the first step toward pain. From Grace's viewpoint, Dani was a very bad gamble. From Dani's perspective, Grace was a chance at the lottery, but could she take the risk?

"O—kay. Unnecessary as it was, thanks for trying to protect me." Grace touched Dani's hand and held it briefly before adding, "I was wondering if you'd do me a small favor."

"Sure. Seems I need to atone."

"Help me get Harry back home."

Not exactly the request she'd expected, or possibly wanted, but easy enough to accommodate. "Sure. When?"

"MJ will have the sunroom ready tomorrow afternoon. Bring him with you from work?"

"I can do that." She wasn't ready for Grace to go but struggled for something else to say, something meaningful that needed saying, but then she nodded and walked toward the diner. When Grace was around, Dani turned into a malleable, eager to please butch, groveling at the feet of her femme Dom—a thought that both excited and terrified her. But Grace deserved more.

Grace forced herself to leave Dani outside the diner, though she'd felt a powerful urge to stay and help Dani tweeze the words she was struggling with to the surface. But she hadn't asked for Grace's help. As she walked toward her patrol car, her walkie-talkie crackled with Jamie's voice. Had something gone wrong with Petunia's exam this morning? When she looked at her watch, more time had passed than she realized while she and Dani chatted. The woman made her lose track of time and herself, probably not a totally good thing.

"Sarge, you on?"

"Yeah, what's up?"

"Can you come by Clay's garage? We've got a situation over here."

"On my way." When Grace pulled up a few minutes later, Trip, Jamie, and Petunia headed toward her. Clay was on the phone and didn't look happy. "What's going on?"

"P alerted on a toolbox in the back of the garage."

Grace took a second to register the information, her mind still partly on Dani, and the improbability of Jamie's words. "Drugs? Here?"

Jamie nodded. "Clay suspects they belong to Bo, one of their mechanics."

Grace turned toward Clay, but the question she was going to ask stalled when she saw the fear on Clay's face. "What's wrong?" Grace took a step toward her.

"Bo, why are you answering River's phone?" Clay said as Grace moved closer and leaned in to hear the conversation.

"Cause me and your girl are taking a little drive." There was static or wind noise in the background. "Let's just say you've got something I need, and I've got something you want."

"I'll bring your shit, Bo. It's not like I want it, but you better not hurt River."

Grace touched Clay's arm, trying to keep her calm so they could get more information. "Where is he?"

Clay punched the button to end the call. "He's got River and wants me to bring the drugs and meet him at the mill to trade." Clay stomped around, dust flying up from her boot falls. "Damn it all to hell." She stopped and looked at Grace. "I'm going."

"No." Grace was firm. These situations could get out of hand quickly enough without a loved one nearby escalating things. Grace needed to focus on River, not divide her attention worrying about Clay.

"He said for me to come alone. He specifically told me not to bring you. So, I'm going." She squared off in front of Grace.

"*No, you're not.* You're staying here with Jamie." She looked at Jamie. "Call for backup. Tell them we have an active hostage situation and drugs are involved. Who knows if Bo is under the influence of something right now."

"It would explain a lot." Clay swept her fingers through her hair. "God, I'm an idiot."

Trip rested her hand on Clay's shoulder. "Leave it with Grace, pal."

"But he'll see her and do something stupid. He said no cops."

"Clay, I've got this." Grace's voice was steady, calm. "He's not going to hurt River. Besides, she's smart and will be trying to escape. At the least she'll distract him, throw him off his plan." She walked toward her patrol car, planning her route, with Clay on her heels. "He'll take the Mill Road, that's fastest and the most secluded, and I'll be on the loop road. Trust me, he'll never see me coming. I'll approach on foot once I get there. Now, let me do my job."

"Aren't you going to wait for backup? Isn't that how this works?" Clay asked.

"I can handle one redneck." Grace closed the patrol car door and backed away from the garage. Dust and gravel swirled as she whipped the cruiser onto the paved road.

Things like this didn't usually happen in Pine Cone, and Grace hadn't expected the adrenaline that flooded her system and made her feel like Super Woman. She stomped the accelerator flat out, lights and siren blaring, and leaned forward as if her body weight would propel the car forward faster.

When she reached the Mill Road fork, she veered to the right following the loop road which would be less conspicuous and have less traffic. Finally, she saw dust clouds in the distance on the main road and gunned the gas again. She caught sight of Clay's old pickup that River drove ahead of her and to the left. The vehicle was weaving in the road, and it looked like the two people inside were fighting.

River was one feisty woman, and she wouldn't give up easily. "Good girl. Keep it up," Grace said as she watched in disbelief as the pickup suddenly swerved off the shoulder of the road, down the embankment, and into the Altamaha River. "Oh, no! This can *not* be happening." She skidded to a stop at the spot where the truck left the road and saw it sinking slowly, water pouring in through the windows.

Grace unsnapped her seat belt while opening the door and ran toward the bank. River popped through the surface and started treading water. "Swim this way, River. Over to me." The top of the truck was almost completely under water and disappearing quickly. River glanced back and forth between the sinking truck and Grace before diving back under. "What are you doing? River, no."

Grace pulled at her heavy utility belt and dropped it on the ground. She'd sink like a stone if she tried to swim with all the equipment around her waist. She stripped off her uniform shirt to release the bulky vest and toed off her shoes. As she started toward the water, River emerged dragging Bo behind her.

"Are you all right?" Grace asked.

"I'm good..." Her breath came in gasps. "But I need...to get away...from him. He's all yours." River swept her hands through her wet hair and started walking barefoot back the way they'd come.

Grace grabbed her gun and pointed it at Bo who was still spitting and coughing on the ground. He wasn't going anywhere. She glanced over her shoulder and saw Clay and Trip pull up in Trip's truck. Clay would take care of River now. Grace reached for her walkie-talkie, canceled further police assistance, and requested an ambulance, non-emergency.

When Bo recovered enough to breathe properly, Grace handcuffed him and pulled her shirt and utility belt on. The only things left to do now were fill out the paperwork back at the office and keep Clay away from Bo until the ambulance arrived.

CHAPTER TWELVE

Dani pulled off her smock the next afternoon and threw it in the laundry bin on her way to pick up Harry. She'd thought about seeing Grace again all day, and Michelle had called her out for being distracted several times.

"So, where you off to in such a hurry? Thought we'd grab a drink on the way home since we're so friendly and civilized now."

"Can't. I'm taking Harry back to Grace's this afternoon. It's time to see what happens."

Michelle cocked a hip to the side. "See what happens with Harry or with Grace?"

"Seriously, it's time for Harry to be resettled wherever he's going."

"Let's keep it real, boss. You're more interested in Grace Booker than you want to admit. I've seen the same look you've got in more than a few women's eyes."

"You're imagining things. I'm taking Harry to the B and B because I live there, for the time being. It has nothing to do with Grace." A tiny flutter inside begged to differ, but what was the point of sharing that? "I'll see you in the morning."

"Whatever, but if you come to work with that fresh-fucked look on your face, I'll bitch-slap you hard with an I told you so." Michelle tossed a flirty wave over her shoulder.

Dani tried to push the image of having sex with Grace out of her mind by concentrating on Harry's resettlement. Being near Grace again was challenging enough physically without fighting her own traitorous feelings, which she hadn't bothered to acknowledge or share with Grace.

She threw a towel over Harry's cage and strapped it in the passenger seat of her SUV.

"On the road again," he chirped happily along the way.

"Yes, my little friend, and I hope you like your new home." She also hoped Harry's sabbatical had somehow resolved his dislike of Grace, or he could end up re-homed, which was not good for a parrot with attachment issues.

When Dani pulled into the B and B driveway, Mary Jane greeted her. "Grace got detained by the sheriff but will be along as soon as she can. They're wrapping up that drug bust and chase from yesterday."

"I heard all the commotion. Is everybody okay?" Dani asked.

"Yeah, just paperwork now. Can I help with anything?"

"I've got Harry. Is his large aviary already in the sunroom?"

"We didn't have time to move it this morning, but Grace said she'd take care of it when she got home. You can just park Harry on the coffee table for the time being. We'll fix him up later. You probably have other things to do."

"I told Grace I'd help get him settled, so I don't mind sticking around." She'd never been alone with Mary Jane without a meal between them. Their only other common topic was Grace, sort of, and she wasn't comfortable having a conversation about her. She followed Mary Jane into the house and placed Harry's cage on the coffee table in the sunroom, taking in the changes Mary Jane had made to accommodate him. "He'll love it out here."

"I think so too. What about a glass of sweet tea while we wait?"

"Sounds good."

"I might even have a leftover slice of peach cobbler from dinner last night, if you're interested."

"I'm always interested in your food, Mary Jane." Her initial caloric concerns about Mary Jane's cooking had faded, along with the weirdness of eating with strangers. She almost looked forward to meal times now, sampling the latest recipes, and chatting with the small group of people who were becoming more familiar every day and the ones passing through.

Mary Jane heated the cobbler, added a dollop of ice cream, and placed it along with a glass of tea in front of Dani at the counter. "Enjoy."

"None for you?"

"I'm watching my schoolgirl figure."

Dani gave Mary Jane a visual once-over. She was verging on being too thin. "How do you and Grace stay so fit eating like this all the time? My grandmother used to say, never trust a skinny cook."

"My motto is never trust anyone who doesn't enjoy their own cooking, and I probably eat my weight in food every day. Just have a high metabolism I guess."

Dani shoveled the cobbler like she hadn't eaten all day and savored the blend of peaches with sugar and a crusty top. One thing Southerners got right was comfort food. Had her mother ever prepared a meal? Nothing about her home life seemed normal— fast food, strangers, and constant bickering over money—not one of her childhood memories was nearly as sweet as Mary Jane's tea or cobbler. She'd gone quiet, and Mary Jane was staring. "This is fantastic, Mary Jane. Really good."

"Please, call me MJ, honey."

"I can see why people keep coming back here year after year. It feels like a home, or what I imagine one should feel like."

Mary Jane's broad smile made her look younger and even more welcoming. "Thank you. That's probably the best compliment you could pay a Southerner." She refilled Dani's glass. "You mentioned your grandma. Is she still alive?" Mary Jane leaned casually against the stove as if she'd inquired about the weather. She had no way of knowing her question cut through Dani like a finely honed blade.

But she'd opened this door and couldn't ignore Mary Jane's question. "N—no." She choked down the unexpected flood of emotions that brought tears. She pretended to sip her tea but couldn't swallow. "Died years ago."

"You were close."

Dani nodded.

Mary Jane moved to her side, rubbing her hand soothingly down Dani's back. "I'm sorry, honey. I didn't mean to upset you." But her kindness did exactly that in the most bittersweet way. Dani wiped her eyes and looked away. "Granny was the best. Caring, understanding, and always on my side. She used to say home was the most important thing in life, whether with blood relatives, family of choice, friends, or lovers. She was the only real family I had, and I miss her every day."

"And your parents?"

Dani shook her head, emotionally unwilling and physically unable to speak.

Mary Jane hugged Dani and held on, probably sensing the subject of her parents wouldn't be covered today. Besides, a woman as compassionate as Mary Jane would never understand her parents' poor life choices and preference for drugs and booze over their only child. She'd tried to erase the painful memories, but occasionally a soft touch or kind word reminded her of what she'd missed.

Grace watched the scene unfold between Dani and Mary Jane from the back door. She desperately wanted to know what they were talking about but couldn't bring herself to interrupt. Dani was more emotional than Grace had ever seen her, so Mary Jane had touched a nerve. She waited until Dani composed herself before making her presence known.

"Hey, sorry I'm late. Is there any peach cobbler left or has Dani bogarted it all?"

Dani finally turned toward Grace, looking almost normal except for her red-streaked eyes. "You snooze, you lose."

Grace feigned shock and fell to her knees at Dani's stool. "Please give me the tiny morsel on your plate. I'll be forever in your debt."

Dani glanced between her last bite of cobbler and Grace with a mischievous grin and then offered her hand. "How can I refuse such a beautiful woman? It's yours." She slid the plate to her left and pulled the stool out for Grace.

"You are indeed a kind woman." Grace picked up the saucer, swiped Dani's fork from her fingers, and raked the last bite of cobbler into her mouth. "Oh my, so good."

"Didn't your parents teach you any manners?" Mary Jane pretended to be shocked, but her eyes glinted with satisfaction.

"Sorry, no breakfast or lunch today." She grinned at Dani and plopped beside her at the counter. "How are you, Doc?" She wanted to touch Dani, to let her know that no matter what she was going through, both she and Mary Jane were there for her, but decided the attention might upset her more.

"Better after my snack. Did you work all night? I heard about the drug bust."

"Pretty much, but it's all squared away now."

"Good. Harry is in the sunroom." She nodded toward Mary Jane. "We were waiting for you so we could move his aviary from the cottage. Are you still up for it?"

Dani's concerned tone tugged at Grace, and she placed her hand gently on Dani's forearm. "I'm fine. Really. Thanks for asking and for bringing Harry home."

"No problem." Dani's voice was thick with emotion as she hurried out the back door toward the cottage.

"What's going on, MJ?"

"Another time, honey. Let's keep it light. Sure you're okay?" When Grace nodded, Mary Jane fell in behind Dani, and Grace had no choice but to follow along.

She'd forgotten how much trouble she and Karla had getting the aviary into the cottage in the first place, so wedging it back through her tight front door took longer than she'd hoped. By the time she and Dani got it to the larger sunroom door, Mary Jane was done.

"Hate to leave you girls, but I need to finish supper or there won't be any tonight."

"We've got it now, MJ," Dani said, giving her a quick hug.

Grace stared at the exchange while Mary Jane gave her a wink over Dani's shoulder. All Grace could do was smile and wonder what had transpired between the two of them to create this sudden bond.

When Dani turned back toward her, she must've had a strange look on her face. "What's wrong, Grace?"

"Nothing."

"You look like it's something."

"You and hugging? MJ? Just surprised."

Dani looked down and scuffed her leather lace-up boots in the grass. "Well, she said I should call her MJ, and we sort of had a moment. She's a really nice woman."

She waited for Dani to expand on the *moment*, but when nothing followed, she added, "Yes, she certainly is. And just so you know, if you ever need anything, we've got your back."

Dani offered a weak smile and her eyes darkened, showing how much Grace's offer meant. The air between them shimmered with emotion until Dani said, "Thanks. Let's get this monstrosity inside."

They positioned the aviary in the space Mary Jane had cleared on the southwest corner, stood back, and assessed their work.

"This looks perfect," Dani said.

Grace tried to scoot around her, placed both hands lightly on her waist to pass between her and a nearby lamp, and stopped when their bodies came together. Dani tensed at the initial contact but relaxed when Grace lingered.

"You're a very touchy person, Grace." Dani's voice was a strained whisper.

"I'm sorry. Does it bother you?"

"Just different. Takes some getting used to." Dani's tone remained soft, almost wistful.

Grace inhaled Dani's special blend of shampoo with outdoorsy cologne and placed a light kiss in her hair. She loved the feel of Dani's body pressed against her breasts and released a contented sigh.

"Uh…Grace?"

"Yeah?" Grace was lost. Her task swept away on a current of emotion. She rested her cheek against Dani's back and wrapped her arms around her waist. A shot of arousal pulsed through her. "Oh God. Why do you feel so damn good?"

Dani moved one of Grace's hands up between her breasts. "Can you feel what you do to me, Grace?"

"I want you, Dani."

"Anytime, anywhere." Dani swallowed hard. "But shouldn't we finish this first?"

Grace returned her hands to Dani's waist, kissed the back of her neck, and finally raised her head. "Oh yeah. The cage. Just one tiny adjustment. The door needs to face this way. Could you turn it a bit?"

"Right." Dani's voice was husky as she made the change and then placed one hand over Grace's and tightened her grip. "How's that?"

"Perfect," Grace whispered and once again pressed against Dani's back. "Just perfect." Whatever had happened between Mary Jane and Dani had softened her, at least temporarily, and Grace soaked up the comfortable change.

"What's perfect?"

A voice from behind shattered the moment, and Grace stepped back. "Hi, Jamie. We're relocating Dirty Harry."

"I see." Jamie's tone implied she'd seen more than a simple birdcage transfer. "It looks great out here. He should like the sunlight and views across the yard."

Grace regained some of her composure but realized one hand still rested at Dani's waist. She pulled back slowly enough to appear casual just as a dreadful odor filled the room. She glanced down at Petunia leaning against Jamie's leg. "You better take her in the front door. MJ won't like her so close to the kitchen while she's cooking."

"Thanks. I forget. She's like an appendage."

"Any results from her checkup with Trip?" Grace asked.

"Not yet. She's still doing tests."

"Well, good luck. Jamie, have you met Trip's new vet, Dani Wingate?"

"Of course. We're both staying here." Jamie gave her a quirky smile and nodded at Dani. "Nice to see you again and thanks for your help with P the other day."

"No problem," Dani replied.

The room grew quiet. Jamie was too discreet to comment on what she'd seen, Dani wouldn't acknowledge what Jamie had walked in on, and Grace was temporarily lust dumb.

"Okay then. I'm going to shuck this uniform. Got plans. See you later," Jamie said.

"Yeah, later." Grace hadn't changed out of her uniform either, so distracted by Dani that she'd completely forgotten. "I should probably do the same."

Dani caught her hand as she turned to go and pulled her close again. "Shouldn't we put Harry in his cage first to let him get acclimated?"

Grace glanced down at their joined hands. "I'd rather stand here and hold your hand for a while, but if you insist."

Dani's cheeks flushed. "Do you always say exactly what's on your mind?"

"Mostly. I quite like the feel of our hands together."

"So do I, Grace, but—"

She placed her fingers over Dani's lips, the soft heat flashing through her. "And that's enough for now. Just let whatever happens happen. Don't overthink it." She kissed Dani lightly and forced herself to stop. "Let's get Harry settled."

Dani pulled the light covering off Harry's cage and lifted it toward the aviary. He spun around in his cage, looked straight at Grace, and squawked, "Man down. Man down." He flapped against the side of the small cage until his outstretched wings became trapped in the bars. "Grace. Five-O."

"Harry, please." Grace stepped closer, and he screeched louder.

"Grace, I think you should go. He's not going to calm down with you here."

The look Dani gave her pulsed with questions Grace had no answers for. The charmed seconds they'd spent together vanished, along with Grace's hope of an intimate evening getting to know Dani better.

Dani closed the sunroom door when Grace left to take a shower, thinking it best to protect Harry from any further upsets tonight. Maybe he'd simply responded badly to his new environment, or maybe not. His reaction to Grace had been just as bad, if not worse, than the first time she'd seen the two of them together. Animals had keen instincts about people. Was Harry's dislike of Grace a warning of some type? Did he sense something Dani had missed?

She glanced at Grace when she returned and pulled out a chair across from her at the table. Her eyes were dark with sadness and confusion. Harry's continued rejection hurt Grace, and Dani didn't know how to help.

"Sorry if I kept you waiting."

"Your timing is perfect, honey." Mary Jane placed a platter of fried chicken in the center of the table. A bowl of green beans, sweet potato fries, and a basket of freshly baked biscuits completed the meal.

"This looks delicious." Dani smiled at Mary Jane and then Grace, trying to engage her.

"Yeah, really good." Grace's usually sincere tone sounded flat and forced.

"Well, I hope you enjoy it because I have to run out for a while." She folded her arms and glanced from Dani to Grace. "I don't know what happened in the last thirty minutes, but you should probably resolve it before you eat or you'll get indigestion, and that would be an awful waste of my food. Grace, you know what to do with the leftovers when you're finished."

"Is anything wrong?" Grace asked.

"Doreen Divine-Dot asked me to come by and give her a hand with arrangements for a wedding this weekend. I shouldn't be late." She waved on her way out.

"Okay, bon appetit," Grace said to Dani.

"I'm sorry about Harry. It must be upsetting not to know why he rejects you, but I'm not sure what else to do."

"I'm starting to get a complex, but thanks for understanding."

The hurt in Grace's voice pierced Dani's heart. If being rebuffed by a bird upset Grace this much, how would Dani's departure affect her? Was it more merciful to eventually leave Pine Cone without further explanation of how she felt or to tell Grace the truth? Her leaving would probably hurt worse the longer they continued this dance. The safe, arousing feeling of Grace's arms around her earlier returned and Dani made a split-second decision. "I can't be with you, Grace. Get involved with you. Care about you."

Grace slid her chair back and moved to Dani's side of the table. "Your eyes are saying something else."

"They are?" Damn it. She couldn't even lie convincingly when Grace was near.

"Your eyes are begging me not to believe what your mouth is saying. They're begging me to kiss you." Grace scooted Dani's chair away from the table so they were facing each other and knelt between her legs. "Am I wrong?" Grace slid her hands up Dani's thighs, kneading her flesh with strong, sure fingers.

Dani swallowed hard and shook her head, unable to admit what she really wanted. But she had to be clear before this went any further. "Grace, you need to know—"

"You're leaving as soon as you get a job up north?"

"Yes."

"I'm aware, Dani, but it doesn't change how I feel. I just don't want to waste any more time pretending. Let's get to know each other and enjoy the moment. No pressure, no promises."

The sharing part terrified Dani, but her choices were to face her fear or push Grace away entirely. The latter scared her more. They would eventually go their separate ways. "We can try."

"Excellent." Grace rose and straddled Dani in her chair. "I'd really like to kiss you right now. May I?"

Dani nodded and wrapped her arms around Grace. "I'd like that." Grace licked her lips and met Dani's with a touch so light she wasn't sure they'd connected until Grace's hot breath brushed the side of her face. "God, Grace."

"Kiss me. Like you mean it."

She cupped Grace's face and slowly brought their mouths together. Determined not to fumble like last time, Dani kissed her lightly, traced her lips with the tip of her tongue and requested entry. The gentleness of their connection set Dani's body on fire. When Grace opened, Dani claimed her, explored the soft heat of her mouth, poured everything she felt into Grace and prayed she wouldn't have to explain it in words. She slid her hands under Grace and pulled them closer, rubbing their chests together but resisting the urge to rock her pelvis. "You feel so good."

Grace kissed the side of Dani's neck and back to her ear, sucking her lobe and rimming her ear with her tongue before dipping inside.

Dani shivered and the sensations swept through her. "Grace, please."

"Please what?"

Grace's hot breath in her ear melted Dani's insides, and she shifted uncomfortably in her seat. She was so out of her element with Grace, letting her take charge, lead wherever she wanted, and she'd gladly follow.

"Do you want me to stop?" Grace asked.

"Never." Dani wanted this, wanted Grace more than she'd ever wanted anyone. Grace was fearless, diving into a situation with no net, no promise of anything, and Dani felt weak by comparison.

"If I don't stop, we might not have dinner." Grace ran her fingers through Dani's hair and sniffed the spot where her hairline stopped at her ear. "This smell is so you. I love it right here." She inhaled deeply and seemed to purr. "So good."

Dani kissed Grace again but this time didn't try to control the shifting of her hips against Grace's bottom. "I need you, Grace."

"I'm all yours."

"Well, is this what's for dinner?" Jamie's amused voice behind them again brought everything to an abrupt halt.

Dani started to get up, but Grace held her firmly and said, "Did anybody ever tell you your timing sucks, Grant?"

"Not until now. I was a basketball star, and my timing was impeccable. As I said, I'm on my way out and thought I'd grab a chicken leg or something to hold me over. Imagine my surprise." She motioned toward Grace and Dani.

Grace waved her hand toward the food spread out on the table. "Help yourself to whatever you want." Then she turned back to Dani. "Are you hungry yet?"

Dani played along. "Absolutely starving." Grace's subordinate had found them in a compromising position, but she remained unfazed, unwilling to relinquish her position on Dani's lap. She had to admire her guts.

"Why don't I make us a plate and we'll go to the cottage?"

"Sounds good."

"Yeah," Jamie said, "That would probably be more appropriate than the dining room table. After all, I have to eat here and I don't want to imagine you two…you know."

Grace gave Dani a quick kiss on the lips and rose as Jamie snagged two drumsticks and headed for the door. "See you lovebirds later."

"Jealous much?" Grace called after her, winked at Dani, and started filling two plates with food. "What would you like?"

"A little of everything and a lot of you."

"Good answer, Doc." She handed Dani her plate, quickly put away the leftovers, and led the way across the yard to the cottage.

Dani followed in Grace's powerful current, oblivious to hazards in the deep emotional waters Grace navigated so effortlessly. How would she communicate the things she'd kept buried for years? Was it even necessary? Grace said no pressure or promises. Her insides tightened the closer they got to the cottage. When Grace opened the door, Dani was in a full-blown panic and faltered at the threshold.

"Relax, Dani. I'm not a black widow and I'm not asking you to marry me. We're just having dinner." Grace waved her inside, threw the sofa cushions on the floor, and turned on a small fan on the corner of the kitchen island. "It's not much, but it'll circulate the air. "Sit. What would you like to drink?"

"Beer, if you have it." Dani chose the cushion closest to the door and set her plate on a small side table. "I don't know why I'm so nervous. I'm usually a…"

"A player, free-range chicken maybe?"

Dani grimaced. The words didn't totally describe her anymore, at least not the way she wanted Grace to see her. Now those descriptors conjured up a sense of being unfinished or lacking, and she didn't like the feeling.

Grace handed her a beer and settled beside her on a cushion, leaned over and gave her a quick kiss. "Dig in while it's still warm." Grace brought her plate closer and started eating. She'd taken a couple of mouthfuls before she noticed Dani watching her. "What?"

"Why do you have furniture if you prefer to sit on the floor?"

Grace's face turned pink as she sucked a fry into her mouth. "Uh-oh, busted. A habit I picked up as a child. Reminds me of happy times traveling the world with my folks."

"It's sort of sexy. I'm a little turned on right now." Grace's blush deepened, and Dani wanted her entire body to feel the heat. "You on the floor, fingers in your mouth, sucking on a fry. Damn hot."

"Thanks?" Grace's face glowed red. Mission accomplished.

"Did you like traveling with your parents?"

"Loved it. Different cultures, exotic foods, unique animals, wearing next to nothing, and all the diversity. Great times really." The laugh lines around Grace's mouth gradually disappeared and a worry line formed above one brow.

"Are you sorry now?"

Grace shook her head. "Sometimes I wonder if the nomadic lifestyle made me want more stability as an adult. I stayed in Pine Cone partly because of the people I met as a child."

"And the other part?"

"The B and B is home. I want to eventually put down roots here. Maybe even have a family." Grace grabbed several sweet potato fries and nibbled. "Do you have any childhood habits that remind you of your parents?"

"You mean other than self-preservation?" She hesitated, unsure if she should or even could say more about her pathetic upbringing. Recalling those times made her sick and weak, but Grace gave her courage to face them. She took a deep breath and steadied her voice. "Are you sure you want to hear this?"

"More than anything."

"My childhood home in the city was a series of crack houses and apartments shared with other addicts. The cops raided our place one night looking for drugs, ripped up furniture, and broke dishes. I was just a kid. They dumped my cereal out of the box all over the floor." Dani paused until the lump in her throat eased. "That was all I had to eat when my parents were drugged out."

"Oh, Dani." Grace's shocked voice was a whisper.

"And then," Dani sounded like the scared little girl she'd been that night, "they tore apart my stuffed giraffe and left his guts everywhere." Dani clasped her hands together until her knuckles turned white.

"I'm so sorry, Dani. No wonder you hate cops."

"I was twelve when we moved from the city into subsidized housing in a smaller town. I hoped for a fresh start, but my mother felt isolated with Dad looking for work all the time. He brought pills home to help her relax at first, but gradually the drugs replaced everything, and they forgot about work and me altogether. I left home at sixteen, and their addictions killed them." She forced it all out and waited for the look of pity in Grace's eyes, but it didn't come.

"Well, at least you didn't pick up those habits, right? You obviously have a lot of drive and determination."

Grace nudged her shoulder, and Dani did something she never imagined doing when she talked about her family—she laughed until tears streamed down her face. Her shoulders relaxed and she felt lighter. When she finally stopped laughing and wiped her eyes, she leaned over and kissed Grace. "Thanks. Guess I really needed to purge."

"That must've been a hard way to grow up. I am sorry about your folks and the things you missed."

"Thanks," Dani said.

"One more question?"

"Depends." Maybe this talking stuff wasn't so bad after all. Was this intimacy? Dani often wondered if she'd ever meet a woman she'd share her stories with and love enough to make sacrifices for. If that woman was Grace, Dani had to risk being totally honest.

"How did your childhood affect how you live your life now?"

"My parents taught me how to hide in the anonymity of the city, dull my feelings with the anesthesia of choice—which in my case was sex—and keep so busy that none of it ever catches up to me. The only thing I really learned was to avoid drugs and personal connections because one way or another they cause pain." Except for her career, she'd summed up the entirety of her life in two sentences. Way too much information. Grace seemed to be thinking about what Dani said, quietly studying her face.

"I'm really sorry, Dani." A progression of emotions played across Dani's face when she talked about her parents—fear, shame, embarrassment, anger, and finally relief. She was heartbreakingly sad, and her expression was like the one Grace had seen with Mary Jane. "Were you and MJ talking about your parents in the kitchen earlier?"

"My grandmother. She was my only close relative, but I didn't see her much because she lived far away. When I did visit, she tried to make up for all the crap in my life. We'd go to the lake for a picnic, or I'd help care for her menagerie of strays, sometimes for her...if she needed me. Other times we'd just sit and talk about life and what I could expect along the way. She helped me win my first girlfriend's heart when I was fifteen. Gran said a home and relationships were the key to happiness..." Her voice cracked. "But I never found that key."

"So, she's the reason you became a vet?"

"Probably. Her backyard was a zoo of cats, dogs, birds, and wildlife she'd taken in to nurse back to health or just feed, and I loved helping, feeling needed. I couldn't have a pet in the apartment."

"Sounds like an exceptional woman."

"She was, but I didn't even know the right questions to ask at fifteen. I'd probably be a better person if I'd had her guidance a bit longer. I still don't know much about relationships."

The sadness in Dani's voice wrenched Grace's heart. She moved their plates aside and shifted in front of Dani. "What don't you know?"

Dani edged closer until their knees touched and took Grace's hands. "This is the hardest thing I've ever done, so bear with me, Grace." Dani clenched her jaw several times before gathering enough courage to speak again. "I like you and I know I haven't done a very good job of showing it. You're fun to be around, easy to talk to, a great kisser, and you're damn gorgeous, not to mention smart, accomplished, and compassionate."

"You better stop, or I'll start believing you. Where's the but in this scenario?" Grace thumbed the back of Dani's hands, encouraging her to continue.

"I don't know how to give you what you want. I don't have a role model for long-term relationships. I've never had one myself. And the need for deep conversation escapes me. What's the purpose anyway, to expose your weaknesses so someone else can exploit them?"

"Not if you're lucky. Haven't you ever heard that two share the pain and disappointments of life and double the fun? If you find someone who's strong where you aren't and vice versa, it's a gift." She rubbed her hands back and forth on Dani's thighs until she looked at her again. "You don't have to tell me anything if you don't want to. I'm just interested in you, in everything about you." Her words registered on Dani's face like a splash of ice water.

Dani straightened and pulled away from Grace. "What if you don't like what you find?"

"I'm an excellent judge of character. You're a good person, Dani Wingate, but for some reason you don't want others to see that side of you."

"How do you know that?"

"You gave money to a homeless man, tried to save me from what you thought was an angry biker, animals love you, and we all know they have great instincts. You've spent your off time figuring out what's wrong with Harry. And you're constantly warning me to stay away from you so I won't get hurt."

Dani rolled off her cushion and stood. "And maybe you're just seeing what you want to see. Maybe you should find someone who can give you the stability you want. Why would you settle for less?" She waved her hand at the discarded plates and said, "Thanks for dinner...and the chat. I'll see you around?"

"Wait. What? You'll see me around?" The transition from intimate conversation and kissing to total shutdown had been a matter of seconds, and Grace felt the loss acutely. "What did I say wrong?"

"Nothing. This just isn't a good idea." Dani didn't wait for her to say anything else.

The cottage door closed softly behind her, and the room was too quiet and empty. Grace heard the disappointment in her own voice when Dani withdrew. Was she imagining a connection between them, heading down a familiar road with a woman who had no long-term potential? Her heart said no, but she'd pushed Dani outside of her comfort zone.

Grace ran her fingers across lips that still burned from Dani's kisses and hugged herself against the absence of Dani's touch. She wanted to understand what had gone wrong. She'd gotten a glimpse of the real Dani Wingate and was hooked. Would Dani take the time to recognize and accept the bond between them?

CHAPTER THIRTEEN

Dani locked the clinic for the day and walked toward her car. She'd showered and changed for her trip to a gay-friendly bar in Savannah. Dancing always took her mind off things. Tonight, it would be Grace and the constant urge to see her again. Grace's delicate handling of their dinner conversation about family and life desires had summoned things from her she hadn't intended to share. Had she already given Grace the ammunition to hurt her?

With every mile toward Savannah, Dani became less excited about the night ahead. She struggled between going back to Pine Cone, finding Grace, and spending the night with her, and getting as far away as possible. Grace stirred desires Dani didn't understand—taking a walk just to enjoy the scenery; sharing a drink on the B and B patio with a crazy parrot squawking in the background; attending a neighborhood cookout; sitting on the floor talking; kissing and more kissing, even if it didn't lead to sex. Grace was seeping into her pores and slowly changing her from a loner to a more engaged person, and she wasn't sure how she felt about that.

She parked across the street from the club's glass façade and shook her head to dislodge her unsettling feelings. Waiting for the line to clear, she scored the steady stream of women entering the club. A curvy redhead wearing an emerald-colored version of a little black dress caught her eye. She had great legs and her hair swung loose at her shoulders. She looked so much like Grace that Dani's stomach clenched and she did a double take. It *was* Grace. And a butch blonde with spiked hair wearing black leather had her hand firmly in the small of Grace's back ushering her into the club. The woman from Trip's cookout, the same woman Grace had held and comforted.

Dani gripped the steering wheel with both hands, willing the image to disappear. She reached for the door handle, released it, started the car, and then turned it off again. She shouldn't be here. Going after Grace or even watching her from a distance felt stalkerish but sitting in the parking lot waiting for her to come out again or leaving felt wrong too. She got out of the car, closed the door, and leaned against the side, weighing her options. A few minutes of dancing to let off some steam couldn't hurt. She had just as much right to be here as Grace.

Dani bolted through the parking lot, flashed her ID, and hurried into the club, but the change in lighting from the outside temporarily blinded her. She stepped to the side, and when she could see clearly again, scanned the ultra-modern interior, the blue-lit bar, and large dance floor, but Grace and her escort had vanished. Dani's chest tightened. What was happening to her? Grace had every right to date other women. So why was Dani so upset?

She moved to the bar and got a beer, refusing to think about what her erratic behavior meant. She was here for a diversion… and apparently so was Grace. Dani circled the club and stopped in the back with a view of the entire space. She downed her beer in a few gulps and ordered another from a passing waiter, the whole time surveying the interior for Grace. A couple of women made eye contact, but she quickly looked away, suddenly having no interest in her initial reason for coming here.

Then she spotted Grace in the middle of the dance floor a few inches from her date, moving to the rugged repetitive beat of DJ-blended dance music. Grace looked free, happy, and engaged in her surroundings, and Dani's heartbeat faltered. The times she'd spent with Grace—sharing breakfast at the diner, talking on the street, discussing relationships, or kissing—she'd been totally focused on her. Dani ached for their closeness again, for the touch of Grace's hand, the softness of her lips, her undivided attention. She'd blown her chance because of fear.

The music in the club changed from the teeth-rattling dance tune to a softer, more romantic one, and Dani's stomach churned. Grace's date stepped closer, slid her arm around Grace's waist, and pulled their bodies together. Dani heated at the thought of dancing with Grace, feeling the press of her full breasts against her chest and the slide of Grace's leg between her thighs. The image shattered as the blonde made the same moves, and Dani looked away. She'd pushed Grace into another woman's arms and couldn't bear to see and feel the results of her stupidity. Every stroke of the blonde's hands over Grace's body was like her own skin peeling off in layers.

She pushed off the wall and started toward them, her eyes totally focused on the lack of space between Grace and the blonde. Halfway across the dance floor, the sound of Grace's laughter cut through the music, and Dani stopped. One of the blonde's hands rested on Grace's shoulder and the other at her waist. Grace was having a good time. She enjoyed the blonde touching her. Dani needed to be anywhere but here. She looked around for an escape route, but the crowd pushed in on her.

She struggled to free herself from the mass of swaying bodies when a brunette shoved her way through the dancers, yelling and waving her arms, and headed straight toward Grace. Dani surged forward to get between them, but the tightly packed crowd pushed her back. The brunette shoved Grace and threw herself in the blonde's arms and entwined their legs. The blonde seemed temporarily shocked but recovered quickly and gave Grace a what-can-I-do shrug. "Real classy, stud," Dani said, trying again to get through the crowd, but was once more blocked. She danced around couples and finally made her way to the edge of the dance floor, but Grace was moving in the opposite direction.

And why shouldn't Grace get as far away from her as possible? She was kind, compassionate, and totally knew what she wanted out of life and deserved a woman who could give it to her. Not Dani. At that moment, she hated her weakness. She gave Grace one last longing glance before slinking back to her dark corner.

❖

"A little air, please?" Grace pulled out of Jay's arms to put some space between them on the dance floor. "You asked me out as friends. I'd like to keep it that way."

"Sorry, Grace. You just look so damn sexy in that dress. What do you expect?"

"A little respect, maybe?" Grace mumbled under her breath. She shouldn't have agreed to go out with Jay before she'd gotten over Cynthia. Pity dates often ended badly. The only woman Grace wanted to be this close to rejected her. Why had she thought going out with another spurned soul would be a good idea?

"We could dance until daybreak. I love dancing, don't you?" Jay yelled.

"Some of us have to work." Grace wasn't about to admit she had the next two days off or she wouldn't be in the bar on a Wednesday night. She allowed Jay to twirl her around the small space they'd claimed as the song ended.

She scanned the congested dance wondering if Dani might be here, and praying she wasn't with another woman. *Hypocritical much?* The parts of the club surrounding the lighted stage were dark and picking out anyone specific would be impossible, but that didn't stop her from trying. What she'd do if she saw Dani wasn't entirely clear.

Jay leaned closer and yelled, "Looking for someone special?"

"Not really, just looking."

"She prefers another club. That's why I chose this one."

"Who?" Grace tried to sound uninterested, but her body tingled at the possibility of any information about Dani.

"Dr. Wingate."

"Jay, really I—"

"You don't have to pretend with me, Grace. I know what it's like to want someone who doesn't want you. Sucks."

Grace shook her head and pretended she couldn't hear, but the statement was one more of the stack of reasons she and Dani wouldn't be together. Dani didn't want her.

"So, are you seeing someone?" Jay asked a bit louder.

Grace shook her head, hoping to end the line of questions heading down a road she didn't want to take.

"Do you think maybe you and me..."

"What?" She pointed to her ears and shook her head again. Jay didn't need another rejection right now, and Grace didn't want to deliver one.

"Love this song, don't you?" Jay asked.

The music changed to a slow tune, and Grace groaned and looked toward the ceiling. "Why are you doing this to me?" She started to leave the dance floor, but Jay caught her hand and pulled her back.

"Stay. Please. Just one slow dance?"

"Jay, I don't think—"

"Just one?" Jay offered her hand and slid her arm around Grace's waist.

Grace let herself be pulled into Jay's arms but said loudly enough to make sure Jay heard, "Only one. I don't want you or anyone else getting the wrong idea."

Jay nodded and led her in exaggerated dance moves, weaving between the other couples. She really was quite a good dancer, and in a few minutes, Grace relaxed and laughed at her flamboyant antics.

"Very smooth. I can see why you're so popular with the girls."

Jay's genuine smile was worth Grace's discomfort. "I do my best, Grace."

The slow song was almost over when Grace spotted Cynthia elbowing through the crowd toward them. "Heads up, your ex is on her way."

"Oh shit. I'm sorry for what's about to happen, Grace. Cyn has a jealous streak."

Jay's satisfied grin indicated she wasn't quite as sorry as she said. Grace stopped dancing and stared at her. "You knew she was going to be here?"

Jay's face turned a deep shade of red that was visible even under the changing dance lights. "Maybe?"

"Seriously?"

"Turnabout is fair play, right?"

Grace started to object, but she'd used Jay as a teaser to get a rise out of Dani at Trip's party. "Fair point." She nudged Jay toward the approaching Cynthia. "Don't worry about me. If you love her, work it out. I'll get a ride home." She barely got the words out before Cynthia shoved her away and wrapped her arms and legs around Jay.

"Get your mitts off my lover. She's spoken for."

Raising her hands, Grace backed up. "We're just dancing."

She waited a few seconds to make sure Jay was okay and then followed the path Cynthia had made through the crowd toward the bar, dancers closing the space behind her as she moved. She edged between two men at the long counter, ordered a glass of merlot, and left it on the bar while she watched Jay and Cynthia dance. They appeared to be very much in love but looks were deceiving. She thought she'd seen a look of love or at least deep affection in Dani's eyes. Maybe it was time to let go of that dream. She was ready to settle down, and Dani wasn't at the same place in her life.

She turned back to her merlot, took a sip, and searched the room for someone she knew to get a ride home. The romantic music changed again to a pounding bass, and the erotic dances of arousal and intimacy morphed into movements of vitality and urgency. Grace swayed to the beat and slowly sipped her wine for several more minutes before deciding to order an Uber.

"Can I get you another drink?" a man next to her asked.

"No thanks, I'm good."

"Would you like to dance?"

Grace shook her head and suddenly felt dizzy and nauseous. The walls of the club vibrated and seemed to contract and expand. She couldn't make out faces or even body shapes. When she tried to grab the bar for support, her arms felt weighted and dropped back to her sides. Her legs shook and threatened to give way. "Wha's long wif me?" Her words slurred.

The man who'd offered her a drink put his arm around her waist. "Why don't you let me take you home? You don't look well."

Grace was vaguely aware of sinking toward the floor. She tried to stop the fall but instead felt strong arms around her. She struggled, but someone picked her up and threw her over his shoulder. She pounded on the muscled back. "Lemme go." A blast of hot, sticky air. Buckled in a seat belt. Total darkness.

Dani searched for a nearby hospital on her phone while Grace mumbled and struggled against her seat belt. Dani's hand ached so badly she could barely hold her phone. It didn't feel broken, but she hoped the guy's nose she punched was. He'd been groping an obviously incapacitated Grace, and Dani hit him without thinking twice.

"Not dunk...drunk." Grace's words were slow and garbled.

"Grace, you're going to be okay now."

"Need hep...help."

"I know, babe. I'm helping you. I'm taking you to a hospital."

"No! No hos—pital. Damn. Who you?"

She cupped Grace's hand where it rested in her lap. "It's Dani."

"Dani?" Grace stared at her hard as if trying to remember who she was but her eyes were glassy and unfocused.

"Yes, I'm going to take care of you. Please, let's go by the hospital for a checkup. I don't know what he put in your drink."

Grace shook her head vigorously and then grabbed the sides as if regretting the intense motion. "Wadder...jus' water."

Dani placed a bottle of water with a straw between Grace's hands in her lap. "The good thing is, you're still conscious, mostly, and you're making more sense than I'd expect. Drink lots of water."

Grace probably didn't understand a word, but Dani felt better saying them. She had to believe Grace would be okay. She couldn't live with any other outcome. When she'd seen the man dragging Grace toward the front door, her whole world shifted. Grace was all that mattered.

"Only two dink...drinks." Grace leaned forward over the bottle and wrapped her lips around the straw, but some of the water ran down her chin. She turned her head slightly and stared as if unsure of what she was seeing. "Dani?"

"Yeah, babe." Dani pulled a napkin from the console and dabbed at Grace's wet chin. "Keep drinking."

Grace took a few more sips, rested her head against the seat, and closed her eyes. She needed a thorough exam by a doctor along with a tox screen but adamantly refused. What if Dani took her anyway? Would being drugged by a stranger in a bar affect Grace's job? Should she at least tell Mary Jane? How about Trip and Clay? Grace deserved the best care, but her friends weren't here. She had to decide what was best for the woman she...the thought froze in her mind as she pulled up to Grace's cottage.

When Dani stopped her car, Grace was still out. Her breathing was steady, not labored or shallow, and her skin tone was good. She simply looked like a sleeping beauty, resting after an evening of dancing. But some asshole had tried to take advantage of Grace, and Dani would find out who he was and deal with him further after she took care of Grace.

As she considered her next move, her headlights cast Grace's cottage in a ball of light. "We're home, Grace." Home. Her growing bond with Grace could hurt her deeply, and she'd taken the coward's way out. She'd run from this place panicked the other night, but now she couldn't wait to get Grace inside and shut out the world.

She riffled through Grace's purse, found her house keys, and once again lifted Grace over her shoulder to carry her into the cottage. Making her way through the space with one free hand, she switched on a lamp in the bedroom, threw back the covers, and eased Grace down onto the mattress. Now what? Grace's emerald dress fit her so beautifully, but she needed to be out of it to rest properly.

Dani had plenty of experience getting women out of their dresses, but not while they were unconscious. She'd fantasized undressing Grace the first time and how exciting it would be, but now her heart ached for Grace's health and her pulse raced with anger that someone had harmed her.

She moved behind Grace and straddled her on the bed, grabbed the hem of her dress in both hands, and worked it up her body— past her shapely thighs, to the edge of her black undergarment, beyond the top of the bikini brief, across her bellybutton, and under her breasts.

"What's happ'ning?" Grace mumbled.

"You're okay, Grace. I've got you. Can you raise your arms for me?"

Grace tried to comply, her arms reaching only shoulder height, but it was enough for Dani to slide the dress off. She threw it to the floor, eased from behind Grace, and lowered her head onto the pillow. Her nearly nude body showed no signs of injury, so Dani leaned over and placed a single kiss on her forehead and covered her. "Sleep now, Gracie. I'll be here when you wake up."

Dani pulled an upholstered chair from the living room to Grace's bedside and placed two bottles of water on the nightstand. She retrieved a blanket from the hope chest at the end of Grace's bed, took her shoes off, and tucked her feet under the edge of the mattress. She'd be nearby if Grace called out or tried to get up. When she woke, Dani would discuss with her what happened next—about Mary Jane, her friends, a doctor, the police, and the two of them.

"D—Dani?"

Grace's voice was scratchy and deep, a sound Dani associated with painful dryness. She must've fallen asleep because when she pulled her feet from beneath the mattress, the muscles behind her knees felt tight and sore from the uncomfortable position. "I'm here."

Grace swallowed hard, winced, and reached for the water on the nightstand.

"Let me." Dani held the bottle close and brought the straw to Grace's lips.

"Why are you here?" She drank deeply and a relieved moan escaped her lips. "So good." She glanced at the bedside lamp and then out the window. "What time is it?"

"Almost daybreak."

"Thursday?"

"Yes."

Grace tried to sit up. "What happened?"

Dani eased her back in bed and pulled another pillow to prop her up. "Don't you remember?"

"I remember you saying you'd see me around and running out of here."

"I was hoping you'd forgotten that part. I'm really sorry."

"I can't forget. So, why are you here, Dani? You're freaking me out a little."

"We were at a club in Savannah."

"Together?" Grace frowned and looked around as if nothing Dani said made sense.

"No. I went alone. You were with some vertically challenged blond butch."

"Jay. So how did *we* get here, and where is Jay?" She grabbed the sides of her head. "I feel seriously hung-over."

Dani stuffed her hands in her jeans pockets and rocked back and forth. "Don't you think we should save this conversation until you feel better?"

Grace placed her hands beside her on the bed and breathed like she was hyperventilating. "If you'd stop rocking, I'd be fine." She sounded harsh, but she searched Dani's face with a pleading look. "Sorry. I don't mean to snap. I just need answers."

"Short version. You were dancing with the butch blonde. A brunette busted in. You went to the bar for a drink. A guy slipped something in your wine and tried to leave with you. I stopped him and brought you home."

Grace stared, her eyebrows scrunched together as if she was trying to recall even a snippet of Dani's story, but then she shook her head. "Nope, I got nothing. So…I was drugged?"

"I'm pretty sure."

"Do you know who did it?"

"No."

Grace pulled the sheets out and looked down at her body. "Did you undress me?"

Dani nodded.

For the first time since she'd woken up, Grace studied Dani closely. "Your eyelids are heavy. You've got black circles under your eyes. And your clothes are a wrinkled mess. How long have you been here, watching over me?"

"A while."

"You saved me from a really bad situation."

Dani shrugged.

"You brought me home. Undressed me. Put me in bed. And stayed with me. All night?"

"You needed me." Dani glanced down at the floor and then back at Grace, her face burning, her heart aching to say the words she'd been thinking since she brought Grace home. "And I liked being needed." The truth of her statement hit Dani full force.

Grace reached out, and Dani took her hand without hesitation. She settled lightly beside Grace on the bed and traced her knuckles with her thumb.

"Thank you, Dani. I don't want to think about what would've happened if you hadn't stepped in. I can never repay you."

"It's not necessary. I care about you, Grace. Really care." Grace appreciated being taken care of, and Dani liked doing it. Was this what a relationship felt like? Give and take? Sharing? Looking after each other in good times and bad?

Grace stroked the side of her face and let her fingers linger near her lips. "Maybe we should talk about what that means sometime."

"Maybe we should just do something about it," Dani said and grinned. "Woman of action, remember?"

"We need to talk, Dani, but when I'm a bit more coherent."

She wanted to tell Grace exactly how she felt, but now wasn't the right time. When she finally said those words, she wanted Grace fully conscious and able to understand what she meant. "You should think about going to the hospital for a blood test. When we catch this guy, you'll need evidence that you had drugs in your system."

"Did you see him put something in my drink?" Grace gave her a skeptical look.

"No, but it had to be him because he tried to make you leave with him."

"Why not someone else close by?" Grace was playing cop, throwing out all the options, and Dani found it both impressive and totally frustrating.

Dani shrugged, and Grace said, "You make a good point, but the law is very specific about those type of charges. We don't have a case."

"Damn it, Grace, I still think you should let me take you to the hospital."

"No way."

"But don't you have to go to work tomorrow?"

"Took a couple of days off. Good thing too. All I need is more sleep and lots of water to flush that crap out of my body." Her eyelids were slowly drooping.

Dani stood and picked up her boots. "Then I guess I better let you get to it."

Grace's expression shifted, her eyes large, scared looking. "I have no right to ask anything after what you've already done, but would you please stay with me? I don't want to be alone after what happened. I'm still groggy and a bit rattled by the whole situation."

Dani grinned and dropped her boots beside the bed. "Do you snore?"

Grace play slapped her on the arm. "What a horrible thing to ask a Southern lady. Of course not."

"Then push over. I'm coming in." Dani set the alarm on her phone so she wouldn't be late for work, shucked her shirt over her head without unbuttoning it, and peeled off her jeans leaving only boxers and a sports bra. "This okay?"

"I'd prefer skin, but under the circumstances that's perfect. Get in." Grace flung the covers back and patted the bed beside her. "You need sleep."

Dani snuggled under the covers but kept a respectable distance from Grace. If she touched her, she'd never be able to stop. "I'm not sure I can sleep like this."

"Give me your hand." Dani complied, and Grace pulled it across her body, bringing Dani's head to rest on her shoulder. "How about now?"

"This is great. I might be able to..." Dani yawned. "You're so...warm. Nice." Grace fit perfectly against her, and Dani felt a tingling of arousal, but it diverted to her heart instead of lower. She sighed, and Grace kissed the top of her head and said something about a shero. For the first time in Dani's life, the woman beside her felt like forever.

CHAPTER FOURTEEN

"Grace, wake up," Dani said, trying to extract herself from the warm tangle of arms and legs. "I have to go to work."

"Not yet." Grace pulled her tighter.

"Trip is taking me on an exotic animal tour this afternoon so I have to do all my regular work and any walk-ins first. I don't want to miss what passes for exotic in Pine Cone."

"She'll understand if you're late."

Grace wasn't waking as quickly as Dani wanted. Damn. What drug had that asshole put in her drink? A normal roofie only lasted eight to twelve hours, but he could've laced it with something else. "Maybe I can put it off. I'm worried about you. Look at me, Grace." She gently shook Grace's shoulders, needing to check her out before leaving her alone.

"I'm fine, really. A bit groggy. Go. Work."

"Are you sure?" She didn't want to leave Grace at all much less if she wasn't well.

"Go." Grace waved her away and almost immediately fell back asleep.

Grace could still give orders so that was a good sign. Dani covered her, kissed her forehead, and dashed across the lawn to the B and B to get ready for work.

The morning passed quickly as Trip chipped in with the usual rounds. More than once, Dani thought about telling her what happened to Grace at the club but changed her mind. She didn't want to blab Grace's business, until they'd had a chance to talk and figure out what Grace wanted to do about it. Around noon, Trip nodded toward the back where her truck was parked and led the way out.

Dani eyed her from the passenger seat. "You're certainly in a great mood. Is that because of Petunia's diagnosis?"

"Some of it. An easily removable benign tumor is a pretty good outcome. Jamie's grateful, Petunia will get better, and it's a beautiful summer day...too nice to be stuck inside." Trip grinned at her. "And today is the day you understand why I picked you over a dozen other qualified applicants." Trip turned off the highway onto a long drive with a black iron sign arched over the entrance that said Green Acres. She nodded toward Dani's swollen and abraded knuckles. "I meant to ask you earlier, what happened?"

Dani slid her hand under her leg, unwilling to share Grace's story until she was ready. "Bar fight. You know how it is."

"Used to." Trip didn't push and pointed toward a pasture to the right. "Isn't this great?"

A dozen bison populated the pasture on one side of the drive, and a mixed herd of miniature cows and horses on the other. "Is this a petting zoo or something?" Dani asked.

"Sort of. Tom and Betty King are the clients. They're partnered with the Livestock Conservancy and raise several old breeds of chickens, rabbits, and other livestock designated as heritage stock. The bison are just a fancy of Tom's. The miniature horses and cows are Betty's indulgence."

As Trip drove past the log-style house and parked beside a large, traditional red barn, Dani took in the rest of the property. Four other long barrack-style barns with signs that identified the residents of each—rabbits, chickens, cattle, horses—finished the complex. "This is a big operation."

"They operate traveling petting stations for county fairs and other venues. Right now, there's a brisk market for the heritage breeds. The free-range and organic farmers like the idea of raising the same chickens their great-great-grandparents did. And they supply zoos all over the country and beyond with some of the more exotic breeds. Today, we're here to see a rabbit."

A woman in a dirty T-shirt, baggy khakis, and knee-high rubber boots emerged from the rabbit barn and walked toward them. Trip waved, and they both got out of the truck.

"Hey, Trip."

"Hey, Betty. You and Tom doing okay?"

"Doing fine." The woman wiped her hand on her pants and held it out to Dani. "I'm Betty King."

Dani shook her hand. "Dani Wingate."

"Dani's my new associate veterinarian," Trip said. "I hired her because of her experience with exotic animals. She worked in a zoo in Baltimore."

"Well, we won't hold being a Yankee against her if she knows her stuff."

"I appreciate that," Trip said, smiling at Dani. "So, who's our patient today?"

"Thumper. I've got him in the red barn. You'll need sutures. His ear is shredded."

"Big Wig get him?"

"Yep. The youngster is full grown now and made the mistake of challenging the old man over a doe. The North Carolina Zoo wants him and a doe, so we'll keep them separate from the others until Thumper's healed and we can ship the pair out together."

Dani marveled at the smooth back-and-forth between Trip and Betty, old friends, familiar with the rhythm and stories of life in a small town. She followed them toward the big red barn where the doors in front and back were open and fans hummed over the pens. It was obviously set up for a petting zoo, but most of the pens were empty.

"We figured this would be the best place for him to recover since school is out and we don't have any groups scheduled for tours until August," Betty said. She led them to a pen in the back corner where a Flemish giant rabbit sprawled on fresh straw and nibbled on a large carrot.

"Wow. That's a big boy," Dani said, not hesitating to enter the pen. Giant rabbits were known for their gentle nature. She approached slowly, then ran a hand along Thumper's luxurious pelt.

Betty beamed. "Big Wig sires them large. He's near four feet long. Thumper is three feet six inches and still growing."

"How about you handle this, Dani. Betty can give you a hand if needed, while I go say hello to Tom."

Betty waved toward the red barn. "He's in the horse barn, waiting. He wants you to look at Ranger's eye. It's better, but still a bit runny."

Trip headed toward the barn, and Dani pulled her kit bag closer. "Betty, would you mind petting Thumper to keep him calm while I sterilize the wound?"

"Sure thing."

Dani cleaned the gashes along Thumper's ear and patted them dry before applying tissue glue. She blew lightly on the area until the glue set and then nodded for Betty to release him. He hopped away, flipping at his ear only once before becoming more interested in a stash of carrots.

"No stitches?"

"I used the equivalent of superglue for skin. No numbing required and no pesky stitches for tiny toenails to snag on while scratching. It'll work better since he's so active. Just keep an eye on the injury, flush it with saline a couple of times a day, and apply this antibiotic ointment. He should be good as new soon. If anything changes, give us a call."

"Will do. Thanks, Dani. I see why Trip hired you."

If only her touch carried over to people. She thought about Grace again for the hundredth time and started to call and check on her, but Trip motioned her toward the truck.

They left the Kings and dropped in on a client whose pet potbellied pig had gotten into a squabble with the neighbor's dog.

Dani cleaned Annabelle's punctures, instructed Mrs. Ludwell how to care for the wounds, and prescribed a course of antibiotics.

Dani had no idea there were so many interesting animals around Pine Cone, but she suspected Trip had planned for her to be surprised, maybe even enough to stay on. They treated a ten-foot albino Burmese python with mouth rot and were headed to a local reptile farm to treat the infected foot of a six-foot alligator when Trip's truck indicated an incoming call.

Jamie's name flashed on the caller ID, and Trip tapped the screen to accept the call.

"Hey, Jamie. Petunia okay?"

"She's home, taking a sick day to rest. The antacid seems to be helping some, and she's eating a bit of that prescription food, the chicken flavor. I just didn't want her out in the heat."

"Good. Make sure she's drinking a lot of water, too."

"Okay. But I'm calling about something else."

Trip glanced over at Dani and quickly added, "Okay. Dani's in the truck with me and you're on speaker."

Dani had witnessed several exchanges between Trip and Jamie, and the attraction was obvious. If they didn't hook up soon, Dani thought Trip might lose it.

"Good. I'm out on the highway at, uh…Big Earl's Exotic Emporium, and we have an animal situation I hope you can help with."

Trip slowed the truck and did a three-point turn in the highway. "Is this an emergency?"

"I think so. Big Earl's orangutan, Kiki, has escaped her enclosure and managed to lock herself into a tourist's car. The car is parked in the shade, and the window's open about an inch, but I'm afraid the interior will heat up quick."

Trip stomped on the accelerator. "We're headed your way, less than five minutes out."

"Jamie, it's Dani. Get a towel or rag and dip it cold water, ice water if there's any around, and pass it through the partially open window. Apes are smart, and Kiki will use it to cool herself."

"Will do. See you in a few."

Trip grabbed the CB radio mic. "Fast Break to Paint Ball. Got your ears on?"

"This is Paint Ball. What's up?"

"Where are you?"

"My place."

"Put your clothes on, grab your locksmith tools, and meet me at Big Earl's pronto. Kiki has locked herself in some tourist's car."

"Paint Ball out and on the way."

Dani raised an eyebrow, and Trip shrugged. "The CB handles are something we dreamed up in high school. They just stuck."

Dani started to comment, but Trip whipped into Big Earl's parking lot. A small crowd gathered next to a luxury SUV, its alarm horn blaring every other second. Jamie stood off to the side, positioned between a middle-aged Chevy Chase doppelgänger and Big Earl, who looked like he'd been an NFL lineman, as they yelled at each other over the racket of the car alarm. Trip rushed toward the crowd closing in on Jamie while Dani went to examine the SUV surrounded by a crowd of children. She elbowed her way through and peered at the orangutan.

"Who owns that Toyota over there?" Dani waved over the woman who raised her hand, ignoring the scuffle and flash of handcuffs where Jamie was between Big Earl and the angry tourist. "Give me your keys." She dangled them next to the window where Kiki sat.

Kiki pursed her lips and made little squeaking noises, but she stared at the keys Dani jangled outside the window.

"She's blowing kisses," one bystander said.

"No," Dani said, still waving the keys in a hypnotic fashion. "Orangutans do that when they're stressed or agitated."

"Aw, baby," Big Earl crooned, moving closer. "Daddy's going to get you out of there."

"Stand back, Earl, and let Dani work," Trip said. "You'll just distract Kiki."

Cahill's tow truck lumbered into the small, gravel parking lot and stopped. Clay hopped out. "What's up?"

"Kiki's locked herself in that car, and we're trying to get her out," Trip said. "Can you unlock that door?"

Clay rubbed her chin and shrugged. "That model is too new to open with a Slim Jim. I'd have to drill out the lock, and he'd have to replace it. Pretty expensive way to go."

"Before we go that route, there might be a better way. Do you have any grapes?" Dani asked Big Earl.

He shook his head. "She ate all of them yesterday, and I haven't gone by the grocery."

"Mom, I've got grapes in my lunchbox," a girl said, tugging on her mother's arm.

"That's right. They're in the car. Go get them," the woman said.

The orangutan touched the window glass next to where Dani held the keys, but Dani concealed the keys in her hand and pointed instead to the keys on the seat next to Kiki.

Kiki pursed her lips again and pointed to Dani's hand. Dani pointed to keys on the seat. Kiki finally followed Dani's line of vision and looked down at the keys next to her, then picked them up. Dani pressed her key fob against the glass, and Kiki did the same with her fob. Dani set the fob on top of her head, and Kiki did the same, beginning to mimic Dani's motions. Dani held the fob up and pressed the alarm button. Kiki did the same to her fob and everyone, including Kiki, seemed to relax in the silence that followed.

"Everybody get back," Jamie said, directing the growing crowd of bystanders to step back about ten feet.

The girl returned with the grapes, and Dani waved her closer. "What's your name?"

"Amy." The girl was bold and confident. Dani judged her to be around eleven years old, and a bit of a tomboy.

"Okay, Amy. I want you to stand here and show the grapes to Kiki, then eat one. Smack your lips like it's really good, but don't smile at her. She'll think you're being aggressive by baring your teeth."

"Okay." Amy lifted the cluster of white grapes to the window than plucked one and popped it into her mouth. She had Kiki's full attention.

"Now eat another and smack your lips. And when I reach to take one, too, don't let me."

Amy did as she was told, pulling the grapes out of reach and shaking her head when Dani attempted to get one for herself.

"Good girl." Dani held up the fob in her hand and pointed to it. "In the wild, orangutans have been observed offering trades for items they want from another orangutan." She pointed to the grapes. "Now I want you to offer the grapes to me in exchange for this fob."

Amy did, and they swapped grapes for fob while Kiki watched. Dani popped a grape in her mouth and smacked her lips. Then she held the grapes near the two-inch opening at the top of the window and pointed to the fob Kiki held. The ape didn't hesitate. She pushed the fob through the opening, and Dani squeezed the remaining grapes through into Kiki's waiting fingers.

"Jamie, can you uncuff Earl? I'm going to unlock the door and I want him to calmly help Kiki out of the vehicle."

"Sure thing." Jamie released Big Earl, and he rubbed the small indentions in his wrists. "Sorry, Earl, but I had to do something to deescalate things."

"It's okay," he mumbled. "I get a little worked up sometimes, and I'm protective of Kiki. She's such a sweetheart and won't eat for days if she gets upset."

Kiki was turning the steering wheel back and forth with her hind feet while she daintily picked one grape at a time from the cluster to eat them.

Dani hit the unlock button on the fob, and Big Earl opened the door.

"Kiki, come to Daddy. Let's go inside and get an orange."

The orangutan held out her hand for Big Earl to take and climbed out of the car. The crowd cheered, and Kiki blew them a raspberry, and waddled inside, still gripping Earl's hand.

"I'm going to get my stethoscope and check her out to make sure she didn't get too overheated," Dani said. "Unless you want to."

Trip waved her on. "You'd know more about what to look for than I would." Dani suspected Trip was more interested in chatting up Jamie than checking on an orangutan.

When Dani returned, Trip and Jamie were standing close, and the look in Trip's eyes said their conversation wasn't professional. Dani pretended not to notice, putting her kit bag and the other instruments back in the veterinary truck.

Trip walked toward the truck but called back over her shoulder to Jamie, "See you and Petunia at seven then. And bring a pouch of her food."

"Making a move on the deputy, boss?" Dani couldn't resist a little jibe.

"A big move. You should follow my lead before it's too late."

Dani thought about Grace and suddenly couldn't wait to get back to her. "Won't this truck go any faster? I've got things to do."

Grace was sitting up in bed when Dani walked in with a food bag in one hand and her gym bag with a change of clothes in the other. She'd been too anxious to see Grace and hadn't wasted time showering at the B and B. "Look who's still in bed. Sleepyhead."

"I'm hungry."

Dani waved the bag of burgers and fries in her direction. "What will you give me for one of these?"

"My body and my firstborn child. You're my shero, again."

"You eat while I shower. Rabbit, pig, python, and orangutan do not go well with burgers."

"Oh, tell me all about Trip's exotic tour."

"So, you were listening this morning. Later." Dani shucked out of her clothes on the way to the bathroom.

"Hurry back." Grace tore the bag open and pulled out a handful of fries.

Grace was fast asleep when Dani returned to the bedroom, her half-eaten burger on the nightstand. Dani crawled in beside her, hungry only for Grace's skin next to hers. She snuggled in and wrapped herself around the body she'd begun to crave. As she drifted to sleep, she whispered, "I think I'm in love with you, Grace Booker, and it scares me to death."

Chapter Fifteen

G race woke the next morning to the taste of stale burgers and greasy fries. She reached for water on the nightstand, but a weight across her body stopped her. Dani. And she was still sound asleep, with one arm and one leg thrown over Grace. Their cocoon was cozy, intimate, and perfect. How they'd gotten in this position was still fuzzy, but she liked it and wasn't in a hurry to move.

She and Dani had been up and down since they met, but her drugging had shifted their relationship in a new direction. But it could just be the chemical effects still in her system. She owed it to herself and Dani to find out when her head was clearer.

"I care about you, Grace. Really care." How had she not seen it before? Dani needed to be needed, to feel she made a difference. She'd admitted as much when she talked about her grandmother and her collection of stray animals. Grace had needed her desperately at the club, and she'd come through. Dani had probably always craved the personal connections she'd missed as a child but didn't know how to truly engage when the opportunity came along.

Beating on the front door brought Grace back to the present. Heavy pounding before breakfast usually equaled trouble in her line of work. The station could've been calling, but she had no idea if her cell was on or even where to locate it.

"Grace, you in there?" Trip's voice was loud and urgent.

"Come on, Gracie, stop fooling around and open up." Clay sounded scared.

"Grace, open the door or we're coming in." Mary Jane joined the chorus of concerned voices. "I left plarn weaving to check on you, so let us in."

She didn't understand the urgency, but something had upset her friends. "Dani?" She committed Dani's sleeping form to memory—innocent expression, mouth partially open revealing the tiny gap between her front teeth, ebony hair flattened on the sides and standing up on top, the musculature of her chest and her strong arm across Grace's body. She could look at her all day, but a stirring in her center said that would never be enough.

"Gracie, honey, this is your last warning," Mary Jane said.

Grace placed light kisses on Dani's forehead and on her lips. "Dani?"

"Uh-huh." She snuggled closer and sought Grace's mouth.

"We need to get up. The cavalry is here."

"Send them away and kiss me again."

"So not a good idea. Bad burger mouth."

Dani pulled her closer. "Don't care. Please."

Everything else vanished except Dani's soft plea and the gentle glide of their lips. Grace wanted to stay here all day exploring and talking, but this wasn't the time. She gave Dani a light kiss and started to get up.

"Well, I'm pretty sure what's going on right now, but are you okay, Gracie?" Mary Jane stood at the foot of the bed with her hands on the foot board, eyes searching the ceiling, flanked by Clay and Trip. None of them looked happy.

Grace pulled the blanket tighter around her and Dani. "What are y'all doing here? It's early and I'm…we're busy."

"We've been calling your cell and no one in town has seen you since Wednesday," Mary Jane said. "What else could we do but launch a full-on search?"

"What's up, Grace?" Trip glared.

"Seriously, dude?" Clay shook her head at Dani and her expression darkened.

Dani jumped up and stood in front of everyone in her boxers and sports bra. "I don't know what you think is happening, but I'm pretty sure you're wrong."

"And I'm pretty sure I'm smart enough to figure out what's going on, and I don't like it, not one little bit, sport." Clay eyed Dani hard.

"Trip, Clay—"

"Hold on, Grace," Clay said, stalking toward Dani like a hunter on safari. "Did you or did you not haul Grace out of the bar Wednesday night over your shoulder?"

"Well, I—"

"Just answer the question," Clay said, moving closer. She and Trip backed Dani into a corner of the bedroom, blocking any escape route.

"Yes, but—" Dani raised her hands in surrender.

Trip shook her head, a look of disbelief on her face. "We spent the whole day together yesterday, and you didn't say one word about...this." She motioned toward Grace.

Mary Jane's hand came to her chest. "I never pictured you as that type, Dani."

"Stop it!" Grace screamed from the bed, and everyone turned toward her. "I never figured y'all as the lynching type either. Get away from her." No one moved, staring at her like she was a mad woman. "I mean it. Move. *Now*." She tried to stand but slumped back on the bed, clutching her head and the edge of a blanket for cover. "Oh crap."

Mary Jane ran to Grace's side and handed her a robe. "Honey, you're not okay. Let me take you to the doctor."

"No, MJ. I'm all right."

"Obviously you're not," Mary Jane said as Grace shrugged into the robe and grabbed the headboard for balance. "We're trying to find out what happened to you Wednesday night. And then we come in and find the two of you like..."

Grace's face flushed. "I'm fine, MJ. I took a couple of days off work, no big deal. I'm not really sure what happened the other night, but I know Dani is the only reason it wasn't worse."

"What?" Clay and Trip said at the same time.

"She basically rescued me from some pervert."

Dani nodded as if validating Grace's statement, pulled on her jeans, grabbed her shirt and boots, and started toward the door. "That's my cue to leave."

"No way, dude," Clay said.

"Maybe we should let Dani tell her side," Trip offered.

"We're all staying until we get to the bottom of this." Clay ushered Dani and Trip out of the room and said, "We'll wait out here until you're ready. Take care of her, MJ."

On their way out of the room, Grace heard Trip mumble something to Clay about owing her ten dollars. She felt comforted that during the craziness some things hadn't changed.

When the bedroom door closed, Mary Jane brushed Grace's forehead. "Your color is bad. Your eyes are bloodshot. You basically look like death warmed over. Why don't you take a quick shower and clear your head? I'll put on some coffee."

"Thanks. I'll be out in a few minutes. Don't let them touch Dani. I mean it."

The hot water pounded Grace's back, relieving the tension between her shoulders, and easing her headache, but the memory of the previous two days blurred. Dani's story about what happened at the club sounded feasible, and Grace really didn't want to doubt her, but she couldn't remember. She pulled on a pair of comfy sweats and joined the others in the living room.

Mary Jane handed her a cup of coffee and she sat at the small dining table, four sets of eyes trained on her. "I believe I was drugged at the club two nights ago."

"Oh, honey." Mary Jane slapped a hand over her open mouth.

"What the…" Trip grabbed the edge of the table, knuckles bleaching from the force.

"Who'd do something like that?" Clay asked.

"Dani can tell you more."

Everyone swiveled, and Dani retold the account of what happened exactly as she'd relayed it to Grace originally. "And that's how I ended up here."

"And how you ended up in bed with a drugged woman? I can't believe you'd take advantage of Grace like that. So not cool." Clay eyed her suspiciously.

Grace placed her hand firmly on Clay's arm. She appreciated Clay's protectiveness, which had lingered since their one and only kiss in high school. "I love you for being concerned, but I asked Dani to stay because I didn't want to be alone."

"And she just saw an opportunity?" Clay wasn't convinced. "How do we know she didn't drug you herself just so she could get you here, like this?" Clay waved back toward the bedroom.

"As if she'd need to drug me. Really, Clay?"

"She makes a good point," Trip said. "Besides, I don't think Dani would—"

"Maybe we should get another version of the story," Clay said, wavering but still not giving up. "Grace went to the club with Jay. Do you think she can verify any of this?"

"Once Cynthia showed up, I'm not sure Jay saw much of anything else. We don't need to involve her in this fiasco. Dani told me what happened, and I believe her."

Clay pulled her cell out of her back jeans pocket. "We should ask Jay." She dialed the number. "Get over to Grace's cottage ASAP. I know what time it is. Well, that's great, dude, but we'll talk about it later. Just get here quick." Clay ended the call. "Now we wait."

"Did you get checked out at the hospital and report this, honey?" Mary Jane asked.

Grace shook her head.

Trip eyed Dani hard this time. "Didn't you think that would've been a good idea?"

"Stop it, Trip. She tried to convince me, but I refused."

"Any idea who this guy was?" Clay tapped her fingers against her thigh.

Grace shook her head again, but Dani said, "I'd know him if I saw him again. He was manhandling Grace, so I won't forget his face. And I might've broken his nose." She raised her right hand, and her knuckles were skinned, bruised, and still a bit swollen.

"What?" Grace stared at her, shaking her head. "You didn't tell me you hit the guy."

"He was trying to drag you out of the club. What was I supposed to do?"

Grace glared at Trip and Clay with her best see-there expression. "Let me get you some ice for the swelling."

"I iced it pretty well after we got home. I'll be fine."

Mary Jane patted Dani's arm. "Well, that's something, honey. You may be able to clear up this whole mess."

"Do you remember what the guy was wearing, Dani?" Clay asked, her tone a bit mellower than before.

"Not specifically, but he wasn't trendy or anything."

"So, fashion fail. Makes sense for someone who'd do something like this."

A knock sounded at the cottage door, Clay opened it, and Jay strolled in. Her satisfied grin vanished when her eyes focused on Clay's tense expression. "What's going on, guys?"

Clay motioned for her to pull up a chair at the kitchen table, and Mary Jane poured her a cup of coffee. The room was quiet for several seconds before Clay spoke. "You took Grace to the club Wednesday night."

Jay scanned the faces around the table, and Grace could almost hear her wheels turning trying to decide what they wanted her to say. If she were a suspect in a crime, she'd fold like a cheap chair. "Yeah...so?"

"Stop hemming and hawing and tell us what happened, Jay." Mary Jane rolled her hand.

"Yeah, Grace and I went dancing, as friends. When Cynthia showed up, Grace told me she'd get a ride home. You guys know how jealous Cyn can be. We started dancing, and one thing led to another. Before you know it, we were in the back room grop—"

"We get the idea." Grace shook her head and glanced toward Mary Jane. She didn't need to hear what happened in the back rooms of clubs.

"She was all over me." Jay's eyes sparkled and her grin widened. She was back in that room, having Cynthia again for the first time in months. "I mean, don't get me wrong, I wasn't complaining, but she gets so hor—"

"For the love of Christmas," Mary Jane said. "We get it. You screwed like wild rabbits in a public place with no sense of decorum. Stay focused, woman."

Jay's face flushed bright red and she nodded.

"Hey," Trip encouraged her, "Did you see what happened to Grace later?"

Jay tilted her head to the side. "I saw her go to the bar and order a drink after Cyn interrupted our dance."

"Did you see her leave?" Clay asked.

"I thought I saw somebody carrying her out later, after Cyn and I...you know."

"And you didn't think that was a bit unusual?" Trip gave her a hard stare.

"Maybe, but—"

Clay shook her head. "You beat all, you know that? Who was carrying Grace out? Damn it, think woman. This is important."

"'Fraid not, Clay." She looked around the room and stopped at Dani. "Could've been her, but I can't be sure. Did something bad happen?"

"No, Jay." Grace took her hand and walked her back to the door. She didn't want another tongue wagging about her Savannah nightmare. "Sorry for the inconvenience. I'm sure Cynthia wasn't happy either. Please don't use my name when you explain why you had to jump out of bed so early this morning."

"Don't worry, Grace. She saw Clay's ID on my phone and knows I'd never be—"

"Whatever." Trip waved her off. "The next time you take a woman out, make sure she gets home safely. Butch rule number—damn it, you should know. Just get out."

"I'm sorry." Jay started to hug Grace good-bye but caught Clay's stare and closed the door behind her.

Grace took a deep breath before facing them. She'd spent enough time reliving a bad dream. "Okay, that's over. As you can see, I'm fine, and Dani has done nothing wrong. I couldn't have asked for a more chivalrous, caring, and devoted guardian the last couple of days. I appreciate your concern, but I'd really like you to leave now."

Dani stood and started toward the door.

Grace shook her head. "Not you." She waved her finger at the others. "Everybody else."

CHAPTER SIXTEEN

Grace closed the door behind them slowly, struggling for a way to keep Dani with her. She'd monopolized her for two days, and Dani was probably itching to get away. When she turned around, Dani was within touching distance. "Oh, hi."

"Grace?"

"Uh-huh."

"Can I go, please? I'd like to take a long hot shower and clear my head."

The hurt in Dani's voice was so evident Grace winced. She wouldn't meet Grace's eyes, shifting back and forth ready to bolt. "I'm sorry about the third degree. My friends are a little overprotective."

"Don't blame them. I'm the outsider. I have a feeling if I stayed here the rest of my life I'd still be an interloper. Why should they take my word about anything?"

Grace stepped forward, but Dani moved back. She traced the frown lines across her forehead, almost feeling the tension underneath her skin. "Southerners can be skeptical, clannish, and exclusive, but you're an honorable woman, Dani Wingate. You were there when I needed you in a big way. They understand that now."

Dani finally looked up, her eyes swirling with pain. "Do they?"

"Yes." Grace eased forward and entwined their fingers. "Stay with me, Dani, if you want."

"Your friends are close if you need anything."

"But they're not you. I need you in a totally different way."

Dani moaned when Grace thumbed the inside of her wrist.

"Can I take that as a yes?" Grace brought their joined hands to her lips and kissed the back of Dani's hand. "Please stay, and not because you think I'm unwell, but because you want to be here… with me."

Dani was quiet too long, but when she looked up again, her expression was a blend of mischief and hunger. "I need a shower."

"I'll wait." She kissed Dani lightly on the lips before shoving her toward the bathroom. "But be quick or I'll have to take matters into my own hands."

"Don't."

Dani stripped on her way to the shower, and Grace paced the bedroom floor. She was attracted to Dani, but she'd convinced herself to move on, and now she was going to have sex with her. Had the drugs scrambled her thoughts, confused her about what was best? When Dani cleared her throat, Grace turned and the answer crystallized, as plainly as Dani's towel-clad body—no matter what happened later, she wanted to be with Dani now. She opened her arms and realized she was opening her heart as well, consequences be damned.

Dani tucked the edge of the towel tighter around her breasts. "Are you sure about this, Grace?" At least one of them should be certain. All Dani could think about was how much she wanted Grace at this moment, like no one before.

"Mostly, but that's okay with me."

Dani needed to say one more thing and hated it, but Grace deserved the whole truth. "I don't know what this means. Yet. You understand, right?"

"Totally. And the good thing is, we don't have to know. Come here, please."

Dani trembled as she closed the distance between them. She was never nervous about having sex, until now. The room with its queen-sized bed closed around her, bringing Grace nearer and heating the air surrounding them, the perfect setting for seduction. It also felt intimate.

"Stop." Grace pressed her forehead to Dani's and whispered. "I see those wheels turning. You're scared as a long-tailed cat in a room full of rocking chairs. Let it go and just enjoy whatever happens."

Dani wanted this so much, but could she stay in the moment? Her whole life had been about planning and execution—escape her horrible family situation, get an education, find a fulfilling job, buy a home, enjoy pleasure when it came along, and keep moving.

Grace stroked Dani's naked shoulders to the top of the towel and then drifted lower until her hands cupped Dani's bare ass. When Grace finally kissed her, Dani lost herself in the softness of Grace's lips, the sweet smell of her perfume, and her own body's reactions. Grace rolled her tongue against Dani's, caressing and exploring. Grace was teasing, and Dani was breathless for more.

"Stay right where you are, Doc, while I set the proper mood."

"Thought we just did that?"

"Patience. It gets better."

Dani tried to kiss her again, but Grace sidestepped. "I don't seem to have any patience when it comes to you or any self-control either. Why do you suppose that is?"

Grace gave her a mischievous smile, ripped the covers off the bed, and threw them in front of the fireplace, followed by the bed pillows and others from a nearby chair. "Because I'm just too damn sexy to resist?"

Grace guided Dani onto the quilt, its deep thickness drawing her in and heating her blood almost as much as Grace's kiss. "Probably."

Grace joined her, gave a naughty grin, and pinched the tucked edge of the towel between her thumb and forefinger. "What happens if I tug this?"

Dani's pulse throbbed between her legs. She'd never let anyone tease her before. Now she wondered why. "Find out." Grace rested her palm on Dani's breast and plucked the towel loose, letting it fall around her. "God, Grace. You're killing me."

"Not my intention at all." She scanned Dani's body bringing heat and moisture so quickly that Dani groaned. "Do you like me looking at you?"

Dani struggled for her usual self-restraint, but Grace reduced her to a mass of uncontrollable need. "Y—yes."

"What do you want?"

"You without these." Dani pulled at the sweats covering Grace's body. Since Grace had given the green light, Dani's hands itched to touch her, to bring her slowly to the edge and then tip her over.

"Do you want to undress me, or should I?"

"You. Slow."

Grace ran her hands under the garment and cupped her breasts, moaning from the contact as if Dani's hands touched her. She slid her arms from the sleeves and into the body of the shirt and shifted it up under her neck. She stared at Dani and teased her puckered nipples. "See how much I want you, Dani? I'm already hard."

Dani squeezed her thighs tight, the image before her too provocative. "More." She sounded urgent. Grace started to shuck her shirt off. "Don't. Just the pants." Dani knee-walked toward her, reaching for her, aching for physical contact.

Grace stuck her arm straight out to stop her. "Not yet." She hooked her thumbs in the waistband of her sweat pants and tugged slowly, past her navel and lower.

"Damn, Grace." Dani scrubbed the heel of her palm between her legs, but Grace gave her an evil eye and shook her head. By the time Grace pulled the pants off her legs and threw them across the room, Dani saw the glistening moisture between her legs and felt it between her own. "Now?"

Grace stretched out on the quilt and the early morning sun cast light across her flushed face and full lips. Dani momentarily forgot her physical discomfort and just stared at Grace's body.

She'd never seen anyone more beautiful or wanted anyone as much. "May I touch you?"

Grace seemed taken aback by the serious tone of Dani's question. Her answer was a whisper of permission layered in need. "I really wish you would."

Dani stretched out beside Grace and propped up on her elbow to watch Grace as she touched her. Did she feel the charged energy between them, the heat surrounding them as Dani did? She traced the outline of Grace's bottom lip and felt it quiver. Without realizing it, she'd hoped for this closeness with someone and basked in the feeling, capturing the image in her mind. Only Grace. "In case I forget later, thank you for this."

Grace's hooded eyes followed Dani's hands and she mumbled something that resembled uh-huh.

"What do you want me to do, Grace?" For some reason, Grace's needs mattered as much as her own, a foreign concept for her until this moment.

"Anything you want."

Grace's words were an instant shot of adrenaline. She kissed the side of Grace's face and down her neck, drawing her own pleasure from the moans they urged from Grace. Dani outlined Grace's puckered nipples, following the rise and fall of her chest as her body responded. She lightly brushed her hand between Grace's breasts, down her torso, but stopped shy of her center. Grace jerked in anticipation.

"Dani."

"Yes, Grace?"

"What are you doing to me?"

"Anything I want, remember?" Dani enjoyed teasing Grace, seeing her pupils dilate and her skin flush as her arousal grew. Nothing was more beautiful.

Grace cupped Dani's hand and attempted to urge it between her thighs. "Touch me. I need...to feel you." Her breath came in hot, jagged spurts, and Dani clamped her legs tighter against another rush of heat.

"Soon."

"Is teasing me…all day…part of your plan?"

"Quite possibly. I love seeing and feeling you respond. Is that okay?"

"As long as you don't mind a little quid pro quo…and stop when I say uncle." Grace started to reach between Dani's legs, but she stopped her. "I need to touch you, Dani."

"Not yet." Dani glanced down, and the image of Grace's hand so close to her crotch ratcheted up the pressure. She wanted Grace to touch her but wasn't sure she could let her. Allowing anyone emotionally close enough to really pleasure her didn't come easily.

"I can't take this anymore. I need skin," Grace said. "And to be out of this damn sweatshirt. I'm dying from the heat."

"Sit up." Grace complied without question, and Dani straddled her legs and skimmed her hands slowly up Grace's sides. How could skin be this soft, this hot? She brushed the fullness of Grace's breasts, and Dani's clit twitched and strained. She cupped both breasts and the tips hardened and teased the center of her hands.

"Suck my breasts, Dani."

Dani tucked her head under Grace's sweatshirt and her distinctive fragrance filled Dani and swirled through her. Inhaling deeply, she committed the scent to memory. Dani captured one breast in her mouth and the other nipple between her thumb and forefinger. Cocooned between flesh and fabric, she ached to devour the soft, delicious parts of Grace, to hear her moan and beg for more, and to finally tease her to orgasm and taste her release. She groaned and slid her center along Grace's leg, the pleasure turning to pain.

Grace pressed Dani's head tighter to her chest, and her hips rose and fell in time with Dani's pulls. "Dani, please."

Dani stripped the shirt over Grace's head, eased her back down on the quilt, and glided down slowly, savoring the scent of her. "Are you ready for me, Grace?"

"So ready." Grace breathed deeply and then seemed to stop breathing as Dani worked her way up her body again. "Tease."

"Definitely." Dani rotated her center along the length of Grace's leg, stopped midway, and rubbed their pelvises together. Grace was so open and responsive that Dani wanted to savor her heat and urgency for hours. Grace groaned and tried to pull her up, but Dani lingered, sucked on Grace's breasts again, and worked their bodies into a heated rhythm.

"Ohhh, Dani." Grace pumped harder and clung to Dani's ass. "Faster."

Dani raised on her hands until only their lower bodies touched and then leaned down to kiss Grace. She poured all her desire into that kiss, trying to convey what she needed and wanted to do next. Her tongue mimicked the rhythm of their bodies as Grace's thrusts became more urgent.

"I need your mouth, Dani."

She kissed her way down Grace's body and spread her legs wider.

Grace squirmed and cupped the back of Dani's head. "Uncle. I need to come."

Dani slid her free hand between her own legs and lowered herself to grant Grace's wish. The first taste of Grace's sweetness exploded on Dani's tongue. She thrashed against her hand and almost came but pulled back in time. She teased Grace's taut flesh back and forth with her tongue and between her teeth until Grace's nails dug into her scalp.

"Fingers. Now."

Dani continued the rhythmic pulling on Grace's clit until she felt her own climax riding her hard. With Grace's taste on her lips, the minute she plunged her fingers inside, she'd pop and she desperately wanted to ride Grace's arousal a bit longer. She'd never been with a woman as exciting as Grace.

"*Please, Dani.*" Grace's voice was raspy with need. "Finger me…but don't stop…sucking. Love your mouth…so fucking much."

Few things turned Dani on as much as a woman who knew what she liked and wasn't afraid to tell her. She tried to keep from touching herself again but failed, forking her clit between her fingers. Dani easily plunged two fingers into Grace, stroked twice, and gave her a final flick of her tongue.

"Oh, my God. Don't stop."

Dani couldn't stop if she wanted to. Her orgasm broke loose and shot through her in waves and she bit her lip to keep from crying out. Her legs tingled, stiffened, and then went numb. She stroked her sensitive clit one final time and then collapsed between Grace's thighs as she heard Grace cry out her release. The walls of Grace's vagina tightened around her fingers, and Dani tumbled into another orgasm.

"Oh fuck. That was awesome," Dani said as another spasm made her shiver.

"Uh-huh."

When Dani looked up, Grace's eyes met hers. Her breasts rose and fell rapidly as she tried to catch her breath, her skin flushed a light shade of pink, and a sheen of perspiration made her glow—so damn perfectly beautiful that Dani's chest ached. "Damn, I'm in so much trouble." Dani hoped she'd thought that last sentence, but Grace's expression told her she hadn't.

Grace gathered enough strength to scoot another pillow under her head and looked down at Dani still resting between her legs. "Why are you in trouble?" Part of Dani's face was covered, but her eyes were wide. One of her hands was tucked between Grace's thighs and the other disappeared between her own. Suddenly, Dani's statement made sense. "Oh...because you didn't come."

"No, not that. I did, Grace. Big time."

"Then why the trouble?" She prayed Dani wasn't already regretting having sex, because Grace very much wanted it to happen again. Dani was an excellent lover—soft, sensitive hands; sensuous, talented mouth; and long, tapered fingers. She was magic. She'd handled Grace like they'd been lovers for years, intuitively touching her in just the right spot at exactly the right time to heighten her desire and ultimately drive her to orgasm.

"Because I liked that, a lot."

"Good." Grace pulled Dani up across her body, flipped her over, and straddled her. "Then you're really going to like what comes next." A look Grace could only describe as panic crossed Dani's face. "What's wrong?"

"Nothing…I…don't…I just need a little recovery time."

Dani couldn't look at her. Something was wrong. Had she misread a signal? "Never figured you for not being able to get it up again." She tried teasing, but the worried look on Dani's face persisted. She stretched out on top of Dani and rolled her pelvis, easing her thigh between Dani's legs. "But I can help with that."

"Grace, no."

"I *really* don't mind." She rose on her hands and knees and started down Dani's body, but she flipped Grace over and plunged two fingers inside her. "Oh…Dani…"

"Shush, please, Grace. Let me."

And to her surprise, within a few delicious strokes, Grace came again. The release was just as perfect as the first time. She stilled under Dani, letting her touch and kiss as much as she wanted. When she finally looked up at her, Grace asked, "Will you let me make love to you?"

Dani buried her head between Grace's breasts, their legs still entwined. "Wasn't it good for you, Grace?"

"It was perfect, *for me*."

"Then what's wrong?" Dani's voice was so low Grace barely heard her.

Grace placed her hands on either side of Dani's face and made eye contact. "Nothing's wrong. I'd just like to touch you, to taste you."

"Not sure I can let you."

"Are you able to tell me why?" Grace ran her fingers through Dani's short hair, praying something hadn't happened in her horrible past that scarred her.

Dani tucked her head into Grace's shoulder. When she spoke again, her words sounded forced, as if they'd been buried too long. "Well…I'm okay giving pleasure, but not so good at receiving.

I'm uncomfortable with touch. The whole intimacy thing. Is there a cure?"

She kissed the top of Dani's head. "Is there a cure for my desire to sit on the floor instead of on perfectly good furniture or for Doreen Divine-Dot's desire to color her cat with food coloring?"

Dani snickered. "You're trying to make me feel better."

"My darling, there's nothing wrong with you. People's sexual preferences are varied as their other personal quirks and can shift over time. Find someone whose idiosyncrasies complement yours and experiment. Does that make sense?"

"Intellectually, yes."

"Just enjoy yourself. You know how to do that, I'm pretty sure. Things will work out as they should."

Dani finally looked at Grace again. "I think I'd enjoy experimenting with you."

"That's very good news indeed." For the first time since she'd met Dani, Grace felt like they might actually have relationship potential. Her heartbeat trebled, but a small voice inside cautioned her to move slowly.

"How do you know so much about this stuff?" Dani trailed a finger along the side of Grace's face, down her neck, and to the top of a breast.

"I read tons of books when I wanted to be a social worker. The material was good training and answered some personal questions too."

"So, you're not afraid of getting hurt?"

"Everybody is afraid of that, Dani. I gave my heart before and was crushed when she went back to her ex in Savannah, but I've decided love is worth the risk. What about you?"

"Never been hurt, not like that. I guess I haven't really given myself emotionally. And thinking about doing it now, when I might not be here long…" But the thought of leaving Pine Cone and never seeing Grace again made her physically ill. She was in so much trouble. "You're amazing, Grace, for putting yourself out there again. Very brave." Dani's phone rang and she glanced at the screen before returning her attention to Grace.

"Need to get that?"

"It can wait. It's taken too long for us to get here," Dani said, kissing Grace again.

"Good answer, Doc. Care to explore just how amazing I can be?" Grace eased her hand down Dani's torso but stopped near her bellybutton.

"Yes. I believe I would."

CHAPTER SEVENTEEN

Grace read Mary Jane's note and grimaced. Clay, River, and Trip were coming for dinner while MJ was at choir practice. No mention of Dani. Mary Jane wasn't the only one unsure about her. They hadn't seen each other since spending the entire day in bed. Dani had opened a bit emotionally, but the subsequent two-day silent treatment worried Grace. She'd sent a text and left a voice mail message, but finally decided to give her space.

She filled the cooler with beer and ice before darting across the backyard to change into a pair of shorts and a tank top. On her way back to the house, Trip pulled up in her huge vet truck with Clay and River close behind on Clay's motorcycle. "Perfect timing, as usual. You guys have the best food radar I've ever seen." She pecked Trip and Clay on the cheek and hugged River like a best girly girlfriend.

"I'm starving," Clay said.

"Got to keep this body in fighting shape." Trip flexed her arms and then lunged forward into a Superman pose.

"Clay, would you get the burgers and other fixings from the refrigerator? Trip, bring out the buns and cooler while I fire up the grill."

"You owe me ten dollars, Cahill," Trip said. "Told you it would be burgers."

"Jeez, Trip. How did you play college sports without getting sidelined for betting? You'd bet on which way the wind blew a fart," Grace said.

When she finished laughing, Clay flung the sunroom doors wide, and she and Trip headed toward the kitchen. Dirty Harry greeted them with a squawk. "Pretty boys. Pretty boys."

"Nice entertainment, Grace," River said. "I've heard about Harry, but we've never met."

"Feel free to introduce yourself while I get the coals going."

"His vocabulary has certainly improved," Trip said as she dropped the pack of hamburger buns on the table and placed the cooler in the shade near two wooden lounge chairs.

Grace laughed. "Yeah, your vet tech taught him a few less colorful phrases. He hasn't been too bad since we moved him over here, seems to have taken to the place nicely. He even lets me near him occasionally without going berserk, though I can never figure out why some times and not others."

"What's not to like about this setting?" Clay set the burger plate on the side of the grill, placed the condiments on the table, and stared out at the backyard, her arm looped around River's waist. "MJ's flowers are awesome, and the view across the fields is pristine. I should paint this someday."

"Yes, you should." River kissed Clay with a tenderness that made Grace ache for Dani.

When they stepped apart, Grace said, "I'd really love to have one of your pieces hanging in the B and B someday."

Clay's cheeks tinged with color. "Really?"

"Absolutely and not just because you're famous, which you totally are."

Trip handed Clay a beer and Grace and River glasses of wine. "To friends, now and forever. Fast Break, Paint Ball plus the woman who tamed her, and Glitter Girl, the modern day musketeers." She raised her bottle and the others clinked against it. "So…is anybody else joining us for dinner?"

"You mean like Jamie perhaps?" Grace asked.

"Shouldn't you know the answer to that question, Trip?" Clay teased her. "You have been spending quite a bit of time together lately."

"Yeah, but we're not joined at the hip."

"Yet." Clay laughed.

"You mean like you and River?" Trip volleyed back and gave River a wink.

"Exactly. You should be so lucky, dude." Clay propped against the deck railing. "What about Dani?"

"What about her?" Grace tried for nonchalance but heard the slight uptick in her tone.

"She was in your bed two days ago. Is she still there? Because she hasn't been at work." Trip started out teasing but ended on a more concerned note. "She's back, right?"

"Back from where?" Grace's stomach churned as she flipped the burgers, turned the foil-wrapped potatoes and onions around on the grill, and avoided Trip's and Clay's stares. The initial connection she'd felt with Dani had grown stronger as they lay together after sex, and she'd thought Dani felt it too. They'd talked, and Grace had opened her heart more completely. Maybe she'd chosen poorly again or imagined something more because she wanted it so much. "What do you know, Trip?"

River moved to Grace's side and rubbed her back soothingly.

Trip took a long pull on her beer. "She called me late Friday and said she had to go out of town, some emergency, but didn't say where or why. Asked me to cover the clinic on Saturday. I owed her one after my cookout binge. That's all I know." Trip shook her head. "You mean she slept with you, said nothing about this, and just left? Un-fucking believable."

"I would've sworn she was totally into you that day at the cottage. She fought for you, Gracie, and the way she looked at you…" Clay's comment hung in the air along with the strong smell of grilling meat.

The group fell quiet except for the occasional new word from Harry in the sunroom, punctuating the silence. She and Dani had shared some intimate and revealing moments, so Grace understood if she needed time to think, but she could've at least told Grace she was going away. Finally, she said, "Dani needs time to figure things out." She hoped she was right.

Clay and Trip exchanged a look, and River shook her head at them, but no one commented on how lame Grace's statement sounded.

"Have you done anything about that guy from the club?" Trip asked.

She drew a heavy breath to calm her emotions and keep her voice even. "Sort of. I can't launch an official investigation since I didn't file a complaint, but I've contacted a cop friend in Savannah who's working a couple of similar cases. She's sending a photographic lineup of possible suspects. We'll see where it leads."

"From the way Dani described him, he's probably some pervert who doesn't have a pot to piss in and gets his rocks off drugging and raping women. Creep." Trip tapped her beer bottle in the wet circle on top of the picnic table.

"Speaking of Dani, do you think she'll cooperate, look at the photos?" Clay asked.

River hooked her arm through Clay's. "Of course she will, love."

"Sure. Why wouldn't she?" Grace had asked herself the same question. Would Dani want to get more involved in Grace's life or in Pine Cone?

❖

Dani cut her car engine and coasted into the B and B driveway, hoping to arrive unnoticed. The cozy setting with Grace's cottage tucked back in the tree line was an oasis after the hectic interstate traffic and the frenetic activity of the city. When had that happened? The city had always been her go-to place to relax and lose herself in the hubbub, but this trip had been different. She'd been on edge and felt herself retreating into her shell but shook it off as just homecoming nerves. Now she wasn't so sure.

For two days, she'd effectively avoided Grace and her protective friends, but she'd also missed Grace terribly, which had been unexpected. She and Grace had connected and it scared the hell out of her. She wasn't ready to face an interrogation about her feelings for or intentions toward Grace, especially not today. The past two nights in her hotel room after the interviews had been quite enough soul searching. She grabbed her overnight bag and crept up on the large wraparound porch, carefully turned the doorknob, and opened the door.

"Trying to sneak in?" Trip sat at the foot of the stairs leading up to the guestrooms. "What's going on, Dani?"

"I told you I needed a couple of days off."

"Yeah, but you didn't tell Grace anything. You should explain this to her and soon. In the meantime, we need to talk about something else."

Dani tried to squeeze past her on the stairs, but she blocked her. "Trip, I just want to go to my room and be left alone."

Clay stepped from around the corner. "And we'd really like to talk to you for a second, on the back deck. Grace is grilling burgers."

She wanted to go to Grace and tell her things—she was a fool for leaving without a word; she missed her; and the city hadn't been as welcoming as she remembered—but not in front of an audience. But how would Grace react? Was she hurt by Dani's absence? Glad she'd gotten rid of an emotional liability? Her mind was spinning, and Clay and Trip were waiting for an answer. "I'm not sure what you want."

Clay stared at Trip as if trying to get her to speak, but when she just glared back, Clay said, "Give us a few minutes?" She turned toward the back of the house and pulled Trip from the stairs behind her. "We'll see you outside and don't try to slip out. It's important."

Dani gave a half nod and bolted up the stairs. Grace had told them what an emotional cripple Dani was, and they were going to not so politely ask her to get lost. Or worse, Grace was having second thoughts, which was probably just as well under the circumstances. She took a quick shower, changed clothes, and decided on her way downstairs that she'd just play dumb. Try levity, and then wait and see what happened.

"I knew this was going to be a strange evening when a van passed me with a cow on the roof. I stopped on Main Street for a double take. A cow's head drooped over the windshield, legs dangled over both sides, and pink udders down the back window like she'd dropped out of the sky. And just when I thought Pine Cone couldn't get any weirder."

The quartet standing around the grill turned from what appeared to be a serious conversation, and Grace was the first to respond. The sound of her laughter cut into Dani and melted everything inside. Her gaze urged Dani forward like a beacon in a sea of uncertainty and made her feel everything would be all right.

"That was the delivery truck for Seward's Butchery. Totally just as you described it." She walked to Dani and placed a light kiss on her cheek. "Nice to see you. Are you okay?"

Dani nodded. Grace's tone was light and non-judgmental, her words sincere, and the touch of her lips warm and welcoming. Dani couldn't wait to get her alone, to tell her what had happened, and to ask…to ask what? Dani's happy image dissolved.

"Have you met Chucky Seward?" Trip asked, grabbing her breasts. "Man boobs for days. I think he might give those udders a run for their money."

Dani relaxed a bit. Nobody questioned her about her absence, a little weird, but welcome. Grace seemed happy to see her, and neither Clay nor Trip had jumped her yet. River Hemsworth, obviously now with Clay, gave her an encouraging smile. Dani tried to play it cool, but curiosity won out. "So, what do we need to talk about?"

Trip looked at Grace and waited for a nod before saying, "A friend of Grace's in Savannah has been tracking the guy who drugged her, and she's come up with some possible suspects. If you're willing, she'd like you to look at a photo lineup." Trip took a sip of her beer and moved closer to Dani. "Hey, I'm sorry Clay and I gave you a hard time the other day. You did Grace a real service, and I'm grateful. No hard feelings?" She stuck out her hand. "Anybody who risks her neck for a friend is all right with me."

Dani felt something shift between them. She'd developed great respect for Trip's professional abilities, but always felt like an outsider, until now. Trip had been a loyal friend to Grace and was now woman enough to admit she might've been wrong about Dani. Would she feel the same way when Dani told her news? She took Trip's hand. "No hard feelings at all. I'd have done the same thing you and Clay did to protect a friend."

Clay slapped her on the back, and then Grace nudged between them. "Okay, give the woman some room." She tucked her arm in Dani's and handed her a cold beer from the cooler. "How do you like your burgers? Wait. Let me guess. Medium rare?"

"Exactly. So, did you decide to report what happened?" Dani asked.

Grace shook her head. "I just asked a few questions. My friend was already working a couple of similar cases. I used the confidential informant angle on my end."

"You being the informant?"

"Right. So, you don't mind looking at the photos?"

"Of course not." She wasn't sure if this development would interfere with her new plans, but she owed Grace this much. Dani joined Clay, River, and Trip at the picnic table sipping drinks while she watched Grace flip burgers and something wrapped in foil.

Grace said, "Don't feel like you have to do this. You've already literally given your pound of flesh for the creep."

"I've got this." Grace continued to surprise her. She'd forgo finding the man who drugged her for Dani's comfort. Where she came from people, not even family, sacrificed for others, but somehow she'd done it for Grace the night she was drugged and felt more herself because of it. And now Grace was willing to do the same for her. *The give and take of relationships? Not so bad.*

"Okay, burgers up," Grace said. "Help yourselves."

Dani spread Duke's mayonnaise, which she'd developed an affinity for, on both sides of her bun, added lettuce, tomato, and a burger, then filled the other side of her plate with grilled onions and potatoes. Everything looked delicious and she was suddenly starving. The last two days had been frantic and she'd eaten and rested poorly. She bit into her burger and moaned with appreciation. "Thanks. I needed this."

The others fixed their plates, and everyone ate quietly. Dani's comfort with the group waned as the silence stretched, and the unspoken hung awkwardly between them. She had to clear the air.

"Sorry I haven't been around the last couple of days. Hope I didn't leave you in trouble at the clinic, Trip." Everybody looked at her, but Grace's stare, full of happiness and hope, squeezed Dani's heart like a fist. "I had business back in Baltimore."

Grace glanced down at her food, but not before Dani saw the spark fade from her eyes. She should've discussed this privately with Grace, not blurted it in front of everyone. She'd hoped by being open, she might gain more of their confidence and trust, but her instincts had been off, again. Would she ever learn the nuances and subtle cues of relationships?

"Job offer?" For all her bravado, Trip was also refreshingly straightforward.

Dani nodded, her throat suddenly too tight for speech. For the past six months, she'd waited for her dream job offer and the chance to return to the familiarity of city life with lots of options and diversions. Now her news had shattered the only real, true thing she'd ever known—Grace.

"I apologize for my delivery." She reached for Grace's hand, but she pulled away.

"Your delivery?" Grace's tone was incredulous. "Not for vanishing without mentioning why? Not for leaving your employer in a lurch? To say nothing of practically jumping from my bed and into your car without a word. That was the phone call you got while we were—" Grace rose from the table but stopped beside Dani. "You really are something, Dani Wingate."

Grace's eyes shone with tears and a deep, unbearable agony Dani had seen often in her parents. And she'd caused it. "Grace, can we talk about this privately, please?" She glanced toward the others hoping Grace would understand.

Grace studied her for several long seconds as if trying to divine her motivation before finally answering. "I don't think that's necessary. I heard you perfectly the first time. Congratulations on getting what you wanted. I'm sorry for my outburst."

Dani listened for any parting comments as Grace brushed by, but all she heard was a clipped exchange between her and Harry as Grace passed through the sunroom.

Trip eyed Dani hard, grabbed her plate, still heaping with food, and tossed it in the garbage. "I took a chance on you, Wingate, and you pull this crap."

"I can work a notice, if you need me."

"Probably best for Grace if you leave right now, but I need your ass at the clinic to handle treatments this afternoon. We'll be busy taking care of our friend." Without another word, Trip followed Grace into the house.

Clay rose slowly from the table, River at her side. "I'm sorry, Dani, for all of us, but mostly for you. You could've had something special." She picked up her half-eaten hamburger in a napkin, disposed of the rest, and fell in behind Trip.

Dani forked a mouthful of potatoes and onions, but her stomach wretched. Some friends. They should be happy for her. She'd been honest about her intentions when she landed in Pine Cone. Why were they surprised? The job offer was a good one with potential for advancement. So why did she feel so awful?

CHAPTER EIGHTEEN

Grace's pulse raced, but everything around her moved in slow motion as she ran from Dani's news. She'd held back the tears until out of Dani's presence, but now they fell freely.

"Hey, Grace. Pretty girl." In Grace's peripheral vision, Dirty Harry danced on his perch like an old reel-to-reel movie about to break.

"Shut up, Harry." He'd said the nicest words to her ever, but she couldn't stop so close to Dani and acknowledge him. She ducked into Mary Jane's room. No one would follow.

She dropped into the upholstered recliner in the corner that was so old dust motes perpetually hovered likes bees around honey. The sides enveloped her the way Mary Jane's arms had when she was a child but offered none of the comfort. And the tears continued.

A light tap on the door preceded Clay's concerned voice. "Gracie, are you okay?"

"We're here, if you need us," Trip added.

"Need...to be...alone."

She'd been wrong about Dani and risked her heart again. Neither their intimate conversations, sharing stories about their lives, satisfying sex, nor deep feelings could hold Dani if she didn't want to stay. No amount of preparation could've eased the ache in Grace's chest or the feeling she might drown in grief. She curled into the chair, pulled a blanket around her to hide from her feelings and the rest of the world, and sobbed.

She woke later to Mary Jane's soft voice laced with worry. "Grace, honey? Are you all right?" Mary Jane shook her gently.

Grace hugged the blanket tighter, refusing to wake up or face anything outside of her fabric cocoon. "Sorry." Her throat was scratchy, and her stuffy nose made her voice sound muffled. Mary Jane didn't need to see her this way again. They'd been here before, and Grace apparently hadn't learned her lesson. "Sorry I invaded your space."

"It's perfectly all right. You know that." She rubbed Grace's shoulder, and then Grace heard her move toward the small kitchenette in the back part of the room. "I'll make us a cup of green tea while you unravel yourself from that blanket. It must be over a hundred degrees under there."

"Thanks." She lifted a corner of her cover, and a blast of cooler air rushed in. She inhaled and wiped her eyes on her T-shirt, the salt of tears making her face feel rough.

Mary Jane took her time puttering with the tea, and when she returned, Grace was sitting up, the blanket once again covering the back of the chair. "I'm sorry again for crashing your place. I know you don't like people in here."

Mary Jane placed the tea on a small side table between the recliner and a cushioned chair she'd scooted closer. "And you're not just anybody, Gracie."

She stared straight ahead not really focusing on anything while Mary Jane patiently sipped her tea. She always seemed to know what Grace needed but gave her time to come to her own conclusions. She reached for her teacup, drew back her shaking hand, tried again with two, and brought the cup slowly to her lips. "Good, MJ. Thank you." She took a couple more sips.

"Well, choir practice sucked tonight. The ladies were more interested in talking about the new mechanic over at the garage than playing cards. You'd think at some point the hormones would level out. I tried to explain that the concept of cougar required mobility."

Grace loved Mary Jane for trying to distract her, even make her laugh, but nothing was going to help her mood right now. "Dani's going back to Baltimore." Her statement hung in the air, making the room feel darker and burying her under its weight.

"Oh, Gracie, I'm sorry." Mary Jane cupped her hand and squeezed. "So very sorry."

"I knew it was going to happen." Grace brushed another round of tears from her cheeks.

"The knowing doesn't make the happening any easier, honey. When did you find out?"

"She announced it at dinner. That's where she's been for two days."

"Any idea when she's leaving?" Mary Jane asked softly.

"No." Grace finished her tea and stood slowly. "I need to get out for a bit, breathe some fresh air." She looked down at Mary Jane and her eyes looked as sad as Grace felt. "And don't worry, I won't do anything stupid, like run after her. Those days are over."

"You want some company?"

Grace shook her head.

A few minutes later, she pulled up to Mosquito Alley, cut the Corolla engine, and waited as it sputtered into silence across the water. She walked to the river's edge and sat on her favorite flat rock overlooking a small waterfall. The last rays of sunlight streaked the surface of the water and brought it to life with color. Clay had painted several beautiful landscapes sitting on the bank while Grace and Trip chatted nearby. Tonight, the muted hues produced only melancholy.

Things with Dani were always going to end badly. But why so soon? She'd hoped for a few weeks, possibly months, of something resembling happiness, but had only gotten a taste. Dani made her feel more deeply than she ever had, and she'd finally opened her heart again. She couldn't regret being with her no matter how painful the outcome.

Grace inhaled the familiar scents of rich river mud, brackish water, and remnants of sweet muscadines and melons decaying and returning to the soil for another season. She listened to the wheezy call of finches, the clicking rattle of scrub jays, and the unique chirping of cicadas as night closed in. The sights and sounds of this place gave her peace, but she'd leave it today to be with Dani anywhere in the world. She couldn't deny it any longer or claim contentment with the temporary. She was in love with Dani. Now what? She bent her legs and rested her head on her knees letting the revelation sink in.

"Hey, Grace." Trip sounded nervous. "Thought we might find you here." She settled on one side of Grace and Clay on the other.

"If you want to be alone, we'll leave," Clay said, her voice thick with concern. We're just worried about you is all." Clay wrapped a light jacket around her shoulders. "The mosquitoes are about to carry you away."

"Hadn't noticed." Grace pulled the jacket tighter, suddenly feeling the bite stings and the crisper night air.

"It's her type O blood. Those females love her," Trip said. When Grace eyeballed her, Trip added, "Sorry. Do you want us to go?"

Grace shook her head. "I've been thinking and I need to tell you something." Clay and Trip scooted closer but didn't speak, letting Grace take her time. "I'm in love with Dani." No one responded. "Well…"

"That's not exactly news, Gracie," Clay said. "But Trip owing me ten dollars is."

Grace laughed out loud and her mood lifted. "It's about time. What was the bet?"

Trip grunted. "That you'd fall for Dani. It's easy to see when you guys are together."

"Hard to imagine you betting against such a sure thing, Trip."

"Yeah, I was hoping I'd lose, but now I'm not so sure. Anything we can do?"

Grace slid one arm around Trip's shoulder and the other over Clay's so they were all connected. "Nothing to be done. I gave it my best shot, and she's still leaving. End of story. I just needed to admit the truth. When will she finish at the clinic?"

"Not sure." Trip looked out over the river and swatted mosquitoes. "I told her she could go now for all I care. Good Lord willing and the creek don't rise, you won't have to see her again." Trip frowned and tucked her head when Grace squeezed her neck. "Sorry, but I'm pissed. She hurt you. Do you want me to ask her to work out a long notice?"

"Don't really see the point. Just be nice and don't make matters worse. And you *will* give her a good, no, make that a great, reference." When Trip didn't answer, Grace added, "Understand me, Tripoli Olivia Beaumont?"

Trip covered her ears. "Keep it down. I don't want the whole town knowing that moniker. I'll give Dani a glowing recommendation. She's an awesome vet. I'd even thought about expanding the business and asking her to become a partner, but she blew that too."

"Pine Cone would never be enough for her." Grace's voice quivered as she watched insects dance above the water's surface. "And neither am I."

Clay patted Grace's arm. "I wouldn't be so sure about that, Gracie. I was lucky enough to entice River away from New York City."

Grace smiled, grateful for Clay's kind words, but Dani was nothing like River.

Trip nodded toward the car. "Come on. My eyeballs are floating. Too many beers at dinner."

"Well, your favorite bush is right over there. Don't let us stop you," Clay said.

"I'm not dropping my drawers out here at night. Those bloodsuckers would latch onto my lady parts and ruin me for life. Let's go."

Grace stood and started toward her car. "Nothing like best friends to put life back into perspective."

CHAPTER NINETEEN

For the next five days, Dani tied up the loose ends of her stay in Pine Cone. She looked at the police lineup and picked out the guy who'd drugged Grace, and he was charged in several cases. She'd just finished her final week at work and intended to leave for Baltimore early the next morning. She cleared out her small locker in the back of the clinic, stuffed everything into her duffel bag and left the door key on the shelf. Trip had been the consummate professional at work, for which Dani was grateful, but had given her a wide berth personally. The separation made Dani feel wretched. So, this was what it felt like to lose friends she cared about.

And Grace was never far from Dani's mind, always arousing feelings she couldn't control. Grace had been purposely absent at the B and B, and Mary Jane's kindness bordered on overkill—cooking her favorite meals, changing her sheets and towels every other day instead of every three, and even offering her a long-stay discount on her bill. They were both probably giving Dani what they thought she needed for a clean break. Grace and Mary Jane were totally that considerate, and their thoughtfulness only made Dani feel worse.

When she pulled into the driveway in front of Grace's cottage for the last time, it was nearly dark. She'd felt more at home in this place than anywhere she'd ever been, all because of Grace.

Dani wanted to see her one last time, to say good-bye privately, but she was being selfish. The least she could do was leave without causing more pain.

She got out of the car, closed the door softly, and started toward the B and B, tugging her emotional baggage and regret like a lead ball behind her.

"Dani?"

She stopped but didn't turn around, afraid she'd imagined Grace calling to her.

"Dani, would you come in for a minute, please?"

She turned slowly and froze again. Light from inside framed Grace in the doorway, penetrating her sundress, outlining her curvy body, and shadowing her expression. Dani licked her lips and struggled for the right words, but everything she considered saying sounded wrong. She walked toward Grace, unsure what to do when she reached her.

Grace offered her hand and led Dani inside to the sofa. "Something to drink?"

Dani shook her head.

"Dani, I—"

"You don't have to say anything, Grace."

"But I want to. You need to know that I'm not angry or upset with you anymore. I was shocked at first, not sure why. You've been honest about what you wanted."

Grace's eyes grew larger as she blinked back tears, and Dani's heart ached. She couldn't outlive this pain. "I'm sorry I hurt you, Grace."

"I knew what I was getting into. I chose to open my heart again and risk being hurt. Don't blame yourself because I fell in love with you."

Grace's words split Dani equally between desire and fear. She wanted to wrap herself in Grace's love, share hers, but she also wanted to run because she'd eventually fail her in some essential way she'd never understand until it was too late. "You what?"

"I'm in love with you."

"But I—"

Grace placed her fingers over Dani's lips. "Shush. I don't expect anything from you."

"Why did you tell me? Wouldn't it have been easier to keep quiet?"

"Not for me. I wanted you to know how I feel and that you'll always have a home here." Grace placed their joined hands over her heart. "Never doubt my feelings. No matter where you are or who you're with. What I feel is forever."

"Grace..." Nothing else was possible, just the sound of Grace's name rolling softly off her tongue like a prayer. Dani touched Grace's face and slid her fingers slowly down the side of her neck, her body heating as Grace's eyes fluttered shut. "You make me feel so...different. May I kiss you?"

Grace didn't answer but closed her lips over Dani's, licking, kissing, and slowly pressing. She couldn't resist Grace's invitation, didn't want to. When Grace's tongue claimed hers, Dani felt a surge of energy from her core break loose and spiral through her, melting and rearranging her insides to accommodate her feelings for Grace. They kissed until neither could breathe and then broke for air.

"Let me make love to you, Dani. Just once. *Please.*"

Grace's plea reduced Dani to a bundle of needy flesh and nerves. "Are you sure?"

"Mostly, but that's okay with me."

Dani gasped at Grace's willingness to step into the unknown so easily. She'd said the same thing the first time they made love, and her words still pulled Dani in, made her weak and empowered at the same time. She nodded.

Grace stood and slowly unzipped her sundress, letting it pool on the floor at her feet. She shimmied out of her bikinis and gradually peeled her lacy bra straps down her arms. Each movement, every tantalizing reveal, brought Dani to life with surges of desire. She stared into Grace's eyes for several seconds before taking in her gorgeous face, full breasts, and the dip of her stomach. "You're amazing, Grace. I need you so much."

"Don't you mean you want me? I've seen that look in your eyes before, Doc."

Dani swallowed hard. "I'm scared to death I might mean more." Her words registered. She needed Grace to touch her, but more importantly, to connect with her in a way she'd never allowed before. Grace stood very still in front of her, searching Dani's face. "You okay, Grace?"

"What you said was beautiful."

Dani flushed and reached to pull Grace closer, but she leaned back. "Please."

Grace knelt between Dani's legs and stripped off her shoes and jeans in a series of quick motions. Next, she opened Dani's shirt, and her eyes sparked when she discovered she wasn't wearing a bra. "I like you like this. Boxers and unbuttoned shirt, exposed, but not completely." She grabbed Dani's hips, urged her closer to the edge of the sofa, and ran her hands up Dani's legs and under the hem of her shorts, gripping the taut flesh of her thighs.

"Oh, God, Grace."

"Will you let me have you tonight, Dani? All of you?"

Grace's throaty tone and quickened breaths made Dani feel like she was the most desirable woman in the world. Grace wanted…and needed *her*. "I'll try." Grace leaned forward and pressed against Dani, the soft weight of her breasts resting just under Dani's.

"I want to touch you, to show you how much I care, and I need you to feel it." Grace kissed her again deeply, bringing her words to life.

"Yes, Grace."

She alternated feasting on Dani's breasts while her thumbs and forefingers teased the juncture between her hips and thighs. "Is this okay?"

Dani nodded, unable to speak.

"Dani?" Grace rested her chin on Dani's thigh, holding her gaze, waiting for a reply.

Dani hesitantly nodded again, desire and uncertainty occupying the same space.

As Grace moved to touch her lower, Dani involuntarily tensed and tried to close her legs. She'd never allowed anyone to caress her so intimately. She wasn't sure she could now, and if she did, what to expect. She hadn't trusted anyone enough to find out.

"Relax, Dani. I won't hurt you. Ever."

Grace caressed Dani's abdomen and pelvis creeping lower, and with each pass Dani felt new sensations fire through her stoking an urgent, unquenchable thirst. The tension in her lower body slowly released. No became maybe, followed by probably, and finally yes. She ached for more direct contact. She squirmed against the sofa and forward into Grace.

"Do you want me to stop, Dani?"

Her eyes shot open. "What? No." She stared into Grace's hooded eyes, desperate for something more meaningful for the first time in her life. But she didn't know how to ask for it, whatever *it* was.

"What do you want me to do?"

Dani encircled Grace's wrist and guided her hand between her legs. "Touch me."

Grace held eye contact as she slid Dani's boxers off and came to rest again between her legs. "Thank you for this." She leaned forward and breathed against Dani's wet center. She fingered the patch of hair just above Dani's clit, and she jerked. "Do you like that?"

"Not sure yet."

Grace added more pressure, and a different kind of tension gathered inside Dani. "Ohh, that's good. More." She loved watching Grace touch her body, worship her like she was special. It was totally erotic like nothing she'd ever experienced.

Grace increased the pace, and Dani rose to meet her. "Yesss." Dani flew apart and came back together every time her flesh disconnected and then rejoined Grace's. The most exquisite pain coursed through her, coalesced around her heart, burrowed lower, and finally curled into a powerful ball in her core. When Grace slid her fingers inside and the warmth of her mouth closed over Dani's center, she shattered into a million shards of pleasure. Only Grace could ever put her back together.

❖

Grace woke as dawn cast light across the floor and onto the pile of blankets and pillows she and Dani had finally claimed as their bed. Dani. Beside her. Holding her. Looking calm, sated, and, dared she think, happy. Last night had been magical. Dani let her in emotionally, but was it too late? Had Dani surrendered because she was leaving today?

Whatever the reason, Grace could live with it. Her friends would think she was crazy for sleeping with Dani, but she'd experienced the real, true passion of Dani Wingate, unguarded and accessible. She'd seen Dani's need and exposed her own. One night like that with the right person could last a lifetime. Was Dani that person? If not, Grace could let her go. She'd never imagined being able to love so completely without having that feeling reciprocated, but she'd had no choice but to love Dani that much. She snuggled into the crook of Dani's arm and feathered kisses along her jawline.

"Mmm. Grace?"

"Right on the first guess."

"Couldn't be anyone else." Dani pulled her closer and kissed her forehead.

Grace slid a leg across Dani's thigh and felt desire building as Dani surged into her. "See what you do to me? I need you again."

Dani's expression shifted, questioning and wanting. "Grace—"

"Don't say it. We both know what happens when you walk out that door this morning."

"And what if I don't...walk out?"

Grace stroked the side of Dani's face, enjoying the flush of heat under her fingers and the rapid pulse at Dani's throat. "You'd be giving up your dream. I can't be responsible for that."

Dani rolled on top of her. "And what if my dreams have changed?"

"Then you have to decide what's next." Dani had to come to her willingly and totally. Grace's love alone wouldn't be enough to sustain their forever. Dani searched Grace's face and started to say something but stopped. "What, Dani?"

"Nothing." She nipped Grace's neck. "So, how about one more time for the road?"

Grace answered her with a deep kiss but pulled back when the air around them turned steamy. "I'd prefer to leave us both wanting more." She pushed Dani off and crawled out of the covers. "Time to face the world again, Doc."

Behind her, Dani groaned. "I'd call that cruel and unusual treatment verging on torture, Deputy Booker."

Grace tossed a pillow at her head. "You haven't seen my cruel side yet. I'm going to take a quick shower and make you breakfast."

"What if I join you?"

Grace held up her hand. "We'd be naked all day, and you'd be no closer to Baltimore."

Grace forced herself to leave Dani nude and willing on her living room floor and retreated to the bathroom. If she could hold it together another hour, she'd be in the clear. She couldn't send Dani off feeling like she'd done something wrong or like Grace would fall apart without her. Dani deserved the opportunity to find her own brand of happiness. She tugged on a T-shirt and jeans and rejoined Dani in the living area.

Dani was sitting up, wrapped in a blanket, bathed in light from the window. She was the most handsome woman Grace had ever seen—pale skin still flushed from their lovemaking, dark hair and eyes, and a thoughtful crease etched across her forehead.

Grace watched her take several long breaths, enjoying the feeling that Dani finally looked content. "Okay, you, time to get dressed. You've got a long drive, and I want you to have plenty of time for rest stops."

While Dani showered, Grace prepared an omelet with ham, cheese, and spinach, and they ate quietly and exchanged looks Grace couldn't quite name. She'd given everything, offered her heart, and now the choice was Dani's. Grace sighed as she put the dishes in the sink. The choice had always been Dani's. Grace had been in love with her since she gave Beetle Bledsoe money in front of the diner. The small things had slowly won her heart without the need for grand gestures. She couldn't help wondering how Dani felt as they walked toward the door.

Dani reached for the handle but turned back to Grace and pulled her close. "I've never met anyone like you, Grace. You've done things to me I don't understand."

"It's called good sex." Grace tried to keep it light so she wouldn't break down.

"No, it's more than that."

She waited for Dani to explain, but when she didn't, Grace kissed her one final, breath-stopping time and opened the door. "Next time you're passing through Georgia, remember we have a great little B and B in Pine Cone."

"You certainly do." She started out but paused again. "By the way, did you notice that Harry spoke to you civilly the other night... the night you grilled on the deck? When you passed through the sunroom, he wasn't freaked out."

"Not really. I might've been a little distracted. If that's true, I wonder why the change?"

Dani shrugged. "Maybe he just doesn't like cops, like me." She winked, looked toward the main house, and stopped. "Oh, shit."

Grace followed her gaze to the back deck where Mary Jane, Clay, and Trip sat drinking coffee and staring toward the cottage.

"Your bon voyage committee, I'm guessing." She took Dani's hand and walked to join the others.

"Good morning, everybody," Grace said.

"You sure about that?" Trip asked.

"Absolutely." Grace squeezed Dani's hand and gave Trip a hard stare, daring her to do anything to upset the smooth send-off she'd planned for Dani.

"Okay, then." Trip stood and offered Dani her hand. "It's been a pleasure. You're an awesome vet." She handed Dani an envelope. "Here's a damn fine reference. If you need anything else, let me know."

Dani looked stunned for a second before she shook Trip's hand and accepted the gift. "Thanks for this, and for giving me a job when I was desperate. I've learned a lot from you."

Clay placed a hand on Dani's shoulder. "We'll miss you, dude. Guess the townsfolk will have to find something else to gossip about now."

Dani laughed and shoulder bumped Clay. "I'm sure you and Trip will keep them busy, especially now that you have River and Trip has Jamie. And I'm glad you got back to your art. I've seen some of your stuff in the gallery. You're good." Grace, Clay, and Trip all stared at her. "Yes, I've been to the gallery. I'm not a complete heathen."

"Who knew you had a sensitive side, Wingate?" Trip asked.

"I did," Grace said, giving Dani a scorching look.

Mary Jane moved closer. "Well, I've packed a few sandwiches and snacks for the road. There's a disposable cooler by your car with drinks." She gave Dani a big hug. "It's been a joy to have you here, honey, a real joy. Come back any time."

"You have no idea how much I've enjoyed being here. You've all taught me a lot." Dani hugged Mary Jane and clung to her as if she couldn't bear to let go, and Grace choked down a sob. Just a few more minutes. "I'll never forget you."

Grace followed Dani to her car and gave her a quick hug, but Dani caught her arm as she pulled back and kissed her, first lightly, and then more urgently. The thin tether holding Grace's emotions in check started to fray. She poured everything she felt into their kiss before pushing away, breathless. "I...love you, Dani."

"Grace, I'm in—"

"Be safe." Whatever Dani was about to say, Grace couldn't hear it and then watch her leave. She kept waving until Dani's car disappeared around the final curve at the town limit sign before turning back to the cottage. Her friends started toward her, but she shook her head and kept walking. Once inside, she closed the door behind her, and collapsed on the tangle of blankets and pillows that smelled of Dani.

CHAPTER TWENTY

When Grace awoke, it was dark outside and she was still wrapped in the blankets she and Dani made love on. Her wet pillow stuck against the side of her face, her tongue was dry from mouth breathing, and she could barely see out of her swollen eyes. The sound of tires on gravel she'd prayed for between bouts of crying never came. Dani was really gone. She flung the covers off and walked out the door, unable to bear the sight or smell of their love nest another second.

The crisp night air stung her skin, confirming that her pain was real. She tugged her T-shirt tighter around her. The moon was nearly full and lit the path to the B and B. She stood on the deck and gazed at the stars. Where was Dani on her journey? Did she drive straight through or stop for a rest? Did she think of Grace on the trip, consider coming back?

She opened the back door slowly, careful of the squeaking hinge on the screen that alerted Mary Jane to visitors. Harry flapped his wings when she entered. "Shush." She gulped a glass of water at the kitchen sink then snagged an orange and returned to the sunroom, curling into the wicker chair beside Harry's cage. "Want to talk?" She was losing it. Talking to a parrot.

"Orange." Harry's squawk sounded more like a request.

Grace peeled the fruit, tore off a small chunk, and eased it under the cover of Harry's cage. If he saw her, he might go ballistic, and wake Mary Jane. "Here you go, boy." Harry nibbled the segment gently from her fingers, and Grace almost burst into tears. "Now I know how you felt when Karla left. Throwing myself against the walls and picking myself bald doesn't sound so bad right now." She slid another piece of orange through the cage.

Dani had spent a lot of time with Harry and cleared him medically. Surely, Grace could figure out why he didn't like her. He'd been nice after Dani's bombshell, but she had no idea why. Had he somehow sensed her despair? "You and I are going to be friends, Harry." She gave him the last segment of orange and headed toward the door.

"Bye, Grace," Harry said as she eased the screen door closed.

The following week, when she wasn't distracted with work, she buried herself in library books and online articles about African grays. She wasn't particularly an animal person, but she was responsible for Harry since Karla abandoned him, and she'd try to make him happy. He deserved a peaceful life and affection like every other creature.

She pulled a spiral notebook from her bookshelf and scribbled Harry across the front. Opening to the first page, she filled in her efforts so far.

Day one—Dani left. Harry spoke to me civilly for the first time. Unsure why. Peeled and ate orange with him pre-dawn. Cage covered. No adverse reaction. Said good-bye to me when I left.

Day two—Talked to Harry quietly while changing his food and water. Cage covered. No adverse reaction.

Days three-six—Sat outside his cage late at night and told him how Dani cared for him when he was sick. Reassured him that he'd always be part of our family. Fed him orange slices. Teaching him a few new phrases. Still haven't let him see me.

Days seven-ten—More of the above.

Day twelve—Took cover off Harry's cage while changing his food and water this morning before work. He went crazy again, but when I put the cover back on and spoke, he calmed down. Remembered something Dani said before she left. Have an idea. Test tomorrow.

The next morning, Grace bounded across the backyard to the B and B. The sun was brilliant and the sky blue with promise. She'd showered and dressed in shorts and a T-shirt to test her theory. "MJ?"

Mary Jane placed the last platter on the buffet table and turned toward her. "What's up?"

"Today is the day I figure out why Dirty Harry hates me and I need a witness." She reached for the cover of his cage and eased it off, holding her breath as he turned and stared in her direction.

Harry bounced up and down. "Hello, Grace. Good morning. Pretty day."

He actually seemed happy to see her, no loud, disturbing response. She cautiously opened the cage door and reached in, offering her finger as a perch. Harry hopped on, and she pulled him out slowly. He was still calm, so she lifted her finger to her shoulder and he stepped over. "Look at that, MJ."

Harry pecked gently at her hair and nibbled the rim of her ear. He'd only ever done that to Karla before.

"Well, I never. He's kissing you." Mary Jane's voice held as much wonder as Grace felt. "He's okay now. What happened?"

"He hates my uniform...just like Dani. Not me. Isn't that great?" The partially bald, neurotic parrot Karla left was becoming part of the family. Grace couldn't imagine the house without his cheerful phrases and playful mocking.

Mary Jane ran her hand down Grace's back. "You've done an amazing job with him, honey. He obviously loves you."

"Yeah," Grace said wistfully. "I guess he does. And I admit, I like having him around. He's a perfect sounding board late at night when I can't sleep. Never talks back or offers a dissenting opinion."

Mary Jane pinched her arm. "In other words, he tells you what you want to hear?"

"Exactly." Grace changed Harry's water and topped up his food dish while he danced and sang on her shoulder. When she finished, she tried a new command she'd been teaching him. "Okay, Harry, cage."

Harry obediently jumped from her shoulder to the cage top and worked his way inside.

"Good boy, Harry." She handed him a slice of orange she'd held back as a reward. "I'll see you both after work." She kissed Mary Jane on the cheek and hurried to change into her uniform. Dani would be proud of her progress with Harry.

On her way out of the cottage, Grace stared at the pile of blankets still on the floor from her last night with Dani. She'd left them there to remind her of what she'd had and what she'd been able to give up for love. Would her life ever feel complete again?

CHAPTER TWENTY-ONE

Dani woke to blaring car horns and an ambulance siren rattling her bedroom windows. She bolted upright, taking a second to get her bearings. The thin futon mattress sagged and slats poked her bottom. She shivered against cold air seeping into the poorly insulated space and wiped the sleep from her eyes. Not Booker's cozy B and B in the Deep South. She'd been back home in Baltimore for a month. Home. The word felt foreign here.

She rolled over and pulled her thin blanket tighter. She'd dreamed about the last time she'd been with Grace and woke in the middle of the night unsettled. She kicked the covers off and checked the time on her cell. Five thirty. Her roommate's deep snoring reverberated through the drafty loft like another siren, making further sleep impossible.

The apartment she'd scored near the zoo with one of the vet techs was convenient but far from comfortable and homey. She dressed quickly and threw the rest of her clothes in a duffel, anxious for the rituals of the day to keep her from second-guessing her decision to return to Pine Cone. Coffee with a bacon and egg bagel from the corner shop first, followed by a brisk fifteen-minute walk to the zoo, check in, review daily schedule, and care for the animals. Then, road trip back to Pine Cone...and Grace.

She'd returned to her professional routine easily but attempts to re-create an active social life failed miserably. Clubbing bored her now. Picking up random women held no appeal. Sex with anyone but Grace just wasn't going to happen. Instead of soothing and shielding her, the city now seemed to claw at her nerves and suck her energy. She'd told herself as soon as the languid pace and lingering memories of Georgia faded, she'd be fine again, but that day never came. She still longed for the comfortable relationships of her friends in Pine Cone, colorful coworkers, and her connection to Grace.

Dani bit into her bagel as she walked, chewed a few times, and tossed the rest in the garbage. It was nothing like Mary Jane's fluffy biscuits that made her mouth water and forced her to work out harder to stay in shape. Her boss was opening the employee's entrance as she approached and finished her coffee. All she had to do was focus on work until noon.

"You're early, again."

"What can I say?" She did love caring for animals, but work wasn't all that mattered anymore. She'd sampled another slice of life with Grace and the hunger lingered.

"Hey, Wingate, there's a supervisor's position opening up in the next couple of months if you're interested. I could put in a good word."

Dani nodded absently but handed him her resignation—something she couldn't imagine doing several months ago now felt not only right but necessary. "Don't think I'll be needing it."

She completed her morning tasks enjoying the verdant surroundings, animal calls cresting and tumbling through the park, and her special link with each creature. When the main gate of the zoo opened, the grounds flooded with people and noise. The air around her shifted, and she flinched. The animals retreated to safe zones in their enclosures as the chaos of excited children and curious onlookers swelled. Dani wanted to escape with the animals somewhere safe and quiet.

People did the same thing—found solace from uncontrollable situations wherever they could. Her parents had chosen drugs and eventually fled city life for the quieter country, but they'd waited too late. The city hadn't been her parents' salvation or hers, only an excuse to isolate and disengage. Her grandmother's wisdom about home and relationships being the key to happiness returned, followed closely by an image of Grace.

The next couple of hours passed quickly, each minute bringing her closer to Grace. Dani had researched the monthly happenings in Pine Cone and prepared what she hoped would be a unique and irresistible reappearance. On the drive, she second-guessed her plan. Maybe it was too wild or too lame. Maybe Grace preferred a more direct approach and wouldn't get it at all. Or maybe Dani was still scared and this was a cowardly tactic. She prayed Grace would focus on the unique and irresistible angle.

Less than thirty minutes now to Pine Cone—the place that felt like home; the place reminiscent of the simpler times before her family fell apart; the kind of place she'd shared and loved with her grandmother and had come back to full circle with Grace. If only she wasn't too late.

❖

Grace waved her arms at a group of people sauntering across Main Street holding up traffic. "Come on. Daylight's burning, and the ice cream's melting." She shooed them toward the big tent in front of the library that served as the check-in point for the Crazy Hat and Ice Cream Day activities. "Herding cats. I swear," she mumbled under her breath as Jamie and Petunia walked up beside her.

"Sounds like somebody needs a break."

"Perfect timing. Good to see Petunia up and around. She totally recovered?" Grace squatted and scratched behind P's ear, and she nuzzled Grace's hand.

"Good as new thanks to Trip and…" Jamie's voice trailed off.

"Okay then. You should be clear enough in an hour or so to close off the street and have some fun. Thanks, Jamie." Grace headed toward the hotdog stand where Trip and Clay were waiting. "Hey, guys."

"You're drenched," Clay said, nodding toward the sheriff's office. "Why don't you go change, and we'll save you a spot on the library steps. Great view from up there. I want to take a few pictures for sketches later."

Grace scanned the large crowd on the way to the station, pleased with the attendance. The town council had considered scaling back the monthly events, but maybe this turnout would save them. The folks in Pine Cone loved a gathering, especially one with a quirky theme and food.

She found Clay and Trip staked out on a raised portion of the library entrance overlooking the festivities. "Perfect perch for girl watching." Clay and Trip raised their hands simultaneously. "Seriously, you two? Pussy-whipped already?" Their wide grins said it all. "So, why aren't you with your *wimminfolk* instead of hanging out with me?"

Trip nodded toward the intersection where Grace had left Jamie. "Mine's working. At least I can enjoy looking at her." Trip threw a mock salute in Jamie's direction. "She's just damn hot, right?"

"River will be along shortly. She's finishing up at the gallery." Clay's eyes held a spark Grace hadn't seen in years. "Besides, what's a celebration without an appearance by Fast Break, Paint Ball, and Glitter Girl? Plus, we're judging this year. Go figure." Clay nudged Grace's shoulder. "We love you, Gracie."

Grace choked up a bit at Clay's sincerity. She and Trip had stuck close over the past month, making sure Grace had things to do while also giving her room to grieve. She kept going through the motions, but nothing felt right since Dani left. The only bright spot had been her bonding with Harry and seeing him flourish. "So, what's your favorite hat?"

"I'm partial to the naked anatomically-correct orgy created out of vegetables, but don't tell Jamie." Trip pointed to Michelle's festive headpiece.

"Figures," Clay said. "I like Connie's version of the crash at the Clip 'n Curl. You should give her points for creativity and highlighting the biggest event of the year. What about you, Grace?"

She scanned the usual collection of flowery, fruity, and agriculturally-themed creations, but nothing stood out as particularly special. Then she spotted a unique costume heading toward the library. "Who's that? There." Grace pointed. "In the giraffe outfit with a cornucopia of animals on his head?"

"No idea," Trip said.

"Nope," Clay added, "and we should know, right?"

"Costumes aren't required, but it's a nice touch," Grace said, returning her attention to the giraffe strolling confidently through the crowd to the registration table. Dani had always liked giraffes, but it couldn't be. "Let's take our seats, judges."

Two hours later, after the parade of entries, she, Clay, and Trip huddled in the library's cool conference room arguing the merits of their choices. "I thought hat judging would be fun and easy. Simple. Lots of free ice cream. Food. Seriously."

Trip leaned back in her chair. "I gave up the vegetable orgy, but I'm not budging on the giraffe with animal menagerie topknot. It's unique, and as you said, Grace, the costume is a bonus. Plus, animals. Duh."

Clay shook her head. "Can't you appreciate the artistry in Connie's creation or Doreen Divine-Dot's flower townscape?"

"Face it, Clay, Trip and I aren't as deep as you." Grace shuffled through the entries they'd already eliminated. "We're down to two. So…I'm sticking with the giraffe and zoo."

"Why?" Clay asked.

"I'm not sure. Something about the whole presentation appeals to me. Or maybe it's the way the giraffe moves. I don't know. Call it a gut instinct."

Clay tossed her ballot on the table. "Fine, but this means you both owe me one of everything at all the food tents. I'm starving. And I think Grace should announce the winners because I just saw River and Jamie coming up the steps."

Trip nodded in agreement and pushed away from the table. "Perfect. I'm off."

Grace stood and said, "Let's do this. MJ packed some Yetis with beer and wine in the cooler. Time to get this party started."

The crowd erupted in cheers when the three of them appeared on the library steps, and the grand marshal handed Grace a microphone. "Welcome to Pine Cone's monthly downtown gathering. Thanks for your attendance and for keeping it lively by participating in our weird and unusual competition. After long and heated discussions, your judges, Trip Beaumont, Clay Cahill, and I, have chosen the winners of the hat contest."

The contestants surged forward, but the giraffe stood off to the side. Grace waved him closer to the group. "In third place, Doreen Divine-Dot's downtown Pine Cone in flowers." Everyone cheered. "Second place, Connie's crash at the Clip 'n Curl." More cheering. "And first place goes to…the giraffe with animal headpiece. I'm sorry, I don't know who you are, but well done. Congratulations to all the winners and participants."

The local newspaper photographer took the mike. "Winners on stage for a photo, please."

Grace motioned to the steps beside her, and the two runners-up rushed forward, but the giraffe hung back. "Come on," Grace said. "Don't be shy." The giraffe stepped up beside her, and they waited for the obligatory photos, before Grace said, "Great outfit. It's a real winner."

"But am I…a winner?"

The deep, throaty voice was unmistakable, and the urgent tone rifled through Grace like a shot to the heart. "*Dani?*"

"Shush. They'll think the contest was rigged." She cupped Grace's elbow and nodded toward the library. "Can we talk?"

Grace couldn't move as she searched the comical creature's face and settled on the eyeholes. Brown eyes shiny with tears and deep with emotion drilled into her. "Dani. It *is* you." Her pulse hammered and she felt lightheaded, nervous about talking to Dani but afraid not to.

"Please, Grace?"

She eventually took one step toward Dani and then couldn't move fast enough. Trip and Clay noticed the commotion and gave her questioning stares, but she gave them a thumb up. Once inside the cool library, Grace stopped, jerking Dani to a halt beside her. "Isn't that thing hot?" Not at all what she really wanted to know, but it just came out.

Dani shucked off the large headpiece and wiped her hand through wet hair. "Fucking A."

"If you were trying to get my attention, you succeeded."

"I was hoping you'd remember I love giraffes." Dani waved her hand down the bulky costume and her forehead crinkled. "Too much?"

Dani's face was bright red and sweat trickled down her neck. Her full lips looked swollen, and when she licked them, Grace swallowed hard. "You've always been a bit much. Why are you here, Dani?" Finally, the real question.

"I'm an idiot, Grace."

Dani's sincere expression registered in Grace's soul, but she couldn't suppress a laugh. "Wearing a full giraffe costume in the heat of a Georgia summer, I'd have to agree."

Dani poked her hands out of the cumbersome faux hooves and took Grace's hands. "I mean about us. I shouldn't have left you." She pressed a hand to the side of her head. "I wanted to ask you to come with me, but I knew the city would suck the life out of you, just like it did my parents...and me. Can you ever forgive me?"

"What are you saying, Dani?"

"That I'm sorry and..." Dani shivered, and Grace realized something wasn't right. "I'm serious, Grace. This is important."

"It's hard to take you seriously right now. You disappear for a month with no contact and then show up looking like *that*. Besides, you're probably suffering from heat exhaustion and not thinking clearly. Do you have a headache, nausea?"

"Little of both, but I haven't eaten much today. Drove straight from Baltimore." Dani wobbled sideways but righted herself. "I'm dizzy and dying for a drink."

"Let's go. You need to cool down, fast." Before she had time to change her mind, she grabbed the front of Dani's costume and pulled her out the back door of the library to her car, picking up a couple of bottles of water on her way. The medical services personnel at the event were overrun with fainters and drunks, and Grace wasn't leaving Dani's care to anyone else. "Drink these while I drive."

She turned the car air conditioning on high, and when they stopped in front of the cottage, she sent a group text to Trip and Clay.

Gone home with the giraffe. Don't worry. Tell Jamie to text if she needs anything.

Trip texted back almost immediately.

Woot. It's all good. Clay owes me $10.

As she opened the door for Dani and waved her inside, she wondered if it really was good. Dani was back, but what did that mean? She couldn't get her hopes up, not again. Behind her, Dani clutched a chair to steady herself. "Here, let's get this thing off before you stroke out." She guided Dani to the edge of the sofa, lowered the costume zipper halfway, and stopped. "You're not wearing anything else?"

"Boxers. It's summer in Georgia. I have other clothes, along with everything else I value, in the back of my car in town."

"You brought everything?" Dani nodded and her breathing became more rapid. Grace settled her on the sofa and knelt in front of her. She finished unzipping the costume and shucked it off Dani's shoulders, focusing on what needed to be done instead of what her body wanted to do. She urged Dani's hips up and slid the outfit and her Wonder Woman underwear down her legs. "You're killing me, Wingate."

"I'm fine. Really. Just a little hot, but…" She touched the side of Grace's face. "I think that's all you."

"We'll see." Grace retrieved a bottle of cold water from the refrigerator and handed it to Dani. "Lie back and drink this while I get a cool shower running. Don't move until I come for you. Promise."

Dani caught her hand. "Anything you want, Grace."

She retreated to the bathroom and turned on the shower, propping against the door to catch her breath. How quickly the jovial hat and ice cream social had turned into a life-changing event. She'd missed Dani so much, unable to sleep or eat properly, distracted at work, but what now. This wasn't the time to worry about her fledgling love life or even consider what might happen next. Dani needed her. Grace shook her head and reviewed the treatment for heat exhaustion. Dani could be in real trouble.

When she returned to the living room, Dani was slouched on the sofa, head back and eyes closed. "No, no, no." She rushed to her side. "Wake up." She tucked her arms under Dani's and tried to lift her. "Help me. I can't do this alone."

Dani slid to the edge of the sofa. "Sorry. Dozed off. I can walk." She launched herself into Grace's arms sending them both wobbling backward. "Maybe not."

"Slowly, please." Grace pressed tightly against Dani's side to keep her upright and guided her into the bathroom. "Step into the shower and hold onto me." She peeled off her clothes and then scooted in behind Dani, urging her farther under the cool spray.

"God, that's cold." Dani tried to back away, but Grace wrapped her arms around her and pinned her directly under the water.

"Relax. You need to cool down. I've got you."

Dani exhaled a long breath and almost went limp in Grace's embrace. "Can I sit down? I feel like I might tip over."

Grace sat down on the tile floor, holding onto Dani's waist. "Can you squat down for me?" Dani complied, and Grace extended her legs out beside her. "Now sit and lean against me." She waited until Dani settled and then wrapped her arms around her. Dani's body was still too hot, and Grace directed water over her head and back with the handheld to speed the process. "How do you feel?"

Dani placed her arms on top of Grace's and rested her head back on Grace's shoulder. "Better. I like this."

Her voice sounded so small and needy that Grace's throat tightened. "What do you like?"

"You holding me, taking care of me. Is this how you felt the night I brought you home from the bar? You needed me."

Grace hugged her tighter, trying to ease Dani's insecurity and make her see just how much she did need her. "Yes, my darling, this is exactly how I felt."

"I'm sorry I just showed up without calling or anything. I'm not good at this. I'll leave if you want."

"Shush. Are you feeling cooler?" Grace touched her forehead. "Yeah, much."

"Let's get you out of here." She helped Dani out of the shower and dried her off.

"I feel really tired. Could I lie down for a few minutes, Grace? Just a few, then I need to talk to you, seriously talk."

Grace led Dani to bed, made sure she was comfortable, and climbed in after her. "How's this?"

"Perfect." Dani turned sideways and snuggled closer to Grace, pulling her arm around her middle. "Thank you for this." In a few seconds, her breathing leveled.

"I love you, Dani. So much it hurts," Grace whispered, certain Dani hadn't heard.

CHAPTER TWENTY-TWO

Grace?" Dani dreamed of being in Grace's arms, warm and content, and snuggled deeper into the covers. Something firm pressed against her back. She wasn't alone. An arm encircled her waist, fingers entwined with hers, and rested between her breasts. "Grace?"

"Right on the first guess."

Dani chuckled. Grace had said the same thing after they made love the first time and woke up together. "The only guess." She rolled into Grace's arms and stared into the emerald eyes she wanted to wake to every morning for the rest of her life. "What did you do to me last night? I feel exhausted and dehydrated."

A mischievous grin sprouted across Grace's face. "Wish I could take credit for that. Giraffe suit. Georgia summer. Ring any bells?"

"Oh…vaguely. Guess my surprise wasn't so great, huh?"

"It was a surprise all right, maybe not well thought out, but it got you back in my bed, so I'm not complaining." Grace stroked her fingers through Dani's hair and her eyes turned darker. "How's your head?"

"Little foggy. I might've dreamed we showered together and then…bed. Did we—"

"No."

Dani felt a surge of disappointment. "Oh."

"I'm not desperate enough to accost an unconscious woman. I have standards." Grace scrunched her face in mock shock.

"I was sort of out of it. In case I didn't say so before, thank you for taking care of me. I wasn't sure what to expect when I left Baltimore."

Grace blinked twice and her expression shifted from open and loving to cautious. "We should probably get moving. I'm sure you have things to do."

She started to pull away, but Dani caught her arm. "Don't go." She'd put that hurt on Grace's face, and it gouged at her own pain. She'd do anything to make this right and to convince Grace her feelings were real.

"This might be a conversation I'd prefer to have standing up."

"And maybe not." Dani drew her close again. "Just give me a few minutes?" She took a deep breath and let the words flow from her heart. "Grace, I'm in love with you." Grace's eyes pooled with tears, and she released a barely audible gasp. She'd never been more beautiful, and Dani had never been so certain of her feelings. "I'm in love with you, and I want a life with you…if you'll have me. If I'm not too late. I realize I hurt you, and I'm so very sorry. Please forgive me and give us another chance."

"What about your dream job? The city? You hate small towns. And cops." Grace scanned the room, ticking off every excuse Dani had ever used to distance from her.

Dani cupped Grace's face and forced her to look at her, afraid with every passing second that Grace was slipping further away. "I was wrong, about all of it."

"That was quick."

"Not really. Everything I thought I wanted means nothing without you."

Grace's lips tightened as she searched Dani's face. "Maybe we should take this slow."

A mixture of emotions played across Grace's face, and Dani was desperate to make her understand. "If I went any slower, we'd be dead before we moved in together. Grace, I'm sure about how I feel, finally."

"And your perfect job?"

"I can help animals anywhere, maybe even here if I do enough penance with Trip."

"She'll throw a hissy fit at first, for show, but you're a good vet, so she'll come around. And you were right about Harry, by the way. I did a couple of experiments. He hates uniforms."

"He's in good company, because I much prefer you just like this." Dani ran a finger between Grace's breasts. "You're too distracting. I have other things to say."

"Sorry." Grace's expression said she was anything but. "Continue."

"I realized the city was just a diversion from my family, painful memories, and my own feelings. I had to decide what *I* want. I needed to find a place where I felt loved and safe. And that place is anywhere you are, Grace. You're my home."

Grace's mouth quirked into a small grin. "Those are deep statements, Doc."

"But also very true. My grandmother was right about home and personal relationships being the most important things. And the right one is everything. And that's you for me, Grace. I want to settle down, raise fur and human babies, and be really happy for once. I'm serious. I brought everything I care about with me in the car. I'm not going back...unless you don't want me anymore."

"And the cop part." Grace's tone was teasing.

Dani skimmed her finger along Grace's bottom lip. "I've grown particularly fond of one cop. In fact, I'm hoping she'll utilize some of her restraint techniques on me very soon."

"You are, huh?"

Dani moved in for a kiss, but Grace pulled back. "What's wrong?"

"Are you sure about this? These are big changes for you." Grace hesitated and looked away, sadness gathering at the corners of her eyes. "And you can't hurt me again. It was too much the first time."

"I love you, Grace. I've never said those words before. Never thought I would, but you blew me away. And I want to spend the rest of my life with you, making up for the hurt and indecision, but I need to know one thing first." Her life hung in the balance. Grace had become essential to her. Could she walk away if Grace rejected her? Could she let her go the way Grace had let Dani go? Her answer came immediately—she'd give Grace anything she needed, even a life without her. "Please, Grace. Do you love me?" Dani's heart felt like it would pound out of her chest as she held her breath and waited for Grace's answer.

"Yes, I still love you, very much."

Dani released a long breath and stared at Grace unable to fully comprehend that this wonderful woman loved her and was willing to take a chance with her. "That's excellent news."

"Ahem, now might be a good time for that kiss."

Dani slid her arm around Grace's waist and pulled their bodies together. When their lips met, she melted into the embrace, pouring herself into the kiss and into Grace completely.

After several seconds, Grace pulled back and planted feathery kisses across Dani's face. "You realize this won't necessarily be smooth sailing?"

"You mean because I'm an emotional moron?"

"No, my darling, because we're both human and will make mistakes. I have no idea how it's supposed to work anymore than you do, but if you're willing to try, so am I."

"I like our odds."

"I'm sure Clay and Trip will place wagers, but they'll also insist on changing some of your citified ways."

"For you, I'm willing to undergo the exorcism." Dani snuggled into Grace's arms, and the sensation that she belonged here settled inside. She sprinkled kisses across Grace's breasts and absorbed the heat that flooded her skin. "So, I'm thinking we should seal this agreement with a ceremony of some sort."

"What did you have in mind, Doc?"

"Maybe not exactly what you'd expect right now." She tucked her leg between Grace's and wiggled suggestively. Grace moaned deep in her throat, and by the time it passed her lips, Dani felt her arousal slick her thigh.

"Tell me," Grace's voice was almost a whisper.

"I've never asked anyone for this before…"

"It's okay, Dani. Ask and it's yours."

"Will you…hold me, Grace? Just hold me for a while…and keep saying you love me."

Grace released a contented sigh. "Nothing would give me more pleasure. I love you so much." She pulled Dani more tightly against her, and Dani settled her head between Grace's breasts, enjoying the steady pounding of her heart and the connection of their bodies.

"Nothing, huh?"

Grace stroked Dani's back and kissed her head. "Maybe an extended game of Operation later where I take my sweet time exploring every nook, cranny, and orifice of your body."

Dani's body tingled at the image Grace's words evoked.

"Is that a yes then?"

"For you, always, Grace. I love you." For the first time, Dani gave her heart and her body without reservation. She was finally home.

EPILOGUE

Grace ran her fingers through Dani's windblown hair and stared up at the cloudless Georgia sky. "Perfect."

Dani grinned. "What's perfect, babe?"

"This. Us. I've got the woman of my dreams. The sky is glorious. The temperature isn't too blazing. And we're going to meet my best friends and their new loves at our favorite spot for a picnic. What could be better?"

"Having you under me," Dani teased and slid her hand up Grace's leg to the edge of her shorts. "I freaking love these shorts."

"You just love the easy access."

Dani parked off the side of the road where Grace indicated and urged her closer, inching her fingers under the short leg of Grace's jeans. "Busted." She cupped Grace's head with her other hand and kissed her until Grace pulled for breath.

"Do...we have...time for a—"

"No, you don't have time for a quickie," Trip said as she walked up behind them. "Should've taken care of that earlier. You're on the side of the road, Grace Booker. Think of your reputation." Trip slapped a hand over her chest, feigning shock.

Petunia collected pats from Grace and Dani while Jamie nudged Trip. "Be nice. You've got no room to talk, stud. Remember last night?"

Trip started to object, but Clay and River arrived just in time. "Who's hungry?" Clay asked, pulling a large picnic basket from the back of the truck.

River tucked her arm into Clay's as they joined the group. "You are, my love, always."

"That I am." Clay kissed River lightly, and they stared lovingly at each other until Grace broke the spell.

"Well, I think the new additions should wait here until Clay, Trip, and I set the stage." When Trip and Clay nodded, the three of them headed toward the river with the picnic baskets and coolers. "We'll call you in a few minutes. No peeking."

"No promises," Dani said.

Clay and Trip spread blankets on the ground at their usual spot near the edge of the water and close to the rope swing while Grace unpacked containers of food and drinks. "How's everything going, Clay?" Grace asked.

"Great. River and I have moved everything we need from New York into Eve's old house. We'll still jet back and forth for shows and such, but otherwise, this is our home."

"Sweet," Trip said. "Jamie and Petunia are moving in next week. We won't even need gas masks for P anymore since her surgery. I'm expanding my business with a new partner. Life is good. What about you, Gracie?"

"Dani and I might need a bigger place than the cottage, but not right away."

"Kids?" Clay asked.

"Cool your jets. That's down the road. Can we have a honeymoon period first?"

When the preparations were complete, they walked toward the edge of the water, Grace sandwiched between her two princes. "Our little Pine Cone corner of the world appears to be growing. Are we ready for this?"

"Totally," Trip said, her expression growing serious. "I've loved Jamie since college, and I'm still staggered that circumstances brought her back to me for a second chance. I want us to experience everything and grow old together."

"I feel the same about River," Clay said. "Gracie?"

She slid her arms around their waists and pulled them closer. "This spot has always been special to us. It's time to share it and the rest of our lives with the women we love."

About the Author

A thirty-year veteran of a midsized police department, VK was a police officer by necessity and a writer by desire. Her career spanned numerous positions including beat officer, homicide detective, vice/narcotics lieutenant, captain, and assistant chief of police. Now retired, she devotes her time to writing, traveling, and volunteering.

Books Available from Bold Strokes Books

Captive by Donna K. Ford. To escape a human trafficking ring, Greyson Cooper and Olivia Danner become players in a game of deceit and violence. Will their love stand a chance? (978-1-63555-215-7)

Crossing the Line by CF Frizzell. The Mob discovers a nemesis within its ranks, and in the ultimate retaliation, draws Stick McLaughlin from anonymity by threatening everything she holds dear. (978-1-63555-161-7)

Love's Verdict by Carsen Taite. Attorneys Landon Holt and Carly Pachett want the exact same thing: the only open partnership spot at their prestigious criminal defense firm. But will they compromise their careers for love? (978-1-63555-042-9)

Precipice of Doubt by Mardi Alexander & Laurie Eichler. Can Cole Jameson resist her attraction to her boss, veterinarian Jodi Bowman, or will she risk a workplace romance and her heart? (978-1-63555-128-0)

Savage Horizons by CJ Birch. Captain Jordan Kellow's feelings for Lt. Ali Ash have her past and future colliding, setting in motion a series of events that strands her crew in an unknown galaxy thousands of light years from home. (978-1-63555-250-8)

Secrets of the Last Castle by A. Rose Mathieu. When Elizabeth Campbell represents a young man accused of murdering an elderly woman, her investigation leads to an abandoned plantation that reveals many dark Southern secrets. (978-1-63555-240-9)

Take Your Time by VK Powell. A neurotic parrot brings police officer Grace Booker and temporary veterinarian Dr. Dani Wingate together in the tiny town of Pine Cone, but their unexpected attraction keeps the sparks flying. (978-1-63555-130-3)

The Last Seduction by Ronica Black. When you allow true love to elude you once and you desperately regret it, are you brave enough to grab it when it comes around again? (978-1-63555-211-9)

The Shape of You by Georgia Beers. Rebecca McCall doesn't play it safe, but when sexy Spencer Thompson joins her workout class, their non-stop sparing forces her to face her ultimate challenge—a chance at love. (978-1-63555-217-1)

Exposed by MJ Williamz. The closet is no place to live if you want to find true love. (978-1-62639-989-1)

Force of Fire: Toujours a Vous by Ali Vali. Immortals Kendal and Piper welcome their new child and celebrate the defeat of an old enemy, but another ancient evil is about to awaken deep in the jungles of Costa Rica. (978-1-63555-047-4)

Holding Their Place by Kelly A. Wacker. Together Dr. Helen Connery and ambulance driver Julia March discover that goodness, love, and passion can be found in the most unlikely and even dangerous places during WWI. (978-1-63555-338-3)

Landing Zone by Erin Dutton. Can a career veteran finally discover a love stronger than even her pride? (978-1-63555-199-0)

Love at Last Call by M. Ullrich. Is balancing business, friendship, and love more than any willing woman can handle? (978-1-63555-197-6)

Pleasure Cruise by Yolanda Wallace. Spencer Collins and Amy Donovan have few things in common, but a Caribbean cruise offers both women an unexpected chance to face one of their greatest fears: falling in love. (978-1-63555-219-5)

Running Off Radar by MB Austin. Maji's plans to win Rose back are interrupted when work intrudes and duty calls her to help a SEAL team stop a Russian mobster from harvesting gold from the bottom of Sitka Sound. (978-1-63555-152-5)

Shadow of the Phoenix by Rebecca Harwell. In the final battle for the fate of Storm's Quarry, even Nadya's and Shay's powers may not be enough. (978-1-63555-181-5)

Take a Chance by D. Jackson Leigh. There's hardly a woman within fifty miles of Pine Cone that veterinarian Trip Beaumont can't charm, except for the irritating new cop, Jamie Grant, who keeps leaving parking tickets on her truck. (978-1-63555-118-1)

The Outcasts by Alexa Black. Spacebus driver Sue Jones is running from her past. When she crash-lands on a faraway world, the Outcast Kara might be her chance for redemption. (978-1-63555-242-3)

Alias by Cari Hunter. A car crash leaves a woman with no memory and no identity. Together with Detective Bronwen Pryce, she fights to uncover a truth that might just kill them both. (978-1-63555-221-8)

Death in Time by Robyn Nyx. Working in the past is hell on your future. (978-1-63555-053-5)

Hers to Protect by Nicole Disney. High school sweethearts Kaia and Adrienne will have to see past their differences and survive the vengeance of a brutal gang if they want to be together. (978-1-63555-229-4)

Of Echoes Born by 'Nathan Burgoine. A collection of queer fantasy short stories set in Canada from Lambda Literary Award finalist 'Nathan Burgoine. (978-1-63555-096-2)

Perfect Little Worlds by Clifford Mae Henderson. Lucy can't hold the secret any longer. Twenty-six years ago, her sister did the unthinkable. (978-1-63555-164-8)

Room Service by Fiona Riley. Interior designer Olivia likes stability, but when work brings footloose Savannah into her world and into a new city every month, Olivia must decide if what makes her comfortable is what makes her happy. (978-1-63555-120-4)

Sparks Like Ours by Melissa Brayden. Professional surfers Gia Malone and Elle Britton can't deny their chemistry on and off the beach. But only one can win... (978-1-63555-016-0)

Take My Hand by Missouri Vaun. River Hemsworth arrives in Georgia intent on escaping quickly, but when she crashes her Mercedes into the Clip 'n Curl, sexy Clay Cahill ends up rescuing more than her car. (978-1-63555-104-4)

The Last Time I Saw Her by Kathleen Knowles. Lane Hudson only has twelve days to win back Alison's heart. That is if she can gather the courage to try. (978-1-63555-067-2)

Wayworn Lovers by Gun Brooke. Will agoraphobic composer Giselle Bonnaire and Tierney Edwards, a wandering soul who can't remain in one place for long, trust in the passionate love destiny hands them? (978-1-62639-995-2)

Breakthrough by Kris Bryant. Falling for a sexy ranger is one thing, but is the possibility of love worth giving up the career Kennedy Wells has always dreamed of? (978-1-63555-179-2)

Certain Requirements by Elinor Zimmerman. Phoenix has always kept her love of kinky submission strictly behind the bedroom door and inside the bounds of romantic relationships, until she meets Kris Andersen. (978-1-63555-195-2)

Dark Euphoria by Ronica Black. When a high-profile case drops in Detective Maria Diaz's lap, she forges ahead only to discover this case, and her main suspect, aren't like any other. (978-1-63555-141-9)

Fore Play by Julie Cannon. Executive Leigh Marshall falls hard for Peyton Broader, her golf pro...and an ex-con. Will she risk sabotaging her career for love? (978-1-63555-102-0)

Love Came Calling by CA Popovich. Can a romantic looking for a long-term, committed relationship and a jaded cynic too busy for love conquer life's struggles and find their way to what matters most? (978-1-63555-205-8)

Outside the Law by Carsen Taite. Former sweethearts Tanner Cohen and Sydney Braswell must work together on a federal task force to see justice served, but will they choose to embrace their second chance at love? (978-1-63555-039-9)

The Princess Deception by Nell Stark. When journalist Missy Duke realizes Prince Sebastian is really his twin sister Viola in disguise, she plays along, but when sparks flare between them, will the double deception doom their fairy-tale romance? (978-1-62639-979-2)

The Smell of Rain by Cameron MacElvee. Reyha Arslan, a wise and elegant woman with a tragic past, shows Chrys that there's still beauty to embrace and reason to hope despite the world's cruelty. (978-1-63555-166-2)

The Talebearer by Sheri Lewis Wohl. Liz's visions show her the faces of the lost and the killers who took their lives. As one by one, the murdered are found, a stranger works to stop Liz before the serial killer is brought to justice. (978-1-635550-126-6)

White Wings Weeping by Lesley Davis. The world is full of discord and hatred, but how much of it is just human nature when an evil with sinister intent is invading people's hearts? (978-1-63555-191-4)

A Call Away by KC Richardson. Can a businesswoman from a big city find the answers she's looking for, and possibly love, on a small-town farm? (978-1-63555-025-2)

Berlin Hungers by Justine Saracen. Can the love between an RAF woman and the wife of a Luftwaffe pilot, former enemies, survive in besieged Berlin during the aftermath of World War II? (978-1-63555-116-7)

Blend by Georgia Beers. Lindsay and Piper are like night and day. Working together won't be easy, but not falling in love might prove the hardest job of all. (978-1-63555-189-1)

Hunger for You by Jenny Frame. Principe of an ancient vampire clan Byron Debrek must save her one true love from falling into the hands of her enemies and into the middle of a vampire war. (978-1-63555-168-6)

Mercy by Michelle Larkin. FBI Special Agent Mercy Parker and psychic ex-profiler Piper Vasey learn to love again as they race to stop a man with supernatural gifts who's bent on annihilating humankind. (978-1-63555-202-7)

Pride and Porters by Charlotte Greene. Will pride and prejudice prevent these modern-day lovers from living happily ever after? (978-1-63555-158-7)

Rocks and Stars by Sam Ledel. Kyle's struggle to own who she is and what she really wants may end up landing her on the bench and without the woman of her dreams. (978-1-63555-156-3)

The Boss of Her: Office Romance Novellas by Julie Cannon, Aurora Rey, and M. Ullrich. Going to work never felt so good. Three office romance novellas from talented writers Julie Cannon, Aurora Rey, and M. Ullrich. (978-1-63555-145-7)

The Deep End by Ellie Hart. When family ties become entangled in murder and deception, it's time to find a way out... (978-1-63555-288-1)